TAYLOR DANAE COLBERT

IT GOES WITHOUT SAYING

Published: Taylor Danae Colbert 2018
www.taylordanaecolbert.com
Editing: Lizzy McLellan Ravitch
Cover Design: Taylor Danae Colbert
ISBN-13:978-1723105289
ISBN-10:1723105287

For you, Little. Thanks for believing in me always, and for pushing me to be fearless.

ONE
Now

Damn, it was a good day. It was like, walk-out-of-the-office-smiling-at-strangers good. First of all, it was Friday. Knowing that within the hour, she could be lounging on the couch with no bra and an open jar of Nutella in her lap was glorious in and of itself. On top of that, Bria just got the promotion she'd been waiting for since she graduated from college. She was finally promoted to junior sales manager, and was going to get some of her own accounts. No more assistant duties. No more getting Benji coffee. Ugh. She hated getting Benji coffee. Every latte she placed on his desk felt like another boost to the patriarchy.

And as if the hefty pay raise and the new office weren't enough, Benji had given her a week off before starting her new position. So she walked with a bounce in her step down the Bethesda streets to the garage where she parked her car every day. She couldn't wait to tell Drew, but he'd be with patients for another hour, at least. Bria had to admit, she was pretty damn excited that she'd be contributing more to their income. Drew might be on his way to being a doctor, but damn if she wasn't working her ass off, too. She scrolled to her favorites in her contacts and dialed her mom.

"Hello?" Louise answered.

"Hey, mom! You're never gonna guess what happened to me today."

"Oh, um—"

"I got the promotion! I'm junior sales manager now!"

"Oh, sweetie, that's. . .that's wonderful." Her mom sounded tired. And unfocused. This wasn't the overly enthusiastic, my-kid-shits-rainbows response that she was expecting.

"Mom?" She heard a sniffle on the other end. "Mom, what's going on? What happened?" There was a long pause, and she knew her mother was gathering herself.

"It's your sister."

"Katie? What about her?" she asked, pausing outside of the parking garage so she wouldn't lose service.

"The Lyme is back. And it's worse this time."

Bria couldn't say anything. She didn't want to. She just leaned back against the brick wall, steadying herself. She watched the other commuters who were still enjoying the day. The dark cloud of the Kreery family wasn't hanging over their heads. They got to have their Friday. They got to take off their bras now. Stupid, happy, braless people.

"B?" her mom asked, after a few moments of silence.

"Yeah, sorry. I'm here. I'm coming home." She dug her keys out of her purse and walked into the garage. She had been so excited when she landed a job in Bethesda, because it was the perfect half-way point between her new life in D.C., and her hometown. Dalesville, Maryland was about twenty miles away from

Bethesda—close enough that Bria could see her family a few times a month, but far enough away that she felt like she could breathe, make her own life. But on nights like this, when her family needed her, she was close enough to make it home in less than an hour.

As Bria sat in bumper-to-bumper traffic on the beltway, she wasn't screaming at the people that cut her off, or banging her hands against the steering wheel, desperate for the cars to clear. Instead, she was actually relieved to be sitting, and to have a few moments to herself before the Kreery madness descended upon her. She wondered how bad it would be this time.

They first noticed Katie's symptoms when she was in middle school. She had debilitating headaches, her joints swelled, and she had random bouts of temporary paralysis. And so, the endless search for answers began. She was misdiagnosed three times before a specialist finally determined that she had Lyme disease.

"Unfortunately, we don't know a lot about Lyme, yet. But there are a few things we can try."

This was the standard response from the six Lyme specialists Katie saw throughout the course of her teenage years. Apparently, Katie had been bit by a tick years before, but they never spotted it. If she'd seen it, and had gotten on antibiotics quick enough, she might have recovered after just a few weeks. But they never saw the tick, never saw a rash. Nothing. Poor Katie. She was forced to quit sports, occasionally needed a walker when her knees would swell, and had to take an abbreviated schedule at school so she could go to the doctors regularly. The first time, she had symptoms for three years straight, no relief in sight. And the bills kept coming. Her mother had gone back to work to chip away at some of the medical costs, while Bria and her other sister, Sam, eventually had to take out loans to pay for the remainder of their college tuition.

But finally, midway through her sophomore year

of high school, Katie saw the light at the end of the tunnel. Her symptoms seemed to be managed, and the doctors she saw seemed to be keeping her pain-free. She finished high school on the honor roll, got into the University of Maryland, and was finally hanging out with people other than their mother and father.

Bria had just FaceTimed her two nights ago. She was going to the doctor that week for a check-up. She never mentioned that she was feeling bad, but now it was clear that Katie just didn't want Bria to worry.

Finally, Bria got off at her exit, and drove the last seven miles into the quiet streets of Dalesville. She swore it was like crossing into another dimension, the second she passed the faded green "Welcome to Dalesville" sign on her right, going back in time forty or fifty years.

Everything was just a little bit slower. She had to admit, though, the sprawling farmland was pretty this time of night, with the pink and orange sky rolling off of it and into the distant mountains.

She pulled onto Main Street, and she felt a familiar calm washing over her. Despite the situation she was headed toward, it was good to be home. She passed the grocery store, where her dad had taught her to drive in the parking lot. She smiled as she passed her high school. Her heart fluttered a bit when she passed the Jimmie Cone sign on her left. She hadn't been there since. . . well, the last time she was with him. That felt like a lifetime ago. She sighed, shaking her head, focusing on the situation at hand.

After sitting through the stop-and-go of the three traffic lights on Route 108, she finally turned onto Connell Street, where her family's house sat at the end of a perfect little cul-de-sac. The houses in her parents' neighborhood were modest, but theirs had been plenty big enough for their family of five. It was a cute little split-level with a front porch and green shutters. Her parents had bought the house shortly before they became pregnant with her. They had a small backyard, but it was fenced in with plenty of room for three little girls to play. As they got older, their dad had built a big patio out back, where she and her friends would sit for hours. She turned off the engine and took a breath. Let the madness begin.

She popped her shoes off in the garage before going in. For a moment, the house was too quiet. Then she was bum rushed by Buster, wagging his tail, barking, and licking her to no end.

"Okay, okay, hi, yes, I see you," she said, patting his head. "Hello?"

"Hi, B," her dad called from the living room. "We're in here."

Bria dropped her keys on the kitchen island, and left her coat on one of the chairs. Her mother sat on the couch, Katie's head in her lap. Her dad sat in his recliner, staring up at the television, peering over the rims of his glasses. Bria was surprised to see Sam home; she had graduated from Salisbury University a few months before, but Bria still wasn't used to her being around. While Sam was in college, she definitely enjoyed her time away. Probably because she didn't have to deal with things like this. But, she was here, sitting on the couch. That's how Bria knew this was serious.

"Hi, sweetie," her mom said, her tone still defeated, but genuinely happy to see her. "Where's Drew?"

Shit. Drew. She had totally forgotten to tell him she would be late tonight.

"Crap!" she said, running back into the kitchen and snatching her phone up before she even kissed them hello. She tapped her foot anxiously, waiting for him to pick up.

"Hey, where are you?" he answered.

"Hey, babe," she said. "Listen, I talked to my mom right after work today, and it turns out that my sister isn't doing so well."

"Sam?" he asked.

"No, Katie. Remember how she was sick a few

years back?"

"Oh, yeah," he said.

"Yeah, well it's back. I had to come home for a bit. I'm sorry, but I won't make it to dinner. Tell everyone I said hello. I'll see you tonight."

"Okay," he said, "so I guess we're not going wedding cake tasting this evening, either?"

Shit. She had forgotten about that, too.

"Shit, I'm sorry, hon. I'll call and reschedule for this weekend."

"Sounds good, see ya later," he said, with a click.

He didn't have to say it; after five-and-a-half years with him, she knew when he was ticked off. But most of the time, she didn't really care.

"Okay, so what's going on?" she asked as she walked back into the living room, lifting Katie's legs up and plopping down on the couch.

"Well, she's been having issues with the paralysis again," Louise said, still stroking Katie's hair. Buster had jumped up on the couch, sprawling out over top of Katie. "Her joints are swelling, her headaches are back."

"Basically everything," Katie said, emotionless, staring at the television. The poor kid. She'd dealt with so much in her short life. Every time she went through this, Bria's heart broke for her. There was nothing she, or anyone else for that matter, could do. They just had to watch her in pain, watch her as her own life passed her by.

"Damn it, Tommy," Bria said, smiling at Katie. Tommy was the name they had given the tick that bit Katie all those years ago. It made it easier to place the blame on someone, or something, when it had a name. Katie smiled faintly.

"I'm tired," she finally said, scooting off the couch, wincing as she bent her stiff knees. "But I need to wash my hair."

Bria looked up at Sam. That was their cue. They'd been through this plenty of times. Sometimes, Katie would get bouts of paralysis from the Lyme so bad, that she could barely move, let alone bathe or dress herself.

They each held out a hand to Katie, helping her up and walking with her up the steps to their bathroom.

"I think I can do it myself tonight, just might need some help after," Katie said, her tired eyes blinking slowly. Sam and Bria nodded, stepping out of the bathroom so that Katie could shower. Some nights, she'd been in such pain, so swollen, so stiff, that her sisters and her mother had actually helped her shower, or wash her hair. A few minutes later, Katie trudged out of the bathroom. Sam combed through her wet strands, and Bria folded them into neat braids. They helped dress her for bed as if she was a child. Bria supposed Katie would be embarrassed by all the help if she weren't so exhausted.

When Bria and Sam made their way back out to the kitchen, Louise and Joe were sitting at the table, Louise with her head in her hands, and Joe rubbing her back. Bria wondered what it felt like, having a child that was perpetually in pain, always living a sub-par life, and be unable to do anything about it. Probably pretty helpless. She put her hand on her mother's as she and Sam sat down with them.

"Well, I think that's what we're going to have to do," her father said, leaning back in his chair.

"What is?" Bria asked.

"I think I'm going to need to look for another part-time job, and your mother is going to have to find something full-time."

Bria and Sam looked from their father to their mother.

"Why?" Sam asked.

"Katie's treatment. Her doctor wants to give her medications through an IV, so she'll need to get a port. It's not covered by insurance. It could cost us anywhere from forty to sixty thousand dollars," Joe said.

Bria said nothing, just stared down at her hands.

She always knew this day could come again, but ever since Katie had reached remission, Bria had blocked the entire illness out of her mind. Bria had told herself that once Katie was feeling better, she'd be fine forever.

Nope. Tommy had other plans.

She hated to see her parents dealing with the same dilemmas they had faced just a few years earlier. They were like hamsters on a wheel, just trying to stay ahead. They were in their fifties now, and it broke her heart that they would be dusting off their resumes to look for more income as if they were new college graduates just starting their lives. They should be reducing stress in their lives, saving for retirement. This, right here, was one of the reasons Bria wanted to get out, stay away, avoid the problem. She never wanted this for herself, or her future kids. No struggling. At least not in this same way. She absolutely adored her family. She was as close with her sisters as sisters could be, and she had a great relationship with both of her parents. But she told herself that putting a little distance between them would make her immune to their same fate.

"I don't mean to scare you girls, but I'm not even sure how we're going to pay the mortgage next month, at this rate," Louise finally said, wiping her nose with a tissue.

Bria felt the lump in her throat rising. The first time she had overheard her parents talking about losing their house, she was about to graduate high school. She had felt useless. She had three-hundred dollars to her name at that point, and knew she couldn't do a damn thing to help. Through a stroke of well-timed luck, her parents had come into some money at the last minute. Bria never asked where the money came from, because honestly, she didn't want to know. She couldn't imagine them doing anything illegal, but in a desperate moment, she knew it was a possibility. Then, Katie had made a turn for the better, and her treatment stopped shortly after. Her parents were able to get back on top of their bills, and all was well. This time was different. Bria doubted money would fall from the sky like it did the last time. But, this time, Bria wasn't useless.

"I'll move back in," she said, squeezing her mother's hand.

"What? No," Louise protested.

"No, B, we can't let you do this. This isn't your responsibility," Joe said, shaking his head.

"Yeah, but you didn't ask for this," she said. "I just got my promotion. I'll be making a lot more money. And my school loans are almost totally paid off. I can help out with the bills around here and help get her to her appointments until her treatment is over."

"Don't be silly," Louise said, "what about Drew? You can't just leave him."

"I hardly see Drew during the week anyways because of his hours. I'll go to D.C. on the weekends. We will be fine."

"Bria," Joe started to interject again, but quickly realized he didn't have another point to make.

"I can try. . ." Sam started to pipe in.

"You'll try nothing," Bria said, looking at her. "You have a new job to get. We will be fine."

Sam nodded. Bria could physically see the weight lift off of her parents' and Sam's shoulders. Joe and Louise hugged and kissed her, over and over, thanking her and telling her how lucky they were to be her parents.

"Stop, guys," she said. "You're my family. It's our job to take care of each other."

They nodded, kissed her and Sam once more and said goodnight. She sighed. Right back to Dalesville. She picked up her phone and went out on the front porch.

"Hello lover," Mari answered on the other line. After all these years, it was still a relief to hear her voice.

"Hi," Bria answered. Even with just that one word, Mari knew something was up.

"What's going on? Spill."

So, Bria took a breath and told her the whole story.

"Wow. I'm so sorry this is happening to your family again, B. And that poor kid. She's had it rough. But I know she will get through it just like she did before."

Bria nodded to herself, her friend's simple, but reassuring words calming her.

"How is Drew with your new living arrangement?" Mari asked.

"Well. . ." Bria started to say.

"Oh, have you not told him yet? That's okay, I know he will understand. He's got to. It's your family, right?"

"Right. Thanks, Mari."

"Any time, babe. Love you."

She sighed. Now it was time to tell Drew. She scrolled through her phone to her favorites, clicking on his name. She had saved a heart emoji next to it years ago, and had never taken it down.

"I don't. . . I don't understand. You're moving out?" he asked.

"No, I'm not moving out. I'm just moving in with them for a few months. Until she's healthy again." There was silence for a moment.

"I'm coming up there."

Click. She waited on the front porch for forty-five minutes until he arrived, just breathing in the Dalesville air. Certain times of the month, it reeked of manure, but luckily, the air was fresh tonight.

Finally, lights in the driveway. She got in, and they drove four minutes to Andy's, one of the only places in town that served alcohol.

Drew didn't seem angry; he just seemed overwhelmed, confused. He barely spoke to her until they got to their table.

"So, explain this to me again," he said, putting the two beers he had ordered from the bar down on the table.

"Katie is sick. Again. My parents can't afford her treatment. So I'm moving back in with them to help out and pay some of the bills until she's healthy."

"Mhmm," he said. Bria knew Drew didn't fully understand Katie's situation. His medical education never taught him about the long-term effects of Lyme, and she always sort of felt like he doubted Katie's symptoms.

"I mean, I get it, but, uh, what about us?" he asked. "What about our wedding?"

"Things will be fine in plenty of time before the wedding," Bria said, over-confidently. The truth was, she had no clue how long Katie's treatment would take. But she had no other option. She wouldn't leave them to struggle on their own.

"I get that your sister's sick, but this is kind of unfair, Bria. I mean, what are we supposed to tell people?" he asked, a little more upset now. His tones were hushed, but his anger and irritation still resonated just fine. But Bria didn't have a pissed-off-in-public voice. That was the problem. She had a one-size-fits all, be-careful-what-you-wish-for voice. Whether they were in the privacy of their bedroom or in the middle of a busy restaurant, like they were right now, provoking Bria had the same consequence.

Luckily for Drew, though, she wasn't angry yet. Mostly, she was preoccupied. She just stared down at her hand, twirling the two-karat teardrop diamond that sat on her left ring finger. Around, and around, and around.

"Are you even listening?" he asked. She sighed and returned the diamond to its rightful position.

"Yes, Drew, I'm listening. But I don't know what you want me to say. They are my family, and I won't just leave them hanging. Unless you'd like the four of them to move into our one-bedroom apartment?" she said, taking a sip of her beer. His eyes widened slightly, the terrifying vision of an apartment full of Kreeries probably forming in his head.

"Does it even bother you that we won't see each

other, but two days a week? I mean, Jesus, we're engaged."

"Of course it bothers me. Are you kidding? I spent my whole life trying to figure out how to get out of Dalesville for this exact reason, only to end up right back up here the day I happened to get the biggest promotion of my professional career." He looked at her, puzzled. "Oh, yeah, I got the promotion."

"Oh, well, congratulations," he said. Yeah, that sounded super genuine.

When she met Drew in undergrad, she fell hard and extremely fast. They were staying together every night by her senior year, and when she graduated, she moved into his D.C. apartment. One night, after he finished medical school and started his residency, he took her to a fancy restaurant in the city, where he proposed in front their parents. It would be a longer engagement, over two years by the time Drew finished his residency and they had the wedding, but she couldn't wait. It was absolutely beautiful, and Bria thought she'd never love someone the way she loved Drew. But right now, she kind of wanted to punch him in the face.

Just as she was getting ready to put up her metaphorical dukes and lecture Drew on the importance of family, the restaurant door opened, and what felt like the whole place rang out into a cheer.

"Knox is in the house!" she heard someone holler. She could have sworn her heart stopped beating. As the crowd parted, she laid her eyes on him for the first time in about five years. God, he looked older.

He took off his black knit beanie, the same one he had had since they were in high school, and shook out his hair, still as thick and dark as ever, framing his glowing, Kelly-green eyes. She knew he did absolutely nothing to style it, but it seemed to lie perfectly every day. He was lucky like that. He was only about six-feet tall, but she noticed now that his shoulders were much more broad than they had been all those years ago.

Bria tried to look casual so that Drew wouldn't notice, but she couldn't take her eyes off of Knox. As he scanned the crowd and gave hugs to a few more people, his eyes finally landed on hers. He stopped in his tracks. For a second, the room was deafeningly quiet.

It was normal for Bria to run into people she knew whenever she was in Dalesville. After all, it was a town of only a few thousand, and most people seemed to migrate back after their time away. But not once had she run into Knox.

Ben Knoxville, known as "Knox" by anyone who knew him from his freshman year of high school on, was her absolute best friend in the world. Or, at least, he used to be. Whenever she was back in town, she found herself subconsciously going the long way to her parents, or to the store, passing by the townhouse development where she had heard he lived. She'd drive past Andy's at night, where she knew his friends used to get drinks after work. But not once had she seen him since her sophomore year of college. Until tonight.

Finally, when the moment of shock passed, Bria realized Knox was walking directly toward her. She played it off like she hadn't been eyeing him down since the second she heard his name, looking down, then up, with raised eyebrows. She practically jumped out of her booth as he reached her, but she was careful not to look as excited as she actually was.

"Hey, you," he said.

TWO
Then, Freshman Year

When she first saw him, she was flat on her back. She was so hot and sweaty, she almost forgot how nervous she was.

Bria had just run her fastest mile ever, trying to score a spot on the varsity cross country team on her third day of practice. In just a few weeks, she'd be starting high school. She was tiny. Skin-and-bones, flat-chested, the epitome of an awkward teenager. Her chestnut brown hair lay in a loose ponytail off of her shoulder as she leaned down toward one leg to stretch.

"Okay, everyone," Coach Boone said, scanning over the clipboard in his hands, "nice work today. Let's go for a cool down, and you're done for the day."

As the seniors jogged to the front of the pack, she made her move up there with them. She definitely didn't want to overstep her boundaries, but she wanted them to know she was serious about the sport. She wanted them to know how badly she wanted to be on that varsity squad with them.

"You're doing pretty well, girl," Marisol, the

captain of the team, told her. "We've all been talking about it."

"Oh, really? Thanks!" Bria said. As they jogged around the fields behind the school, Bria noticed they were headed down toward the football practice fields.

"Stay to the right, ladies. Don't want to get in their way," Marisol called back to the group. Bria tried to be a part of their conversation, laughing and joking, without seeming like she was trying too hard.

"Let's go, ladies, keep up!" Christa called. She and Marisol had been on the team all four years, and it was clear to Bria that they took it very seriously. As the other freshmen giggled at the back of the group, she was determined to stay separate from them.

"So, how long have you been running, Bria?" Christa asked, as they rounded the end zone. Just then, she heard a bunch of voices.

"Look out!"

"Duck!"

BAM.

When she came to, Marisol was fanning her while Christa was holding people back. The school trainer was running across the field toward her.

"You okay, kid? Sorry about that!"

Bria didn't recognize the voice. As she rubbed her head, her vision became clearer. A football player was standing over her. He reached up and took off his helmet. When he shook out his shaggy mane, as dark as black coffee, she recognized him immediately. Ben Knoxville, the junior running back. His name wasn't known all across town like some of the other guys, but the announcers did call him out over the loudspeaker now and then for a good play. Even dripping in sweat, with his wild hair sticking to his face, he was pretty beautiful. He was sweaty, but not the kind of sweaty that smelled of souring food. He was the other kind of sweaty—the intoxicating, slow-motion, *Baywatch* kind of sweaty. It was in that moment that Bria realized she was still flat on her back with a knot the size of a golf ball growing out of her forehead, in the middle of the high school football practice.

"Oh, no, my bad, I'm sorry," she said, hopping to her feet without allowing anyone else to help her up. "I'm good, really. Let's finish that cool down!" she said. Marisol took the cue and regrouped the pack.

"Do you want some ice?" the trainer asked.

"No, thanks," Bria said, desperately trying to get a move on.

"Sorry, again," Knox said. "Hey Mari," he waved to her in a sing-song voice. Marisol laughed.

"Hey, Knox," she said. "Long time no see."

"Yes it has been. Let's not make it so long next time, my love," he said. Marisol rolled her eyes playfully. "You too, Christa. I miss my running ladies. We need some cuddle time, soon."

Christa giggled like a schoolgirl, blowing him a kiss as they ran by.

"Okay girls, let's finish up!" Mari called. Bria could feel her heart racing. She couldn't imagine him saying something like that to her, but Marisol and Christa seemed to just let it roll right off.

"Oh my gosh, hon, I'm so sorry that just happened!" Marisol said to her, once they were back on the track.

"Yeah! Are you sure you're okay?" Christa asked. Physically, she really did feel okay. The bump would go down soon. But her ego was bruised, and at the same time, her curiosity was piqued.

"Yeah, yeah, I'm good. So, are you two. . .?" she started to ask, eyeing the football field. Marisol and Christa both looked at her quizzically, then followed her gaze to the large mass of boys running each other into the ground. Bria wasn't surprised at Knox's interest in Mari; she was tall and slim with long, mocha-colored legs, and wavy chocolate-colored hair that touched the middle of her back. She could definitely be on the cover of some magazine, one of those ones where the girl is bikini-clad, kneeling in the sand, her eyes squinty, probably biting her lip as she gives the camera "the look." But then, Knox had moved on, waving his fingers in Christa's direction.

"Wait, are you asking if me and Knox. . .? No!" Mari said, breaking out into a fit of laughter. Christa joined her. "No, no. Rule number one of Dalesville High: if you are female, Ben Knoxville will find you. And he will flirt with you."

"Well, with some girls he does a lot more than flirt," Christa said, eyeing the cheerleaders across the field.

"True," Marisol nodded. "But physical intentions or not, that's just how Knox is. He's a mess. He's never had a girlfriend, but he's had *plenty* of girls. But, he's a sweetheart, honestly."

"Yeah, he really is. He's just a goof," Christa agreed.

"Got it," Bria said, pulling her arm behind her back into a stretch. She pretended to focus on wherever their conversation was going next, but her head was still on the field, golf ball knot and all.

As the first few weeks of practice passed, Bria quickly became not only a varsity runner, but the fastest runner on the team. She was placing in the top ten in every race, and she was surprised to find that the other girls on the team were nothing but ecstatic for her. Marisol had totally taken Bria her under her wing, and Bria was surprised at how quickly they had become close friends. She truly felt she could confide in Marisol about anything, and she knew any advice Marisol gave was worth following. Having always served the role of older sister, Bria enjoyed having someone she could look up to and goof around with.

By November, when the state meet rolled around, Bria was expected to finish in the top five, based on her record-smashing season. She couldn't focus all week long.

She sat in her classes, staring out the window, picturing the last four hundred meters of the state course. When the final bell rang Friday, she walked like a zombie to her locker. Her nerves were kicking into high gear, and they weren't going away. As she stood on her tip-toes to reach her science book on the top shelf, she clumsily knocked it further back in, and just out of her reach. Great. She climbed into the locker, stretching as far as her limbs could go, but it was no use.

"Let me get that for ya, darlin,'" she heard a male voice say. She froze. It was Knox.

"Oh, thank you," she said with a nervous giggle.

"Hey, you're the kid who took the ball to the head a few weeks back, right?" he asked. She was slightly irritated by his use of the term "kid," but she couldn't help but be excited they were conversing at all.

"Yep, that was me," she said. "That's why I stick to sports that don't require much hand-eye coordination."

He laughed, and she felt herself shamelessly glowing with pride.

"You're running in the state meet tomorrow, right?" he asked. "I heard you were pretty fast."

She blushed. "Uh, yeah, I guess so. We'll see how it goes!"

"Well, I think a bunch of us are coming out to watch. I'll be there cheering you on."

"Oh, cool!" she said, trying not to sound too excited, then realizing suddenly that her bus would be leaving soon. She shut the locker door, flashed a quick, nervous smile at Knox and threw her backpack on. "See you there!"

By the next morning, Bria had forgotten about anything that wasn't the state meet. She barely spoke to anyone. She just glanced around the course, taking in all the inclines, all the turns, all the spots where she might be able to gain some position. Before she knew it, it was time to get to the starting line. She eased the tip of her toe up to the line, bending her knees slightly. Her heart was beating so hard, she could actually hear it. Three, two, one. Bang.

The course was deadly. Some of the biggest hills she had ever seen seemed to pop out of nowhere, and just when she had finished climbing one and caught her breath, another appeared. But she periodically counted the girls in front of her—always fewer than 10. She could see the finish line, now, about four hundred meters away. All that was standing between her and it was one more monstrous hill. As she approached it, she felt every ache and pain that she had been fighting through the entire race. She felt the lactic acid weighing down her legs like they were a thousand pounds each. She felt the breath escaping her lungs, and she felt herself unable to take in more air. That's when she heard him.

"You got it, kid! Push yourself! You're so close to the finish!"

Bria looked up. Knox was on the side of the hill, surrounded by more of the football players and other kids from their school. He had a bandana tied around his head, and his shirt was off. He and some of his teammates had painted their bodies in Dalesville green. But she didn't notice any of that. All she knew was that he was there, cheering for her. That's when it kicked in. She felt an uncontrollable urge to lift her legs higher. She almost didn't notice how badly they were burning. She got to the top of the hill, and passed one girl. Eighth place. But all she saw was the back of the next girl. Seventh place. Sixth, fifth, fourth. Third was a few yards ahead, but she didn't have the kick that Bria did. Boom. Second place. As she zeroed in on the finish line, she saw the girl in first place a few more yards ahead. She kicked it in hard, but it was no use. The girl had been first place all along, and she wasn't about to lose in the last twenty meters. Second place finish. Not bad, but she was so close to first that she could taste it.

Despite Bria's slight disappointment, her family,

and what looked like half the school, could not have been more excited. They came around the side, screaming and hollering, chanting her name, waiting for her to come under the other side of the orange tape that separated the spectators from the runners.

"You did it, girl!" Marisol called to her a minute or two later, when she finished. "I am *so* proud of you!"

"Yes!" Christa called, running toward her with open arms. As the rest of the girls surrounded her, the crowd parted again as the football players made their way toward her.

"Not bad, kid!" she heard Knox call to her. He, too, walked toward her with open arms, and she almost didn't know what to do. He picked her up and swung her around, but instead of putting her down, he popped her up onto one of his shoulders with absolutely no effort at all. The rest of the group surrounded them, chanting her name and congratulating her. She couldn't remember a time when she had felt so good. Not just because of her doting crowd of fans, but because he was the one holding her up.

As the meet drew to a close, Bria was packing her track bag when she felt an arm around her shoulder.

"Hey, freshie, some of the kids are celebrating at my house tonight," Knox said. "Come on by."

Bria looked up at Marisol.

"Christa and I are going," she said, "if you want a ride."

Bria nodded with a nervous smile.

"Sure, yeah," she said.

"Don't worry," Marisol said, "I'm not going to drink tonight, so I can drive you home, too."

It was clear that Bria had never been to a real party before; she wore baggy jeans and a t-shirt with her hair tied back in a pony. Marisol and Christa were dressed in short sundresses, their hair curled, and their makeup done perfectly. *Shit*, she thought, getting into the back of Mari's car.

"You ready for your first party, hon?" Mari asked, backing out of Bria's long driveway.

"Yeah, what did you tell your parents?" Christa asked, curling her eyelashes in the passenger overhead mirror.

"Uh… I just told them I was going to a party with you guys," she said.

"What? And they were cool with that?" Mari asked.

"Yeah, I guess they just. . . trust me. I don't know. My parents are kind of hippies. Not much worries them."

Christa and Mari laughed as they made their way down the back country Dalesville roads.

She had to admit, she was definitely nervous. She was okay talking to Knox when there wasn't a big crowd around, but she hadn't been around him yet when he was in his element, like Mari and Christa had told her about. She had no idea how to act around him.

It was obvious he liked being the center of attention. And it was even more obvious that he preferred that attention come from a female, or, better yet, multiple females. He was so charismatic and charming. But that was all the more reason for her to be cautious. She was trying to be painfully realistic. He was one of the most popular kids in school, and he was only a junior. She was a lanky freshman who hadn't quite grown into her knees. The girls he was actually interested in were older, and had boobs, and had experience. All things that she was still *very* much lacking.

She didn't want a guy like that, anyway. At least, that's what she was going to keep telling herself. But it didn't mean she couldn't revel in it when he did happen to notice her.

When they got to Knox's house, she was surprised at how few cars there were.

"It doesn't look like anybody's here," she said.

"Most people walk here since they'll be drinking,

or they get rides," Mari said.

Bria nodded. She had so many tricks to learn. As they walked up the front path, the front door burst open.

"Hey-ooooh!" Knox shouted, the smell of beer sliding off his breath. Mari laughed and shook her head.

"Hey, Knox," she said, letting him wrap a sloppy hug around her. He pulled Christa in for the same.

"Look who it is! The champion!" he called out, swooping in and picking Bria up with little-to-no effort, yet again. When he put her down, he pulled her head into his chest, stroking her hair gently. "I'm so proud of my little baby," he said, with a fake whimper. Again, with the baby, kid shit, but still, she could get used to all the touching. She giggled.

The party was surprisingly pretty tame. People were drinking, but they weren't belligerent. So *this* was a high school party. Some people were out on the patio, some were in the basement. Bria sat between Christa and Mari at a bar table in the corner of the room. Christa was telling Mari about how she had caught her boyfriend Tucker making out with another girl. While Bria was pretending to be enthralled in the drama, she also couldn't help but notice Courtney Blake, freshman star of the soccer team, all over Knox in the corner of her eye. Her legs were draped across his, and she kept resting her head on his shoulder, then popping it off to flick her long, bleach-blonde locks behind her shoulder, then rest it again.

Bria didn't know why she cared. She didn't know why it bothered her. But it was annoying as hell. Maybe it was because Courtney was her age. And Bria liked being the young one of the crowd. She felt like she was crossing some border into the world of upperclassmen that other underclassmen never got to cross. Except for Courtney. Courtney with the boobs she had since the sixth grade. As Bria regained focus on Christa's saga and rubbed her arm sympathetically, she saw Courtney and Knox stand up from the couch. He took her hand, and began leading her down the hallway to the guest bedroom.

Bye-bye, Knox, she thought, as an inexplicable wave of disappointment fell over her. As much as she told herself she didn't give a rat's ass, a small part of her wondered what was *actually* happening in that room. Of course, they were hooking up. But *how* was it happening? Was Knox making the first move? Was Courtney? How far were they going? What was it like? Honestly, she wasn't even sure if she knew what "hooking up" meant. Was it all the way? Half of the way? Regardless, it was all *way* past her level.

Ugh, come on, Bria. Get it together. She knew he was a player, and she wasn't even *close* to being in the game. Since she stepped foot in high school, she prided herself on being smarter and stronger than some of the other girls around her when it came to guys like this. She wouldn't fall victim to some sort of man-trap in high school. But, to be fair, she had never really had to put her man-fighting skills to use yet. Guys weren't exactly lining up to get a glimpse of her knobby knees and sixth-grade-boy body.

After a few more minutes, she was ready to go. The Sprite in her red cup was flat, and frankly, so were most of the conversations going on around her. But Christa and Mari seemed to be having a decent enough time, and weren't ready to go. Bria excused herself and headed out to the back patio, if for nothing more than to enjoy the quiet. Most people were leaving by now, so she sat quietly by herself, playing Tetris on her flip-phone, looking off into the woods. The back door slid open, and to her surprise, Knox himself stepped out.

"Oh, hey," he said. None of his usual pet names, probably still in his post-coitus haze.

"Hey," she said, trying to stay casual. *That was quick*, she thought.

"What are you doing out here all by your lonesome?" he said, situating himself in the chair next to her.

"Ah, just enjoying the fire. It's a nice night," she said.

"Yeah, it is."

Ha. It was a nice night for him for a totally different reason. Bria wasn't sure what had made her so bold, but she was, and so she asked, "Where's Courtney?"

His eyes grew wide. He wasn't expecting to get called out by the little freshman. Well, the *other* little freshman.

"Uh, I think she's uh inside, getting ready to leave," he said, trying to hide a sly smile in the corner of his mouth. Bria couldn't help but smile back.

"Guess you caught me," Knox said.

"Guess so," she laughed.

"You sure don't seem like a freshman," he said.

"But I guess Courtney does?" she asked. Of course she did. That's why it was so easy for him to get into her pants. He shrugged. "Well, you don't seem like the player everyone talks about, but here you are, unzipped fly and all."

He quickly looked down at his crotch, then back to her when he realized she was joking. She had said it playfully, but she also wanted to let him know she was onto him. Not that he gave a shit, she thought, but still.

"Hey, hey now," he said, gently shoving her shoulder, "that's not nice."

She shrugged.

"The truth hurts, honey," she said. He looked at her, laughing again. It felt good to make him laugh.

"You're okay, Bria," he said.

She smiled. Approval from him felt good, and though she told herself it shouldn't matter, it totally did. She also couldn't help but notice that he seemed to have finally dropped the "kid" thing.

"Man, I'm starving," he said.

"Me, too, actually," she said. "I was just thinking that."

"I could use a Maggi's pizza," he said. Maggi's was the family-owned pizza shop up town. They were the only place open past 9 p.m., when the rest of the town shut down.

"Yum, that sounds good."

"Let's go," he said, popping up from the chair. She looked at him quizzically.

"Can you drive?" she asked. He chuckled.

"Yeah. I only had one beer, and it was about five hours ago. I don't drink as much when parties are at my house. I like to keep my eye on everyone else."

Bria nodded. So the whole loud, drunken Knox was just an act. Interesting.

"In that case, yeah!" She followed him around the side of the house to the driveway. He unlocked the driver side door, then reached over and unlocked her door from the inside. His red Chevy sedan was probably older than she was. There was a dent in the bumper, and the passenger seat belt had to be yanked with extreme force in order to click. But she didn't care. She liked being in his car. As he backed out of the driveway, her favorite T-Pain song came on the radio. Without thinking, she reached to turn it up, but she caught herself. This wasn't her car, or her radio.

"No, go ahead," he said. "This is my favorite song."

THREE

Now

As Knox made his way toward Bria and Drew, she remembered the last time she had seen him. She had come home one weekend during her sophomore year at Maryland. As she was walking into Maggi's to pick up her pizza, he was walking out. His eyes had grown wide, and he had wrapped his arms tightly around her. But he didn't hold on as long as he used to. They caught up for a few moments, and she was quick to mention Drew. And then he gave her a quick smile, told her it was great to see her, and he was gone. She had tried getting back in touch with him after that, texting him occasionally, even calling when she was home on weekends. But Knox replied less and less frequently. And it got to the point where Bria forgot to even try.

Five years. *It had been almost five years.*

Her heart raced faster with every step he took toward her.

He didn't sound as excited as she had hoped, but when she finally got her arms around him, she felt how tight he squeezed her, even lifting her an inch or two off the ground. He still smelled exactly the same. His own musky scent mixed with whatever shampoo he had in the house. She remembered when it used to be her favorite scent, and she was surprised how it knocked her back about ten years with the first sniff.

"Knox!" she said, once he put her back down. "My God, how are you?" She could feel their eyes lingering just a little too long on each other; she could feel Drew's confused eyes move from her, to Knox, back to her, trying to figure out what was going on. She reached for Drew's hand. "Honey, this is Knox, my friend from high school."

Drew's baby blue eyes widened. He knew the name. When he and Bria first got together, she talked about Knox a lot. But that dissipated as their relationship blossomed, and Drew figured Bria's friendship with Knox had just fizzled out.

"And Knox, this is Drew, my fiancé," she said, stumbling over the last word a bit. Knox smiled with his lips, but his eyes didn't follow. He turned to Drew.

"Hey, man, it's nice to meet you," he said, sticking out his hand. Drew took it, hesitantly.

"Yeah, you too," he said.

"Congratulations! I thought I heard you were engaged," Knox said. "When's the wedding?"

"This coming April," Drew said, in such an unenthused tone that she was actually embarrassed.

"Awesome, that's. . .that's great, you two," Knox said. "Well, I'm going to go catch up with these guys," he said, jutting his thumb back toward the bar, "but it was great running into you." He said it to both of them, but he looked only at her.

"You, too, Knox, really," Bria said, suddenly overcome by a wave of inexplicable sadness. She instinctively reached for his hand, but stopped herself. She didn't know him like that anymore. And Drew was sitting right there.

As Drew pulled cash from his wallet and laid it on the table, she casually glanced around the restaurant to see if she could catch one more glimpse of Knox. As they made their way to the door, she saw him laughing hysterically, his hand on Teddy Bill's shoulder as he told whatever story had the whole place so enthralled. She loved Knox's laugh. And she loved when she was the source of it. Man, it had been so long. If it were a few years earlier, she would have run to them, jumping on Teddy with a big old hug. But now, she felt like she needed to duck out as fast as possible, before she got sucked back into the Dalesville High School time warp.

"Look, we weren't done talking before your buddy there walked in," Drew said, unlocking the car once they got to the parking lot.

"Oh, Jesus, Drew," she said, rolling her eyes. "Please just drop it. At least for tonight."

"Fine," he said. "But we need to talk about it. I mean, I hate to think this way, but what if she's not better in a few months, B? What do we do then? Just get married and live thirty miles apart?"

She sighed as she pressed her temple against the cool glass of the window. He was right. And *damn,* she hated that so much. But she couldn't think about it. She couldn't think about her sister not getting better. Katie would be fine in a few months. He'd see.

That night, as he dropped her off, he pulled her in close to him.

"B, I'm just . . .I'm just going to miss you, okay? I understand they need you here. I just don't want you to forget that I need you, too." He looked down at the ground, his arms around her waist as they stood in the driveway. She cupped his face in her hands.

"Drew, you know I don't want to be away from you, right?" she asked. "I've been waiting so long to be your wife. I *love* my life with you, you know that. But I have to be here right now. Just let me get them through this, and I'll be back in the city before we know it. I love you."

"You know, Bria Kreery, your family, me, anyone who knows you, really, we are all so damn lucky to have you in our lives. I'm sorry for how I reacted. I guess this just feels like. . . I don't know, like a step backward for us, I guess. But I understand. I love you, too. I'll call you when I get home."

The week off before starting her new position couldn't have come at a better time. That Monday, she'd been able to go back to their apartment and grab things, only the necessities though, since she'd be back in D.C. on Friday.

Tuesday, she'd slept in and gone for a long run on her favorite path, the one that cut through all of Dalesville, and spent the rest of the day lounging around and watching movies with Katie.

The next morning, as she flipped an omelet in its pan, her mother almost jumped with excitement.

"Oh B, I forgot to ask you! Did you know that Dalesville has a home meet today? I think it's the regional qualifying meet," her mom said. "We should all go, for old time's sake!"

Bria hadn't been to a cross country meet since she last ran in one. She still held records at Dalesville High, or at least, that's what Katie had told her the year before she graduated.

"Coach Boone is still there," Katie said.

"Coach Boone? I haven't seen that man in *years*. Let's do it!" Bria said.

Later that afternoon, as Bria and her mom walked down to the fields behind the school where the cross country course was set up, Bria spotted her old coach. Without hesitating, she ran to him, jumping into his arms.

"Well if it isn't miss B Kreery!" he said, his hearty laugh making his belly jiggle. His hair had a few traces of gray in it, and his face a few more wrinkles. But overall, he was the same old coach. She hadn't seen him in a long time, but they'd kept in touch through the years.

"Hey, old man! I can't believe you're still doing this!" she said.

"Hey, hey, watch that 'old man' stuff. But you know it. They can't get rid of me," he chuckled. "What are you doing here in the middle of the week?" he asked.

Her eyes darted toward the ground. "I'm, ah, back for a little while." Coach Boone raised an eyebrow at her.

"Oh? And why is that?" he asked.

"It's my sister," she said.

"Ah," he said. "Sis is sick again, huh?"

Bria nodded. Coach Boone's deep gray eyes were filled with sadness now, and she couldn't stand that. She hated the pity. And she knew Katie did, too.

"Yep, so I'm living at home for a while, helping my family out some," she explained.

"Well, that girl's as tough as they come," Coach Boone answered, nodding his head as if agreeing with himself. "Don't worry. She'll be fine. But say, if you're gonna be around for a while, you should help me out! I could use an assistant!"

Bria pictured herself running through the fields again.

"I'll think about it," she said with a smile.

"That's fine, but since you're here today," he said, tossing her a stopwatch, "catch their mile times, would ya?"

Bria laughed and shook her head. He got her.

When the gun finally went off, she made her way to the other side of the course, so she could record the runners' times.

"How are they this year?" she heard a silky, familiar voice say. It was Knox. He caught her totally off guard.

"H-hey! Uh, I'm not sure, I just got here, but I

think both the girls and guys have a good shot at states if they can get through this race," she said, fumbling with the stopwatch. "What are you doing here?"

"Grady told me his sister's on the team?"

"Oh, gotcha," she said. Grady was one of Knox's best friends from high school. "That's nice of you to come out and support her."

"Yeah, well, you know. I'm a nice guy," he said with his sly, dangerous smile. He looked down at the ground and kicked a pebble. "I also ran into your mom yesterday, and she said you might be here."

Bria looked up at him. Did he really come to see her, too? Probably not, she told herself. She had tried to stay in touch with him. He was the one who had made that so difficult, after all. He would have come anyway, she was sure.

"I haven't been to one of these since I used to come watch you all the time," he added, making Bria's cheeks flush. She used to love hearing him cheer for her as she pushed up a tough hill, and running into his arms after she crushed a race.

"Hey, honey!" she heard her mom call from across the path. "Oh, oh my gosh! Is that Ben Knoxville I see? Twice in one week; how lucky am I?"

He laughed, jogging across the path to her. "Hey, Mrs. K!" he said, bending down to give her one of his famous bear hugs.

"We didn't get to catch up much, the other day," her mother said. "Tell me what you're up to!"

Bria smiled as she watched them catch up, and eavesdropped as she heard Knox say he was teaching at a middle school just outside of town. He had heard a job was opening up at Dalesville the following school year, though, and he was thinking about applying. Bria smiled to herself. It took him a few tries to figure out where he wanted to be in his life, but he had made it. And she was proud of him. She was pretty sure he would be the most fun teacher ever. And she was also pretty sure he was the heartthrob of the school.

Geez, if he ended up at Dalesville High, he would be the new Mr. Thorn, the insanely hot physics teacher that everyone, including Bria, drooled over in high school. Oh, Mr. Thorn. He had been the subject of many of her teenage fantasies—like the one where she accidentally got locked in the science closet with him. She almost laughed out loud, thinking about the desperate, totally fictional situations she had drummed up as a hormonal teenager. But for half-a-second, she pictured herself back in that storage closet. Only, this time, the teacher was Knox.

Nope. *Nope, nope, nope.*

Just then, she felt her phone vibrating in her pocket, and she jumped as if she had been caught.

"Hey, babe," she said, quietly, stepping a little further away from her mother and Knox.

"Hey. I got off early today," he said, "so I was thinking maybe you could come home for the rest of the day? We could order in, spend the rest of the day naked." Bria giggled quietly.

"That sounds nice," she said, "but I sort of already promised Katie that I'd hang out with her tonight. You know she's so lonely, and I—"

"Oh, okay. I get it. You two enjoy your night." But it wasn't a sweet sentiment. This was a sarcastic, whiny, "pay-attention-to-me" comment. She didn't turn down sex a lot, and it was definitely something that got to him when she did.

"Seriously? You're not actually mad that I'm spending time with my sick sister, are you?"

"I said I got it. Do what you have to do." Ugh. She hated when he played that passive-aggressive shit. She was *not* here for it.

"Can you please act like a grown-up? It's not like I left and am never coming back. And I've only been gone for a few days." She was trying to keep quiet, but she could feel pissed-off Bria rising to the top.

"Whatever, Bria. I'll just talk to you later." As her fingers fumbled to dramatically press the "end" button, she looked up to see Knox coming closer.

Oh, God, Knox. She had forgotten for a brief moment that he was there. She wondered how much he heard. She used to go to him whenever she and one of her boyfriends argued. Knox was Bria's shoulder to lean on, the subject of her boyfriends' jealousy. But now, she didn't know if she wanted Knox in on the secret that she wasn't living a life of pure bliss. She wasn't sure if she wanted to be vulnerable with him anymore. She looked down as he made his way toward her.

"Hey," he said. She looked up at him. "Jimmie Cone?"

Even if she was embarrassed, there was nothing that could stop the huge smile from taking over her face.

"Jimmie Cone," she said.

FOUR

Then, Summer Before Sophomore Year

Her phone buzzed on her bed as she dug through her dresser, trying to find just *one* clean pair of socks. Bria had come to learn that being a runner meant a permanent shortage of socks. Finally, jackpot. She sprang to her phone.

"Hey, sorry! I'll be down in a sec," she said, hanging up as quickly as she had answered. "Mom, dad, Knox is here, we're going to Jimmie Cone."

"Okay, hon, see you later," her dad called.

"Careful," echoed her mom.

Her parents were so laid-back, she could probably kill someone and they wouldn't even bat an eye. Okay, maybe not *that* laid back, but still. She never got into much trouble, so they never really had a reason to impose any rules. She came home early enough on her own account, got straight A's, and kept generally good company. She had never had a boyfriend, or even gone on a real date, so they hadn't really had to worry about her getting knocked up, or dealing with heartbreak.

It had been almost a year since she first went to Knox's party, and since then, they had rarely gone a week without hanging out. They drove around town together in his car, grabbed food during lunch, and even ran together when Mari or Christa wasn't available. Although, Knox bitched about it pretty much the entire time. But to Bria, that just showed that he wanted to spend time with her. He wanted to be around her enough that he was willing to struggle through the endless miles she put on his best basketball shoes.

But Knox was still Knox. There was a different girl almost every week. He was never alone, but she sometimes got the sense that he was lonely, like when he texted Bria late at night, just to talk. She was a few years younger than him, but he leaned on her a lot.

Their relationship definitely wasn't one-way, though. Bria depended on him for entertainment, and even though they were strictly platonic, she couldn't help but live for the feeling his attention gave her. So many times, she'd hear him call her name down a crowded hallway. He would hug her whenever he saw her, petting her hair, holding her close, making her underclassmen friends jealous, their jaws to the ground. Although she and Knox had spent a lot of their summer together—she suspected that his weekly callers were away on vacation somewhere—they hadn't seen each other in a few weeks because of their own vacations. She was excited to sit in his beat-up old car, listening to music so loud the windows shook. They'd stuff their faces with soft serve and she'd laugh at his endearing foolishness. As she walked out the back door and around the house, she could hear the bass in his car thumping.

"Hey, hey, baby cakes!" he said. He held his arms out as she ran to him, her usual full-on collision hug. It might have been a bit dramatic, but she really had missed him. He hesitated for a moment, holding her up in the air. When he did put her back down, she noticed he was looking at her longer than normal. She was tan, with more natural highlights in her hair, her freckles a little more prominent. But more than that, she knew she had. . . developed a bit this summer. She didn't feel as awkward in her own skin; clothes fit her better, she felt more like herself than she ever had. Maybe he had suddenly taken notice. For a second, she actually felt a little self-conscious, something she hadn't felt around him since the first time they met. She tucked her hair behind her ear and crossed her arms across her chest. He cleared his throat and looked over at the house.

Desperate to change the unspoken subject, she reached for the car door.

"Hold on there, killer. I can't come by without saying hi to the mama."

Bria smiled as she watched him walk to the back door, letting himself in. "Hi, sweetheart!" she could hear her mom calling from the house. Bria rolled her eyes to herself, but the smile didn't leave her face. What a suck-up.

They pulled into Jimmie Cone, and as expected, it was packed. Knox drove around to the backside, where the locals knew to park because it was way less crowded. As they walked up, Bria couldn't help but soak it all in. Walking there, next to him. Kids ran around the parking lot, families and circles of teenagers huddled around the wooden picnic tables on either side of the ordering window, the big ice cream cone glowed bright in neon lights on the Jimmie Cone sign that hung over the awning. The air was still warm, but as the sun was going down, she felt a little shiver. Before the chills even popped up on her skin, Knox had pulled his sweatshirt off over his head.

"Here," he said. Just as she reached for it, she heard a screech from across the parking lot. Ugh. Courtney. Bria quickly pulled the hoodie on over her head, as if Courtney was going to try and steal it, claiming Knox as her own.

"Knox!" Courtney cried, running across the

parking lot, diving into his arms, practically knocking her out of the way. So dramatic. That was only okay when Bria did it.

Of course, right behind Courtney was her band of followers, just as expected. And Knox had his moment with all of them. Laughing, smiling, letting his arms dangle around their shoulders just a *little* too long. This wasn't exactly the reunion she had pictured. She sighed. This was pretty typical. As she let him dwell in his ultra-feminine circle, she walked under the awning, getting in line. She'd be damned if she wasn't getting her ice cream. That was the thing about Bria. She didn't *need* his attention like a lot of the other girls in his life did. She liked it, yes. But she wasn't afraid to walk away from him. She supposed that that was why he kept coming around. She didn't need him to fawn over her; she was low-maintenance.

She stood in the extra-long line, tapping her foot while she squinted to see the menu that hung over the ordering window. She didn't know why she even bothered; it wasn't like she was going to get anything other than a chocolate-and-vanilla swirl with rainbow jimmies. But, she looked anyways.

"Damn, speedy, need glasses?" she heard a voice say. She turned to see Brett Balkner, the quarterback, standing unusually close to her in line.

"Hey, Brett," she said, a little weirded out. She was pretty positive that they had never spoken before. With her running success, she had become somewhat famous around school, so she guessed that's how he knew who she was. But all the millions of times she had walked by him in the hall, he never batted an eye. Guess it was the new hips and boobs that Knox had so awkwardly noticed earlier. Thanks a lot, puberty.

"How has your summer been?"

"Oh, good, ya know. Just got back from the beach last weekend," she said, nervously tucking her hair behind her ear.

"Oh, nice. Running a lot, I'm sure," he said.

"You know it," she chuckled. Finally she was at the window. "Can I get a small swirl with rainbow jimmies, please?" She rummaged through her bag, grabbing her wallet, but Brett stuck out his hand.

"And I'll take a chocolate shake," he said. "Both of these are together."

"Oh no, you don't have to—"

"Nonsense," he said, "gotta get the State Champ's ice cream."

"Runner up," she said, laughing. "Thank you." Brett's name was the one you heard all over town; he was a Dalesville celebrity in his own right. The younger kids in town would make t-shirts with his name and number on the back, and even the other parents swooned over him. After a few moments, their ice cream was ready.

"You wanna sit down?" Brett asked, pointing to an empty table. She looked around the parking lot for Knox. There he was, still surrounded, flocks of girls still hanging off his neck.

"Sure," she said, still a little skeptical. Guys didn't just buy her ice cream and ask her to sit with them. This never happened.

"How did you get up here, anyways?"

"Oh, I came with Knox," she said, eyeing the group across the lot.

"Ah, good ol' Knox," Brett said with a chuckle. "Never without a female companion. Although, I don't really get why he's wasting his time with them, when he came with you."

She looked up at him in between licks of her cone. Brett was dangerously good-looking. His dark, curly hair was trimmed tight to his head, and his tan skin glowed, even in the dark. He wore a tight t-shirt that did wonders for his football muscles, unlike the baggy shirts Knox usually wore. He wore bright white sneakers, and smelled like some sort of expensive cologne. He was delicious.

"Ooh, nah. We're not like that," she said, looking across the parking lot again. "He's just my best friend."

"Well," Brett said, moving in a little closer to her, "that's lucky for me, then, I guess."

Bria smirked a little—he was laying it on thick, but she didn't mind—then she scooted even closer to him.

"Yeah, I guess so," she said.

She wasn't doing her due diligence with the licking of her cone, and hardly noticed when a drip of her melted ice cream landed on her sweatshirt.

"Oops," Brett said, pointing to it.

"Ah, it's okay. It's Knox's anyways," she said, and they both laughed. With that, she took the hoodie off, setting it down on the bench next to her.

An hour or so passed, and she still sat at the wooden table with Brett, listening to stories about his summer, and all the colleges he had visited up and down the East Coast. He asked her about her summer, her parents, her younger sisters, how running was going. It wasn't until Knox showed up in front of them that she noticed Brett's arm around her shoulder.

"Hey, you ready?" he asked. "Hey, Brett, what's up?"

"Hey, man," Brett said. "Actually, Bria, I can take you home, if you want?"

She looked back at Knox. The smug look on his face told her he was expecting Bria to reject Brett's offer; he was expecting her to hop up and run to his beat-up old Chevy. Now that his fan club had dissipated, it was Bria's turn again. But for some reason, she didn't feel like popping up tonight. Not when she had the quarterback draped around her, his cologne getting into her hair. And not when Knox had stood her up for an hour.

"Yeah, that sounds great," she said. "I'll see you later?" Knox tilted his head back slightly, his eyebrows raising in surprise, and nodded slowly.

"Alright, see you later, baby cakes," he said.

"Peace, Brett."

For just one second, Bria felt a pang of guilt watching Knox walk across the parking lot by himself.

"'Baby cakes?'" Brett asked, as Knox walked to his car, swinging his keys from his lanyard.

"He always calls me that," she said. After a few more minutes, Brett walked her to his car, the brand-new Camaro his parents bought him after he received his first college offer. When they pulled up into her driveway, he cut the engine off.

"Well, this was really fun," he said. "I'm really glad I ran into you."

"Yeah, me too!" she said, feeling her palms begin to sweat. Holy shit. Was she about to have her first kiss? Jesus. What was she supposed to do? Lean in, or let him come in all the way? Or maybe nothing. But before her thoughts could make her head explode, he leaned over, cupping her cheek in his hand. He laid the most gentle kiss on her lips, no tongue, no intense face-smushing, just a perfect, innocent, just-long-enough kiss. The kind that makes your stomach flip over completely. For a moment, she forgot to open her eyes.

"Sorry," he said, "but I've been wanting to do that all night."

"Don't be sorry," she said. "I'm glad you did."

"Look, can I, uh, can I take you out sometime soon? Like, really take you out, not just run into you at Jimmie Cone?" he asked. She giggled.

"Yeah, I'd really like that."

As she walked into the house, Bria could still smell Brett's cologne lingering in her hair. She said goodnight to her mom and dad and walked up to her room in a haze, falling softly into her bed. *Buzz*. She rolled over toward her phone.

Did Balkner get u home? The text said. It was Knox. She rolled her eyes.

Yep, safe and sound. Instantly, he responded.

Good. Sry about tonite. Hadn't seen them in a while. Hang tmrw?

She paused for a moment. Never had he apologized for letting her disappear. Never had he even seemed to notice that he had forgotten about her. Until now, coincidentally, when someone *else* noticed her.

No worries. Not sure. Might be going out with Brett, she typed, feeling inexplicably triumphant.

She waited patiently for a text back, but nothing. Shit. Was he mad? Did she hurt his feelings? But as she closed her eyes and replayed her kiss over, and over again, she forgot to care.

FIVE
Now

"Thanks," Knox said, reaching through the window and grabbing two chocolate-and-vanilla swirls from the teenage kid who was working. He licked one, and handed her the other. In their younger days, he would lick one, go to hand her the other, but sneak a lick of hers first. She'd roll her eyes and shove him, pretending to be grossed out. But secretly, she had liked the idea of her tongue having been somewhere that his had. It was only an ice cream cone, but there was something sweet about sharing it, intimate, almost.

"Thank you," she said, quickly licking the sides before the ice cream dripped down to her hand.

"So, how are *things?"* he asked with a sly smile as they made their way toward one of the old wooden picnic tables in the parking lot.

"If by *things,* you mean my fiancé," she said, choosing her words carefully, "things are going well."

"Uh-huh," Knox said, his voice weighted with skepticism. Bria felt her defenses going up.

"No, despite what you may have heard today, things are fine. Really. He treats me great. We're looking into rowhomes in the city soon, and the wedding planning is all coming along wonderfully."

"Well, that's great," he said, popping the last piece of the cone into his mouth, and she couldn't help but let her eyes linger on his lips just a little too long. She used to love running to Knox with any relationship issue she was having. She knew anything she said would never get any further than the two of them. And he never really offered great advice, but he listened, something that her other friends tended not to do.

"How about with you?" she asked, cheekily. "How are the ladies in your life?"

He shot her a look, and cracked that half-smile she had loved so much.

"Ah, you know, some here, some there. I'm sort of seeing this one girl, but it's nothing serious," he said, clapping his hands together to dust off the crumbs. She smiled. Same old Knox. She knew he probably still had his fair share of hookups. But something inside her was selfishly happy that he still didn't have anyone steady in his life, and she wasn't quite sure why.

"Sounds like the Knox I know," she said, smiling.

"Mhmm," he said. "So, if things are going so well, why are you home in the middle of the week?" he asked. She looked down at the ground. Knox was the only friend who knew all the intimate details about Katie's illness, and her family's financial struggles. And even though so many years had passed, she still didn't feel like she could lie to him. "Oh, no. Is it Katie?"

Whoa. He knew. She couldn't believe he had figured it out so easily. She nodded, looking up at him.

"Is it bad?" He leaned back against the table as she told him the situation—Katie's symptoms returning, the treatment she needed, Bria's decision to move home to help with the finances.

"I'm so sorry, B," he said, gently brushing her hand with his, sending some sort of weird jolt through her body. "Tell the family that if there's anything I can do, I'm always around."

As they walked back to his car, she smiled as she got in. He had a shiny new Malibu. A definite step up from the beat-up old cars she'd ridden in as a teen.

"Much different than good Old Red, or your dad's old pick-up," she said with a smile.

"Yeah," he chuckled. "Lots of memories in those cars."

As they started down Main Street, turning onto the backroads, Bria heard an old T-Pain song—one of their favorite jams in high school—come on the radio. She instinctively reached for the dial, but stopped herself.

"No, go ahead. I love this song," he said. She smiled and turned it up full blast. As the music reached her soul, she put her window down and stuck her arm outside, waving it along to the beat. Something came over her; maybe it was the warm August sunshine, or maybe it was being Knox's passenger again. But she suddenly felt light as a feather, carefree. She stuck her head out the window, belting out the words, as tone-deaf as ever. She stopped when she heard a familiar, beautiful sound: Knox's laugh.

"If you're gonna put on one of your famous performances, you might as well do it right," he said, reaching up to open the sunroof. She unbuckled and stood up, letting the wind whisk her hair all over the place. As the song ended, she slumped back down into the seat, laughing hysterically.

"Some things never change," he said with a grin.

They pulled up to her family's house a few short minutes later. The screen door burst open, Buster running and jumping on him, lapping him with the most disgusting, wet kisses. Bria's heart warmed; it was almost like the dog remembered Knox, even in his old age. Knox dropped to his knees, letting Buster maul him with love. A half-a-second later, Katie burst through the door, sprinting off the porch toward them.

"Holy shit!" Knox said, standing up and opening his arms. Katie jumped into them from what seemed like fifty yards away, but he caught her with no problem, swinging her in circles before placing her back down to get a look at her.

"You are so *old!*" he said. She laughed.

"We miss you around here!" Katie said. "Just because *she* ran off to the city doesn't mean you can't still come around, ya know."

Knox's eyes flashed to Bria, then back to Katie.

"That's true. I'm so sorry I've been gone for so long, my dear," he said, pulling her head into his chest for another hug. "You know, you and Sam were always the real reasons I hung around here, anyways."

Katie giggled while Bria playfully rolled her eyes.

"Whatever, you two," Bria said, walking toward the house.

"Me and mom are getting ready to start *Dirty Dancing,*" Katie said. "You coming?"

"Yeah, I'll be right in," Bria said. Knox smiled.

"Is there ever a time when that movie is *not* on in this house?" he asked.

Bria smiled and felt her cheeks blush. She wasn't sure why, but each time he brought up something about their past, about their history, it made her stomach do flips. It was like she had assumed he'd forgotten all about it, but with each little quip, he reminded her that he remembered.

"Bye, Knox!" Katie called.

"Bye, Kates!" he said, calling after her. "Wow, she's so grown up. She looks okay, today."

"Yeah, today. Hopefully she has more good days than bad this time." They both stood in the driveway for a minute, both seemingly searching for something to say. "Well, thanks for tonight," Bria said, breaking the silence.

"Course," he said. They stood awkwardly for a moment before he looped an arm around her waist and pulled her in for a hug. She inhaled deeply as her cheek rubbed against his chest. Same old Knox. She let the hug last longer than she probably should have, but the truth was, she wasn't sure when she would see him again. It took her *years* to run into him this time, and who knew how much longer she'd have to wait now.

SIX

Then, Sophomore Year

She stood in the mirror for a little longer than usual, curling her eyelashes and blending her foundation. Tonight was the six-month anniversary of her first date with Brett, and he was taking her somewhere special. She felt her nerves welling inside of her, but she wasn't sure why. Okay, that's not exactly true. She knew why, and it was because of the words Marisol had said at practice that afternoon.

"You two are totally hooking up tonight." Bria almost spit out her water.

"Wha, what?"

"Oh, come on, B. You've been dating for six months, not including all that time you were talking beforehand. That's practically a decade in high school years. It's not like it won't be good," Christa said.

It became clear early on in their friendship that Christa was very much in tune with her sexuality. A few guys around school were in tune with it, too. Bria swallowed hard, and Mari could see the anxiety that was practically leaking from her pores.

"Calm down, B. If you want to do it, do it. If not, don't. He likes you. He will understand," she said. Sweet Mari. She literally had *all* the answers. She was like a walking guide to high school for Bria. Still, she couldn't help but wonder if what Christa said was true. Maybe Brett was expecting it.

Later that day, as Bria walked down the long hallway to the locker room, she almost didn't see Knox a few yards ahead of her. He didn't see her, either. Instead, his gaze was on something, someone else around the corner. Just then, Christa came out of a classroom. Just as Bria was about to call out to them, Knox wrapped his arms around Christa's waist, and pushed her up against the lockers. She wrapped her arms around his neck, and he went in for a long, hard kiss. There had to be tongue. It actually stopped Bria in her tracks. She knew Knox was kissing a new girl every week, on average. But Bria had never actually *seen* him in action until right now. She didn't know if she should pretend not to see them and turn back, or keep walking and act as if it didn't just blow her mind. She couldn't believe his next catch was Christa. Just as she made up her mind to turn the other way, Christa saw her.

"Hey, B!" Christa called. Damn. Spotted. She turned around.

"Hey, guys!" she said. Knox was wiping his mouth, his eyes down at the floor. "I didn't, uh, didn't know you two were. . ."

"Yep," Christa said, smiling up at Knox. "Looks like your boy can be tamed, after all."

Bria wasn't expecting it, but that sentence sent a blow to her heart. Maybe he wasn't just kissing Christa. Maybe there was more. She always knew there was a possibility of Knox actually entering a stable relationship. But she hadn't realized until now how much she didn't want that to happen.

"Well, I gotta get going. AP Chem test tomorrow," Christa said, standing on her tip-toes to kiss him one more time. Bria looked away.

"What are you up to tonight?" Knox asked her as he pulled his backpack up over one shoulder.

"Brett's taking me out. It's our six-month anniversary," she said, matter-of-factly.

"Oh, wow. Guess you two are pretty serious, hey baby cakes?" he said.

"You sure you want to call me that? I'm not sure if your girlfriend would appreciate it."

Knox turned around to face her, so that he was walking backwards in front of her.

"She's not my girlfriend. And you are *always* my baby cakes." He didn't say goodbye, he just turned around and walked away.

Bria heard the knock on her front door as she ran her fingers through her hair just one more time. Katie answered it, excited as always that the town heartthrob was at her door.

"Hey, Brett!" she said.

"Hey, little one. This is for you," he said, handing Katie a single rose. Ugh. Brett was always so cute with her. Bria felt her heart pounding in her chest. She made her way down the stairs.

"Hey, you," Brett said, reaching for her hand, and handing her a bouquet of roses. "Happy six months." She could feel her cheeks flush.

"Hey, yourself. These are so pretty! Sam, can you put this in a vase with some water for me? Mom, dad, we're heading out!"

Ever since she had started dating Brett, she found herself in a hurry to get out of her house. She couldn't bear watching her parents engage Brett in some sort of painful small talk.

Dinner was awesome. He took her to Regal's, the only high-end place in town. They splurged, ordering appetizers *and* dessert—he was on a high school budget, after all, but it was a special occasion. They held hands practically the whole night, and when they got back in the car after their meal, he turned toward her. He leaned in for a long, drawn out, soul-zapping kiss. She returned the favor. Suddenly, she couldn't stop her fingers from running through his hair. She couldn't stop her chest from pushing against his.

"Do you wanna get in the back?" he whispered, in between soft kisses of her neck. She paused. Damn, Christa was right. Bria had to admit, she was curious. But right here, finally in the moment, she realized that she was also one-hundred-percent not ready. No way. She had just recently become comfortable with his hands slipping under her shirt when they made out. She couldn't imagine taking such a grown-up, permanent step right now, when it took her this long to get to second base.

"Uh, I. . .um," she stuttered. He stopped kissing her and pulled back.

"What? What is it?" he asked.

"I just, I don't feel fully. . .ready," she murmured. He sat back in his seat for a moment, likely fighting off the worst case of blue balls he had ever had.

"Okay," he said. "That's cool. Whenever you're ready."

She could tell he wasn't happy, but he wouldn't dare verbalize it. As she let out a silent sigh of relief, an overwhelming feeling of doubt came over her. She wasn't sure that she'd actually ever feel ready with Brett. And she didn't know why.

The ride home was quiet. She turned the radio up a few times, but each time, he turned it down after only a second or two. She asked how practice had been going, and if they were ready for the big game next weekend. One-word answers were all she could seem to pull from him. She guessed his ego was bruised pretty badly at this point. They turned onto Main Street, riding through the busiest intersection in town. Christa's house sat on the corner. As they pulled up, a car pulled out of her driveway, right in front of them. She'd recognize that old beat-up bumper anywhere.

"Hey, that's Knox," she said.

"So it is," Brett said, still seething about his poor blue balls.

"Honk," she said.

"What? No."

She sat back in her seat. He was clearly not in a playful mood tonight. Although, he rarely was when it involved Knox. Pretty much every argument they had somehow involved him. Brett and Knox had been fine before Bria had begun dating him; they were actually friends. But soon after Brett had officially asked her out, something happened. Brett was no longer interested in being friends with Knox, and Bria knew that if Brett had his way, Bria wouldn't be friends with Knox, either.

"What's your deal with him, anyways?" Brett asked. Oh, for the love of God. The blue balls had now gone to his head.

"What?"

"You just. . . I don't know. You just care about him, a lot."

Bria thought about it. Yeah, she did. And until she had a boyfriend, it had never been a problem. Just as she was about to rebut with her standard "you're my boyfriend, you're the one I care about" response, bright lights flashed in her eyes. A car came flying through the intersection, spinning once, then slamming into the passenger side of Knox's car. The beat-up old Chevy spun through the air before landing on its side in the middle of the intersection. She had never heard such a deafening sound as that of two cars slamming together, one going upwards of forty miles an hour. And time had never seemed to stand so still. All of a sudden, they could smell smoke. Orange flames began to spill out from the passenger side of Knox's car.

"Jesus," Brett muttered, his eyes wide. She swore her heart was beating so hard, she could actually hear it. She didn't even think; she just reacted. She sprung from the car, running into the intersection. Suddenly, she heard a shrieking scream. Christa ran from her driveway, stopping next to Brett's car, totally hysterical.

"Bria! Don't!" Brett cried. "You're gonna get hurt!"

But she didn't even hear him. Instead, she ran to the car, getting on her hands and knees at the sunroof. She knew that it never fully closed, despite the fact that it was winter. It had broken almost a year before, and he had never bothered to have it fixed. Bria reached her fingers through the small crack of the opening, and pulled as hard as she could. To her relief, it slid back. The asphalt tore at her knees, and the freezing winter air bit at her face. She looked inside. Knox was still in the seat, blood streaming from his head, his body slumped down over the steering wheel.

"Knox!" she called, but nothing. She could hear the sirens in the distance, but the flames were spreading. She reached inside, grabbing hold of his jacket and pulling. He moved the slightest bit, but he was too heavy. Just then, Brett reached in, grabbing onto his other arm.

"On the count of three," she said. He nodded. But before they could actually count, a burst of flames came dangerously close to Knox's side, and Brett jumped back.

"Whoa! Get out of there, Bria, we can't!"

Bria felt Brett grab her arms, but she instinctively shook him off. She put a foot on either side of the sunroof, looped her hands under Knox's arms, and pulled as hard as she could.

She managed to slide him out of the sunroof, his body limp on top of hers, and his clothes soaked with blood. She heard Brett yelling to the oncoming cars to halt, holding back traffic as she cradled Knox's head in her hands.

"Oh, Jesus, Knox!" she squealed, surveying the blood matting his hair. She tore off her sweater, rolling it into a ball and placing it on her lap as a makeshift pillow for him.

"Knox! Oh, Knox!" Christa cried, running to Bria and kneeling over him. Finally, the ambulance, and what looked like fifty police cars, arrived. The red and blue flashing lights against the black night sky were starting to make Bria dizzy. She let a paramedic take over caring for Knox, as her whole body began to shake. She was soaked in his blood, but she didn't care.

"Please, help him! Please!" Christa shouted, tears streaming down her face. Bria barely noticed Brett's jacket around her shoulders. Several paramedics stopped to see if she had been injured, too. No, Brett explained, it was all Knox's blood. Bria said nothing, she just stared ahead, watching an EMT do chest compressions on her best friend.

"We have a pulse! Let's get him in!" the EMT called. Bria stood at the ambulance doors as they slowly lifted the stretcher.

"Is anyone riding with him?" the driver asked.

"I will," Christa stepped in. Bria didn't even notice the tears streaming from her eyes. Everyone stopped when Knox moaned.

"B," he said. He opened one eye, and held out his hand toward her. "Stay."

Bria paused to look back at Christa and Brett. Both looked dumbfounded. She took Knox's hand and brushed his hair off his forehead. She turned to Brett.

"My phone is in my purse," she said. "Can you call his parents? Their home number is in my contacts."

Brett said nothing, he just nodded.

She climbed into the back of the ambulance as the paramedics rolled in the stretcher. And as Knox's eyes closed again, she covered her mouth to muffle the sobs she had been holding in.

SEVEN

Now

"Come on, kiddo," Bria said, putting her foot up on the kitchen island to tie her shoelaces. Katie trudged through the doorway with a sour look on her face.

"Ugh. I don't feel like it," she said, slamming her sneakers down on the ground. Her doctor had suggested weekly exercise, "especially when she didn't feel up to it." But it was a battle. Bria remembered this from the first time around. Katie was constantly in pain, and even when she wasn't, her energy levels were slug-like. But Bria and Sam had pushed her to go on brisk walks around the neighborhood, or to the path, or a short bike ride around town. To Katie's surprise, it had actually made her feel a little bit better. But today, she had just started treatment, and the first dose of her medication only added to her grogginess.

"Come on, you know you'll feel better after, okay? Here, I'll tie them for you."

The Kreery sisters rarely fought. Even Sam and

Bria, who were closer in age, didn't really fight, even as children. They were each other's best friends. Katie was Bria's baby, in her mind. They were seven years apart, and Bria had always taken to her like a second mother rather than an older sister. And Katie didn't seem to mind, for the most part.

They got in Bria's car and drove a few minutes to the path. The weather was still warm, despite the fact that autumn was now in full effect, so they were making the most of it.

Once they were on the shaded path, Katie's mood seemed to change immediately. She was laughing and joking, telling Bria about the boy she had met in her Biology 101 class. He had asked for her number so they could study together. But then, Katie explained with sadness in her eyes, she got sick and had to leave school. And Bria watched as Katie's brain went somewhere else. Probably thinking about the life she could have had, the life so many other people had, if it weren't for Tommy the tick.

Before they knew it, they reached the other end of the path, one-point-four miles down.

"Whoa, time to turn around already," Bria said.

"Thank God," Katie said, breathless, "I'm ready to call it quits."

Katie sat on a stump at the end of the path, taking a drink from her water bottle. Up ahead, the silhouette of a jogger approached them, growing larger each second. And as it got closer, Bria knew just who it was. She'd recognize that gait anywhere. It wasn't the gait of a runner. It was that of another type of athlete—like, a football player—who just happened to be running.

"Hey, ladies," Knox said, running his forearm across his dripping brow. He was shirtless in the summer-like heat, and Bria couldn't help but get a good look. He had clearly aged, with a few more freckles dotting his shoulders and a bit more hair across the top of his chest, but he still had most of the muscle definition of a high school running back.

"Hey, Knox!" Katie squealed happily.

"Hey," Bria said, "you're still running?"

"Yeah, I guess that's one of the things you got me stuck on," he said with a half-smile. "You still running?"

"Oh yeah, all the time," she said. They both paused for a moment, awkwardly looking down on the ground.

"You guys should go together, like you used to!" Katie said. She meant it innocently, but Bria was glad someone else said it, so that it didn't have to be her.

"Yeah, that would be cool," Knox said. "Well, I'm gonna head on back. See ya."

He turned around and began running back toward the trail head. Bria and Katie started back that way too, at a slower pace.

"How come you guys haven't hung out again since the other day?" Katie asked once Knox was out of earshot.

"I don't know, I mean, we're not that close anymore," Bria said, shrugging it off as if the same question hadn't been weighing on her too.

"That's sad. He was so fun," Katie said. They walked in silence for a bit, Bria soaking in Katie's words. About a quarter-mile from the car, Katie turned noticeably pale.

"You okay, kiddo?" Bria asked, rubbing her shoulder. Katie nodded. "Do you need to take a break?"

Katie shook her head, but stopped. She wobbled from side to side for a moment, and scurried off the path into the grass. She vomited forcefully as Bria held back her hair.

"Oh, man, Kates," Bria said, "let's get you home."

Poor kid. The medicines always messed with her stomach. She had lost a ton of weight as a kid because of it. They started walking again, but after only a few steps,

Katie stopped. She took a few steps forward, and a few back, before collapsing completely in Bria's arms, her eyes rolling back in her head.

"Katie! Katie!" Bria shouted. She panicked. There was no cell service in the woods, and of course, not a single walker, jogger, or bicyclist to be seen. "Help! Hello? Anyone around? Katie!" she cried, tapping her sister's cheeks lightly.

"B?" she heard him say, emerging from the trees like some sort of woodland animal. "What happened?" Bria had tears streaming down her face now.

"She just. . .passed out!" she cried, shakily holding her sister. Knox knelt down, gently scooping Katie out of her arms.

"You go run up ahead and call for help. I got her," he said calmly. She nodded and took off, staring at her phone, stopping to dial 911, then her mother, as soon as she saw she had a cell signal. She ran the rest of the way to her car and paced along the driver's side, gravel rocks crunching beneath her running shoes. Knox stepped out of the woods just as the ambulance was pulling up, with Louise's car right behind it. Katie was cradled in his arms, her head limp on his shoulder.

"Oh, Katie!" her mom gasped as she ran to them. She looked at Bria. "Your father is leaving work now. He's meeting us there."

Bria babbled, tears welling up in her eyes again, "I'm sorry, mom. I don't know—"

"I can bring Bria to the hospital, Mrs. K," Knox said, interrupting. She wasn't exactly in the state to drive.

"Thank you, Ben."

The drive was quiet. God dammit. Why did she push Katie to go for a walk? She said she was tired. Bria should have listened.

"I shouldn't have made her go for a walk," she finally said, barely above a whisper.

"Hey, you didn't know this was going to happen.

You were just trying to help her," Knox reassured her, reaching over to give her hand a quick, but firm squeeze.

When they got to the hospital, Katie had already been taken back to a doctor. Louise came out to the waiting room.

"They think it was just exhaustion, and a reaction to her medications," she said. "She's sleeping right now, and they are just waiting for the blood work. Her kidney function is a little questionable right now, so they want to look more into it." She paused. Louise was seasoned at memorizing a doctor's words and repeating them calmly. Bria wondered how her mother resisted the urge to panic, to break down. "Ben, thank you so much for your help today, sweetie. I'm so glad you were there." Louise gave him a hug before ducking back into Katie's room.

"I'm really glad you were there today, too," Bria said shyly, looking down at the ground.

"Me, too," Knox said. "I'm just glad I could help." Bria sighed and looked around, her racing heart finally starting to slow.

"Wow," Bria said, looking around the waiting room.

"What?"

"I just didn't even realize it when we first came in, but I haven't been back in this hospital since. . ."

"Oh, wow," Knox said. "Yeah, me either."

"I think even to this day, that was still one of the worst nights of my life," she said, this time looking him in the eye. He flashed a nervous smile, and looked down at the ground.

EIGHT

Then, In the Hospital

Bria sat in the waiting room alone, still in her bloody clothes. A few moments later, Mr. and Mrs. Knoxville burst through the emergency doors, with Louise and Joe not far behind. Just as Bria stood up, Mrs. Knoxville enveloped her in a tight hug.

"Oh, Bria. What are they saying? Where's my baby?" She stepped back, bracing herself for the facts.

"He's in the operating room right now, Mrs. Knox. He has a broken femur, and a fractured wrist. His head was bleeding, and they are checking for a concussion." Mrs. Knoxville gasped as Mr. Knoxville held her.

"Bria, we can't thank you enough," he said. "I'm so glad you were here tonight. You are his guardian angel."

The doctor walked out of the room, and pulled the Knoxvilles to a quieter nook in the hall. Out of the corner of her eye, Bria saw her mom slide in, looping her arm around Bria's waist.

"Honey, are you okay? It's going to be a while...

Why don't we head home? Dad will stay here in case Ben's parents need anything," Louise said, gently stroking her hair. Bria lay her head on her mother's shoulder.

"No, I want to see him first," she said. "I'm going to wait here."

Louise nodded, looking unsurprised by that answer.

"Okay, honey. I'm going to go get you some fresh clothes. I'll be back."

Bria sat in silence for a while, hating the drunk idiot who flew through a red light on a Thursday night. Hating the inebriated jackass that almost killed her friend. The cops had told Knox's parents that the driver had somehow escaped with a broken big toe and a scrape to his face. Bria drifted off into an exhausted, anger-induced sleep.

After four hours of half-sleep on a slopey, uncomfortable waiting room chair, Bria saw Knox's doctors reappear in front of his parents. He was still resting, groggy from the anesthesia, she heard them say. He needed stitches in his head, and staples in his leg. He had bad whiplash from the airbags, but miraculously, no burns.

"How can that be? Wasn't the car on fire?" Mr. Knoxville asked.

"Well, it seems he had a quick-acting friend on the scene who pulled him out before the flames reached the driver's side."

The Knoxvilles, and her own parents, turned to her.

"Oh, Bria," Mrs. Knoxville whispered, her lip quivering.

"Can we see him?" Bria asked.

"Yes, absolutely. Right this way."

Bria stood back, giving the Knoxvilles some time alone with their son. After twenty minutes or so, Mr. Knoxville appeared in the waiting room again.

"Hey, Bria? He's up. And he asked for you."

She stood up, her heart racing. Mrs. Knoxville

came around the corner.

"We're going to get some coffee. Go on in, sweetie."

Bria walked slowly to the door, taking a deep breath before she stepped inside. He lay perfectly still, eyes closed, looking surprisingly peaceful. The hospital gown was only on one arm, leaving part of his chest, and the broken arm exposed. She cringed at the sight of the stitches on his forehead, and his leg lie straight out in a white cast. She pulled the scratchy-cushioned side chair up close to his bedside, and gently placed her hand on his. The tears pricked the back of her eyes again, threatening to spill over any minute. He was a big boy, he could generally take care of himself. But right now, she wanted to cover him, protect him from everything.

"Hey, baby cakes," he said, his voice coarse and crackly.

"Hi," she said, wiping the tears quickly from her face. "Look, I know you were pissed at me for not hanging tonight, but this was a little extreme, don't you think?"

He smiled, letting out a small chuckle, and his eyes closed again. He opened his hand.

"Come here." Without hesitating, she did just what he said. Bria carefully climbed into the bed.

"I don't want to hurt you," she said, afraid to put all her weight on the bed.

"Pshh," he said, waving his cast in the air, "you could never hurt me. Besides, I'm on enough drugs right now that you could cut off my foot and I wouldn't even know."

She chuckled. But she couldn't hold a smile for long. She kept seeing him, slumped over the steering wheel, lifeless. She kept thinking about what she would be doing now if he hadn't woken up. God, what would have happened if she and Brett hadn't taken Main Street home?

She wasn't sure exactly what she had with Knox. But it had never crossed her mind that she could run out of time with him.

"Baby cakes," he whispered, opening his eyes. "B? Why are you crying? Please, no."

But she couldn't help it.

"B," he said, gently nudging her head with his shoulder. "I'm here. I'm all good, see?" he held up his casted foot and arm. He reached across and wiped her tear with his unbroken hand.

"I saw you in the car, and I thought you were dead," she said. He didn't say anything. He just stroked her hair.

"Bria Kreery," he said. "You can't get rid of me that easily." But he realized she wasn't in the mood for jokes anymore. "Hey, look at me."

She did what she was told, again.

"My parents, they said you pulled me out of the car?" She nodded. Suddenly, she wasn't the only one with tears in her eyes. "I don't know what I did to deserve you, but I hope I never screw it up."

A few hours later, Bria woke to someone gently shaking her foot.

"Sweetheart, we have to check Mr. Knoxville's vitals," the nurse whispered.

"Oh, yes, so sorry!" she said, jumping from the bed. Knox didn't budge. He was still sleeping off the night before. She was in such a frenzy trying to get out of his bed, that she almost didn't notice Brett in the corner of the room. She paused.

"Babe," she said. He just stared at her, then headed for the door. She followed him out.

"Well," he said, "Looks like you had a rough night."

She couldn't tell if he was being sympathetic or sarcastic.

"I'm so sorry I didn't call."

"Well, how could you? You left your phone in my car," he said, handing it back to her. "Did you sleep with him all night?"

She looked down at the ground. "I didn't sleep *with* him. We were just talking and we just fell asleep."

"Bria, you were practically on top of him when I came in here this morning."

Okay, now she was sort of pissed. Was he really picking right *now* to fight about this?

"Seriously, Bria, this is an issue. I get that you wanted to see if your friend was okay, but he is. He's gonna live. So it's time to take a step back from him. It's not fair to me."

Bria looked through the window slot on the door into Knox's room. He was awake now, holding up his unbroken arm for the nurse to slide on the blood pressure cuff. How dare Brett come here, and demand that she give up the truest friend she had ever had. How dare he come here, and give this ultimatum *today,* the day after she almost lost Knox.

"'Take a step back from him?' Who do you think you are? He almost *died,* last night, Brett. Don't ask me to choose," she said, looking him dead in the eye, "because it'll be him."

Brett's eyes opened wide. Now *he* was the one taking a step back.

"Wow," was all he said, before he turned and headed out the big brown doors. And if she was being honest, that was the last moment she felt anything for Brett, at all. She could say she was sad about the break-up, but she would be lying. After the overwhelming amount of pressure she felt with him the night before, and the shame she felt for not following through, this was actually a bit of a relief.

Later that day, Bria walked out into the hallway to raid the vending machine. She had picked at Knox's hospital food, but they had both agreed that Snickers bars, Doritos, and coffee would be a more well-rounded lunch. His parents were bringing them dinner later, but for now the vending machine would do. She had watched all day as kids from their school paraded in and out, bringing flowers and hugs—and dramatic tears from some of the girls who swooned over him. She rolled her eyes as Courtney Blake recounted her own tale of when she heard about the accident, wiping tears from her cheeks. "I can't believe we almost lost him," she had whined to her friends. Oh, for Pete's sake.

As Bria turned back toward Knox's room, she collided with Courtney, sending the snacks and coffee everywhere.

"Oh, sorry," Courtney muttered, quickly returning her eyes to her phone, without bothering to pick anything up.

"Hey," Bria heard someone say, "let me help you with that." He was tall and broad, with sand-colored hair, and big, dark eyes.

"Thanks," Bria said, taking the Snickers back from him.

"You're Knox's girl, right?" he asked. She shot him a look. She wasn't sure how to answer. "Sorry, I should have said. I'm Johnny Ridges."

Ah, she knew the name. He was the quarterback for the Centerville Eagles, their rival school. Johnny was the Brett of Centerville, his name was all over town.

"Oh, hey," she said. "I'm not his girl, but I'm here with him, yeah. He's my best friend."

"Well, I'm glad to hear he's doing better today. I came to drop these off," he said, holding up a stack of greeting cards. "We made them at school today."

"That's really nice of you," she said.

"Yeah, well, rival or not, he's a good guy." She looked toward Knox's door, feeling her stomach do a flip.

"Yeah. He is."

NINE

Now

After a few more tests, the doctors cleared Katie to go home. Fighting a sinking guilt, Bria waited on her for the rest of the week, bringing her treats and trashy magazines, and watching all of their favorite movies on repeat. She took her to her doctors' appointments and out to eat at all of her favorite restaurants. It had been nice, but Bria's week off was almost over. She'd be starting her new job the coming Monday, but for some reason, her excitement about the promotion had faded significantly.

As she got up to rinse out their ice cream bowls in between episodes of *Jane the Virgin,* her phone buzzed. Drew.

"Hey, babe," she said, holding the phone between her ear and her shoulder as she scrubbed.

"Hey, how's she doing today?" Drew asked.

"Much better. I think the chocolate ice cream is helping," she told him.

"Cool. Are you coming home for the weekend?" he asked. She was caught off-guard. It was Friday. Why wouldn't she be going home? After all, she hadn't seen her fiancé in almost a week. She thought quickly if there was any reason she would need to stay in Dalesville, but she had none.

At least, none that she could say out loud, especially to Drew.

"Yeah, definitely. I was going to leave around four to head back, so I'll get there around the same time you do."

"Perfect. Tara and Cody wanna go out to that new Indian place I told you about in Dupont," he said. Bria sighed to herself—she didn't really like Indian food.

"Great," she said, her voice dripping with phony enthusiasm.

"Okay, well, break's over. I'll see you in a few hours. Love you!" he said.

"Love you, too."

After she and Katie finished their TV binge, she got up to pack up a few things for the weekend.

"Where are you going?" Katie asked.

"I'm going to head home for the night," Bria called from Sam's bedroom, where she had been sleeping.

"Oh," Katie said. She could hear the disappointment in her sister's voice, even from three rooms away.

"I do need to see my fiancé *sometime,*" she said, lifting Katie's chin with her finger. "But I'll be back Sunday."

Just as Bria kissed Katie goodbye and headed to the screen door, Knox appeared on their front porch. She felt her heart pounding into the walls of her chest like a bowling ball.

"Hey," he said. He held a bouquet of roses, and a stuffed bear.

"Hey," she said, quizzically.

"Is Katie home?" he asked. She smiled.

"Kates," she called over her shoulder, "door's for you."

"Hey, Knox!" Katie cried, her mood instantly changed as she ran through the door for a hug.

"Hey, kiddo! So glad to see you feeling better. Last time I saw you, you weren't the most talkative," he said. "These are for you," he said, handing her the gifts.

"Thank you, so much!" Katie said, giving him another hug.

"Of course. You headed out?" Knox said, looking to Bria.

"Oh, uh, yeah, headed back to D.C. for the weekend," she said, lifting her bag up slightly. He nodded slowly.

"She remembered she's engaged and thought she should probably head back to see her fiancé every now and then," Katie giggled.

"Katie!" Bria said, in a shut-your-mouth kind of way.

"Yeah, don't wanna keep him waiting," Knox said, looking right at Bria. "Well, I gotta get going. . ."

"Are you sure? I was getting ready to watch *Impractical Jokers*, if you want to join." Katie said. He paused, one foot on the porch step.

"Well, I always have time for one episode of *Impractical Jokers*," he said, smiling as he stepped inside.

"You staying, B?" Katie asked. She wanted nothing more than to say yes. Just a half-hour. Just thirty minutes on the couch with her sister and Knox. Laughing and watching. She wanted to say yes so badly.

"No, I can't, I'm sorry," she said. "I'll see you Sunday. Bye, Knox."

"Bye, Bria."

Hearing him call her by her full name was still weird for her. It used to be "B," or "baby cakes." It had been a long time since she'd been called that.

She stepped off the porch and got in her car, and drove off to the city.

When she arrived back at the apartment, she

quickly dumped her shitty attitude at the door. Drew deserved more than a dull, pouty version of her. She stumbled through the door, her bag dropping to the floor.

"Hey, babe!" he said, floating across the floor to her. He grabbed her bag and pulled her in for a long kiss. She felt how much he missed her. She wrapped her arms around his neck.

"Reservations are in an hour. But we don't need to leave for another twenty minutes," he said with a sly grin. She smiled back at him. She really wasn't in the mood, but it had been over a week since she had seen him. Over a week since she slept with him. She pushed him away lightly, slipping her shirt off over her head, and letting her jeans fall to the ground. She let out a devilish laugh, and ran to the bedroom. He followed after her.

Sex with Drew had gotten pretty monotonous over the years, but it was still pleasurable. It wasn't every time that she lie there, staring up at the ceiling. Sure, she knew just what to expect: on her back, her on top, back to her back, and boom. Done. But, for the most part, it *was* good. If it ain't broke, don't fix it, right?

As they finished, he kissed her shoulder, her collar bone, the nape of her neck, and her other shoulder.

"I hate not seeing you every night," he whispered.

"Oh, honey, I hate it, too. Thank you so much for being so understanding," she whispered back, pulling him in for a long, naked hug. He laid on top of her for what felt like hours. As he lay, her mind wandered to *Impractical Jokers*. And she thought about how comfortable she was being naked around Drew now. And she wondered if she would be that comfortable being naked around Knox. Holy shit. She was thinking about Knox while she was lying *naked* underneath her *fiancé*. She felt her cheeks blush as she shooed the thought from her mind.

"You okay, babe?" Drew asked, clearly sensing something was on her mind.

"Huh? Oh, yeah, sorry."

"You worried about Katie?" he asked.

"Yeah, I guess so."

"I'm sure. I'm sorry, babe. She will be okay. I still can't believe you carried her out of the woods."

"Huh? I didn't carry her. Knox—"

"Knox?"

"Y-yeah, he happened to be running by, and thank God he was. He heard me screaming and found us. He carried her." Bria felt Drew's whole body tighten on top of her, then he quickly rolled off.

"I'm sorry, I thought I mentioned that," she said.

"No, you, uh, conveniently left that out."

"Drew. . ."

"Just forget it. We have to get ready."

That night at dinner, everything was fine. At least, the show they put on for Tara and Cody was fine. Drew held his arm around Bria her most of the night, and she fed him spicy cauliflower off of her fork. They laughed as Cody and Tara recounted stories of the worst apartments they had seen on their quest to buy property in the city—their standards were high, as they were already planning around the big law firm salary Tara would get once she finished law school the next year. Cody and Drew went way back. They had been friends since childhood, and went to all the same schools, even Georgetown for undergrad, where Cody met Tara.

"So, have you guys been house hunting lately? There's some really great stuff coming up on the market right now," Tara said, sipping her chardonnay.

"No, we're a bit. . .stalled, right now," Drew said, looking down at his plate.

"What do you mean?" Cody asked, his strawberry blonde hair shimmering in the dim restaurant light. Bria cleared her throat.

"My sister is sick," she said, taking a sip of her water. "She's been sick for years, but she recently got worse. She has to get IV treatment, so I'm actually living at home with my folks during the week, so I can help out during the evenings."

She didn't want to add in that she was footing half the bills in her parents' house. And she shot Drew a look that told him he better not mention it, either.

"Oh, wow," Tara said, eyes wide. "I'm so sorry to hear that."

"Yeah, that sucks. I can't believe you had to move back in with them," Cody said. She looked up at him.

"Yeah, I mean, it's not that bad, really. Aside from being away from Drew," Bria said.

"Yeah, but, like, you had to move back out of the city, into your shitty old farmtown, right? Come on, that sucks." Cody laughed as he sipped his beer.

"It's really not that bad." She was getting a little irritated now.

"Yeah, Bria's not minding it at all, are you, B?" Drew said. She shot him another look.

"You know that's not true," she said. "I just also don't mind being around my family. My sisters are my best friends. And it's good to see my parents more than a few times a month."

"Yeah, and Knox, right?" Drew asked. She was seething now. She could feel Tara and Cody's eyes scanning back and forth between her and Drew.

"Who's Knox?" Tara asked.

TEN

Then, Knox's Graduation

The months after the accident were a struggle for Knox. He was in physical therapy three times a week. The staples were out of his leg, but he was still in pain. He had to hobble around school, but on the bright side, Bria got to leave each class five minutes early to help him carry his books.

But it was more than just frustration with his injury, as Bria soon noticed. He couldn't drive, so he wasn't able to be as social as he was used to. And his doctors and physical therapists had rendered his football career over. After a few weeks, she noticed his mood changing. Then one day, when he still hadn't shown up at the front of school when the warning bell rang, she started to worry.

You coming to school?

Nah, not today.

Oh, okay. You alright?

No answer. The day seemed to drag on longer

than normal, and she couldn't wait for practice to finish up. And then three more days passed. She had texted him a few more times, calling him in between classes and after school. While she waited outside for her dad to drive up on the fourth day, she picked up her phone and dialed Knox again.

Still no answer.

"Hey, kiddo," her dad said, pulling up to the curb and putting the car in park. "How was practice?"

"It was good," she said, unfocused. Normally, she'd give him more of a thoughtful answer, but she was distracted. "Hey, dad, can you drop me of at Knox's? I was going to do homework there for a bit tonight."

"Sure."

When she got there, the driveway was empty, per usual. His parents worked a lot, and after all the time they had taken off right after the accident, she knew that they'd probably had to get back to their jobs by now. Bria walked around to the back of the house and let herself in the back door.

"Knox?" she asked. No answer. She expected the bedroom door to be locked, but to her surprise, the knob opened. She pushed the door open and saw him lying in his bed, facing the wall. He had on a hooded sweatshirt, and the covers pulled up around him. "Knox?" He stirred gently, and turned slightly to see her, his eyes squinted. "Are you okay?"

"What are you doing here?"

"You wouldn't answer me. I got worried."

"I'm fine. I just don't feel well." He rolled back over. She sat down next to him.

"Are you sick?" He shrugged. "Well, what's bothering you?" Shrugged again. "Knox?" He turned back over slowly to face her. "Please, tell me what's wrong. You're scaring me."

He closed his eyes, rubbing them with his fingers. After a few minutes of deafening silence, he finally sat up, and scooted next to her on the bed.

"I just. . .I don't feel. . ."

"Like yourself?" she asked, not wanting him to have to finish the sentence. He nodded slowly.

"I'm sick of being here. I'm sick of sitting around doing nothing. I'm sick of depending on my parents to bring me anywhere. And I'm also sick of . . ."

"Of what?"

"Of. . . of being alone." Her eyes widened. Why didn't she come earlier? She squeezed his hand in hers, fighting back tears.

"Knox, I'm so sorry. I had no idea—"

"I'm fine. This happens sometimes. And then I get over it. Just like my parents always say."

"Knox, it's okay for you to feel like this. You don't have to 'get over it.' But you also don't have to deal with it alone. I'm here." He looked up at her.

"You don't need to be stuck here, too."

"Yeah, well, I want to be. I'll come here after practice. And we can just sit here and do nothing, or, I don't know, do a puzzle or something, until you feel like doing something else."

He chuckled, and she felt a weight lift of her shoulders. It was possible for him to smile still. It was possible for her to *make* him smile.

"Thank you, B."

She stayed with him for a few hours, watching movies, eating a frozen pizza, and sharing a milkshake they had whipped up in the kitchen. When it was time for her to go, she didn't want to leave him.

"My dad's here," she whispered in his ear, his head on her shoulder, almost asleep.

"Okay," he whispered back.

"Knox?"

"Hmm?"

"Promise you'll call me if you need anything? Even if you just want to talk? I don't care what time it is."

"Promise. Night, baby cakes."

After a few months passed and Knox had done his time in all his casts and bandages, his attitude started to change. He seemed to be more like his old self, but Bria was still cautious, and spent a great deal of time observing him, making sure that Knox was still, well, Knox. She found herself dying to hang out with him as much as possible. Maybe it was because of the fact that he almost died in front of her eyes. Or maybe it was some other reason that she would absolutely never, under any circumstances, say out loud, or even let herself think.

Since the accident, things between Bria and Christa had been weird too. Mari had warned Bria to "let the air clear a bit." Christa was not all too happy about the fact that Bria was the "chosen one" during Knox's recovery. So Bria did as Mari suggested. She didn't want to hurt Christa. Bria wasn't a girl of faith, but she did follow the commandment "chicks before dicks" pretty religiously.

By the spring, Knox was back to driving, and Bria was back in the passenger seat.

"So, my parents are gone this weekend. I'm having a little grad party at mi casa," Knox said, one hand on the steering wheel, the other tilting a bag of chips into his mouth. Whoa. Graduation. Knox would be graduating in less than a week. She knew it was coming. He was two years older than she was. She also knew he wouldn't be going far; he had planned on sticking around town and going to community college for a year or two. No one was surprised by this decision; it wasn't a secret that Knox didn't take school as seriously as he took sports or his acquisition of female companions. Bria still remembered when he got the rejection letter from Frostburg, the one state school he had applied to. He had opened it, read it for half a second, then quickly stuffed it back in the envelope.

"Yep, two-year-degree for me!" he had said with a smile.

But it still felt weird. He wouldn't be in the halls, he wouldn't be at all her meets. She felt like a chapter of their friendship was ending.

"Yeah, awesome. I'll be there," she said. He gave her a look.

"I didn't say you were invited," he said, "I was just telling you about it."

She shot him an evil eye, and playfully punched his arm.

"You ass."

Bria went over to Knox's house early the night of the party. He had asked her to help him get set up. She couldn't help but feel a little bit like co-host; people were asking her where to put their coats, and where to get drinks. She liked it.

Mari, who would also be done with high school in a matter of days, showed up shortly after most of the other guests arrived, greeting Bria with a big hug. In behind her walked Christa. Bria paused awkwardly, unsure of how to act. But Christa greeted her with a big, overdramatic hug.

"I'm so happy to see you, Chris," Bria said, holding her hands. "I thought things might be weird between us. I'm so sorry if I upset you." She looked right into Christa's eyes as she spoke. Christa smiled warmly and waved her off.

"Look, B, it's no big thing," she said. Bria sunk back on her hip. Hmm. It sure seemed like a big thing the night off the accident, when Christa was throwing herself onto the pavement in a dramatic fit, and the few times afterward when all she had to offer Bria was the stink eye.

"Well, I'm still sorry that things didn't work out with you and Knox, and I hope you know it wasn't my intention to cause any—

"Ha!" Christa exclaimed, actually breaking into a visible smile.

"What?" Bria asked.

"Look, Bria, no hard feelings, honestly. But let's

call a spade a spade. You're not sorry things didn't work out between us. And it may not have been your intention to come between us, but you definitely didn't mind that he let you," Christa said in such a casual tone that it made Bria uncomfortable.

"What. . . what do you mean? I—"

"Bria, I know you and Knox are just 'best buds,'" Christa said, using air quotes, "but I can also see right through that. And I can see that you've *never* liked when he's been with any other girl. But what I don't get is what you really want. I mean, you went out with Brett for so long, and I know you've been interested in other guys. So I don't really get what you want with Knox."

She looked up at Bria, and Bria could feel her nerves spinning. Luckily, Christa kept talking.

"But honestly, it was exhausting to figure out whatever you guys have. And after everything else between you two. . . I'm really fine. But there is something I wanted to tell you."

Before Bria could digest all that Christa was laying out, or ask what the "everything else" was that she was referring to, in walked Brett, reaching for Christa's hand.

"After we both saw you and Knox in his hospital bed together, we sort of bonded over our. . .betrayal, I guess," she said with a sheepish smile. Shit, Christa had been there, too. "Look, is this weird for you?" Christa whispered in Bria's ear, nodding toward her's and Brett's clasped hands. Brett stood there clueless and laughing, distracted by another football player shotgunning a beer out on the patio. Bria almost smiled at the irony. It seemed like such a desperate, childish move, but hey, if Christa was happy, Bria was cool with it.

"Not at all. You two make a great couple," Bria said, smiling at Brett, who had just turned his attention back to the interaction between his girlfriend and his ex. He responded with a blank expression, nodded, and walked toward the bar.

"I have to say," Christa said, taking a swig of her wine cooler, "I'm not surprised it was Knox, but I am surprised you did it so quickly after holding Brett off like that. . ."

Bria looked at her, puzzled. "Not surprised that what was Knox?"

"That he was your first," Christa said casually. "I mean, like I said, I always knew you two had, I don't know, this weird thing going, but I just never thought *you* would join the club and sleep with him." Bria's head spun.

"What are you talking about?" she asked.

"Wait, is it not true?" Mari asked.

"No, I didn't sleep with him. Why would you think that?" Bria asked. She could feel her heart pounding.

"Well, some of the guys on the football team had heard you were hooking up with someone. Well, actually, I heard it was a few people," Christa said. "But then Knox told them all it was him."

Bria froze, in complete shock. Her eyes searched the room for him. He stood in the corner of the room by the pub table, beer in hand, arm around a cheerleader. He could sleep with any girl in the Goddamn school. Why would he use her?

"Oh my," Mari said in a hushed tone. "It's not true, is it?" Bria shook her head.

"No. Excuse me," she said. She made her way across the room, making a b-line directly toward him.

"Hey, baby cakes," he said, as she got closer, an unsuspecting smile on his face. Without stopping, she shoved him with pretty impressive force. "What the hell?" he asked, his beer spilling on himself and his posse, the girls shrieking as if it were a snake.

"So we slept together?" she asked, loudly. He looked around, trying to pretend like there weren't thirty pairs of eyes on him.

"Come outside," he whispered, taking her hand. She yanked it away and stormed out the back door. She flew past the patio, past the pool, and into the garage.

"Speak," she said, arms crossed.

"I didn't want to tell you because I knew you'd get upset," he said, holding his hands up.

"You're damn right, I'm upset. You sleep around with every girl in school," she said, "but you have to pick *me* to start shit about? Why?"

For a moment, he just hung his head.

"I guess Brett didn't take you dumping him so well," he said. "So he told some guys on the team that he broke it off because you were hooking up with other guys. He made it seem like you were some sort of tramp. So I just started telling people it was me. They weren't going to believe that a sophomore dumped him, so I thought it might sound better if it was one person you were hooking up with. It made sense that it was me. People know we're together all the time. I'm sorry. I was just trying to help."

She didn't know what to think. She looked at him, then down at the ground, then up at the ceiling. She wanted to go inside and punch Brett in his stupid face. She wanted to take him by the ear, and make him tell the truth to everyone inside. But a stronger part of her wanted to wrap her arms around Knox's neck. So that's what she did. He held her tight. The more she thought about it, the less it bothered her that people might think that she and Knox had been. . . together.

"Knox?" she asked, her face still buried in his neck.

"Yeah?"

Her heart jumped all around her chest. She wanted so badly to ask him what this was. What they were. Why he cared about her so much. But she couldn't. What if it was nothing? What if they really were just *friends?*

"Feel like giving them a little show?" she asked. He raised an eyebrow at her.

"How so?"

"Well, if Brett's gonna make shit up about me, we

might as well play him on it."

A devious smile spread across Knox's face that heated up Bria's insides like a freaking microwave. They walked back inside, his arm draped around her shoulder.

"Damn, that was *hot*," he said, just loud enough to catch everyone's attention in the room. Bria felt all eyes on her, but she didn't care. She winked at him, and he pulled her in closer, laying a long kiss on her cheek. She actually heard someone in the back of the room audibly gasp.

And from the corner of her eye she saw Brett, his arm around Christa, but his eyes on Bria, burning a hole right through her. She smiled, and reached around and grabbed a handful of Knox's butt.

"Hey, now!" he said, jumping forward just a bit. She laughed. He pulled her in again, leaving one more kiss on her cheek, this time, a little bit closer to her mouth. She felt her legs tingle.

"You better be careful," he whispered into her ear, and she felt one million goosebumps rise up all over her skin. He winked at her and walked toward the bar, just grazing her butt with his hand as he walked by.

"What was *that?*" Mari said, after the show was over. "I thought you said it wasn't real."

"It wasn't," Bria said, taking a swig of the beer Mari was handing her. "But Brett doesn't need to know that." Mari gave her a look.

"You may have thought that was all for show," she said, looking over at Knox, "but I don't know that Knox did."

Bria's eyes trailed over to Knox, and to her surprise, he was staring at her while he sipped his drink.

The next morning, Bria laced up her shoes and hopped down the porch steps, heading out for Knox's. Their houses were just over four miles apart, so she often ran to his house and hitched a ride back. She figured he'd still be sleeping off the night before, seeing as he had a red cup in his hand the whole night.

When she finally got to his house, her jaw dropped at the sight of countless red cups, piles of food, and trash that littered the Knoxvilles' backyard. She didn't understand how people could just trash someone else's home, but she guessed they were drunk enough to truly not give a shit.

She sighed, finished stretching, and got to work, scooping up every ounce of trash, occasionally gagging as she dropped it in the can. After almost an hour, a sleepy, hungover Knox appeared at the back door. He wore long black basketball shorts, and a sweat jacket with no shirt. Her knees went a little weak, and she quickly looked away.

"B, what are you *doing?*" he said, shielding his eyes from the sun.

"I'm almost done cleaning up," she said, matter-of-factly. "We have a busy day today."

"I can't believe you cleaned this all up," he said. "We do? What are we doing?"

"We're celebrating."

"Celebrating what?"

"Your graduation!" she said. He chuckled.

"Is that not what we did last night? And what I'm paying for today?"

"No, that was just the pregame," she said. "Today is the real celebration."

He gave her a perplexed look. She smiled back. "Go get dressed."

After a few minutes of Knox dilly-dallying inside, he finally reappeared at the back door, this time wearing a red t-shirt under the jacket. They got into his car, and she began directing him.

"First stop, Tom and Ray's," she said. They had had about a million breakfasts here before school, and today would be no different.

Bria snagged a hashbrown off of Knox's plate while he guzzled down his orange juice. The waitress came over and slapped their check down on the table. Knox reached for it, but Bria snatched it away.

"Ah, ah, ah," she said, wagging her finger, "this is *your* day." She slipped a few bills from her bag under the receipt and popped up. "Okay, next stop."

"Where to, captain?" he asked with a look of excitement, clearly tickled by her master plan. Bria beamed, pulling out of her bag two tickets to that day's Nationals game against the Phillies. Knox's eyes widened.

"No!" he said.

"Yep," she said. "To Nats Park!"

After the game, as they made their way back to town, he smiled at her as they stopped at a red light.

"This has been. . .awesome, baby cakes," he said. She smiled at him. She loved seeing him so happy.

"It ain't over yet," Bria said. "Jimmie Cone!"

After they grabbed their cones from the window, instead of taking their normal seats at one of the wooden picnic tables, Bria led him back to the car.

"And for the last stop," she said, "the swings."

By the time they pulled up to the park, their cones were completely gone. When he parked, she jumped out of the car, racing him to the swings so that she could get the one with the longer chains that swung further out. But he didn't try to keep up, happily giving up the better one.

"B, seriously, this is . . .today was really great."

"I'm so glad you had fun," she said, pumping her feet in and out, in and out. But after a few seconds, he grabbed the chains, bringing her swing to a stop. She looked at him.

"I mean it. No one's ever done anything like that for me before. I'm not even sure if my parents know I graduated," he said with a half-smile. "But I guess a 2.75 GPA isn't anything to celebrate."

Bria's heart sank. She knew his parents would be at graduation, but hadn't planned anything else after the fact. They couldn't wait for Knox to be done with school, to relieve them of anything else that may have been tying them down. And she hated the way he talked about himself. She hated that he saw himself as a joke, as a failure. She reached out and covered his hand with hers.

"Benjamin Andrew Knoxville," she said, looking straight into his eyes, forcing him to look back at her. "You listen to me. Twenty years from now, no one will give a shit what your GPA was, not even you. No one is going to care that you couldn't play football anymore. The important thing is that you change people's lives, Knox. You make them *better.* You make my life better, every time I see you. And the truth is, I'm so sad that I won't see you around every day, because you're the best part of high school. And I just. . . I want you to know I'm so proud of you. I'm so proud of everything you've done, and how much you've conquered, and just, how you treat people. I don't care if you go to Harvard, or community college, or no college at all. None of that makes you who are. None of that matters." She paused for a moment, feeling herself starting to choke up. And if she didn't know any better, she'd say he was fighting back tears of his own. "Now, for my last gift. . ."

"What? Jesus, B, you've done enough," he interjected. But she reached into her pocket and pulled out a folded piece of paper. She took a deep breath before she handed it over to him.

She had been stressing over this letter for weeks. She knew she needed to get it out, write it down, see the words, have *him* see the words. But she wasn't exactly sure *what* words she wanted him to see. He reached out and took it with a perplexed look, and unfolded it.

To My Knox on Your Graduation Day

I can't believe this is it. I can't believe the day has come for you to leave me!

Just kidding. We both know I'd never let you go far.

But in all seriousness, I need to say something. I need you to know that you have changed my life. And I am so beyond grateful that I have you. I'll miss not seeing you every single day. But please know that no matter where the next few years of life take us, you'll always have me. I'm so proud of you.

Love, Your Babycakes

As Knox's eyes made their way to the bottom of the page, he cleared his throat a few times and straightened up. Bria didn't know what she wanted his reaction to be. She had worded the letter so carefully, so as not to include "friend" or "friendship," and to innocently insert the word "love" at the end. God, she had agonized over that for days.

She was sort of hoping he might, maybe, read between the lines. See what she was getting at. See that she had written *so* much more than what was actually in the letter.

He looked down at their hands, now, hers still on top of his. Then he covered her hand with his other hand, and they sat for a moment. Finally, he looked up at her.

"I'll miss you too, B," he said. "You're the best part of all my days." Then he unclasped their hands, hooking his arm around her neck and pulling her in for a long hug.

"I don't know what I did to deserve you," he whispered, "but I hope I never screw it up."

ELEVEN

Now

"What the *fuck,* Drew?" Bria enunciated, throwing her purse down on the table as he slammed the apartment door behind them. "Why would you say that? And in front of them?"

"Because it's true."

"It is *not* true! You know it's not!"

"No, actually, I don't. I'm not there. You could be living with him during the week for all I know."

"Oh my God. You are so overdramatic. And maybe if you'd make the fucking trip to Dalesville every once in a while, you'd know where I was. But God forbid you drive out to the boondocks."

"When the hell am I supposed to do that? I'm a little busy paying the bills for *our* apartment here, remember?" he asked. Wow. She knew he would eventually throw that in her face. Since she moved back in with her parents, she wasn't really shelling out much to help with expenses at their apartment.

"Okay, fine, Drew. You know what? You tell *me*

what to do. Should I just leave? Come back here? Let them lose the house? Make my dad take a second job? You tell me the solution. I'm waiting."

"That's not. . .ugh," he said, walking over to the window, clutching his head with both hands.

"It's not *what?*"

"That's not what this is about. Obviously I don't want you to abandon your fucking family. It would just be nice if you weren't also rekindling some sort of old flame or whatever it is while you were doing it."

"Oh my God! Drew! I'm not going to keep repeating myself. There is *nothing* between Knox and me. There never was, either," she said. It wasn't a lie. They were never a couple. "He was just one of my best friends. And we drifted apart over the years. And that's it. Jesus."

"Okay," he said, in a hushed, defeated tone, his back to her. "I guess I just feel like we are taking the backseat to everything else in your life right now. And I know that sounds selfish and childish, but, I'm sorry."

She felt her furrowed brow smooth out, and her shoulders sink. She walked over to him, pushing her arms through his and resting her head between his shoulder blades.

"Drew Baker, I love you. You are the man I'm going to marry. This is just a little bump in the road," she said. She heard herself saying the words, but it felt almost as if she was reading them from a script. "And I'm sorry my family comes with some baggage, but I have to be there for them."

"I understand," he said, turning around to face her. "When I found out he was there in the woods, I don't know, I guess just felt replaced. Like he got to be there for you instead of me."

She sighed. Well, that's because he was.

"It was nothing, Drew. Just right place at the right time."

TWELVE
Then, Junior Year

"Uno!" Katie called, slapping her cards down on the coffee table as she did a little dance around the living room.

"Dammit!" Sam shouted, throwing her cards dramatically into the air.

"How does she keep *doing* that?" Knox said, exasperated, throwing himself back onto the couch. Louise chuckled.

"I'm going to make more popcorn. Who wants more?"

"I'll have some!" Katie said.

"Me too," said Joe. Bria smiled as she watched her sisters laughing and playing, Knox at the center of it all. Here they were on a Friday night. He could have been out at a party, but he wasn't. He was here, with Bria and her family, playing Uno. And he seemed to genuinely enjoy it.

"So, Mrs. K," Knox said, snatching up a handful of popcorn, "my parents are letting me and some of my friends take the lake house next weekend. They are supposed to get a big snow up there, and Teddy wants to go snowboarding. We'd love to have Bria, if you and Mr. K are okay with that?"

Bria swallowed audibly. He had mentioned the trip to her earlier that day, but she wasn't sure what her parents would say. Generally, they let her do just about anything, but she had never stayed overnight with boys before. She turned to her parents expectantly. Louise looked at Joe.

"Will your parents be there?" Louise asked Knox. Bria rolled her eyes. Her mother always forgot that Knox was a few years older. He was in college, for heaven's sake.

"Ah, no, they'll be skipping this trip. I guess they figure I'm finally responsible enough," he said, with his killer smile. Louise looked to Joe again, who shrugged his shoulders and cocked his head.

"Well, I think that would be okay, as long as you take care of my girl," her mother said.

"Oh, you know I wouldn't let anything happen to her," he said, winking at Louise. Bria felt her cheeks flush.

The next week at school actually went faster than Bria had expected; usually when she was anxiously awaiting something, time seemed to slow down ever so inconveniently. But to her pleasant surprise, she had made it through the week quickly and painlessly, and it was time to pack for the weekend. Knox would be picking her up right after school.

"What will you do there?" Sam asked, sitting crossed-legged on Bria's bed, watching her throw clothes into a big duffle bag.

"I'm not sure, just hang out, I guess," she said.

"But, where will you sleep?" Katie asked, twirling her ponytail.

"I dunno," Bria said. "The house has lots of bedrooms."

"Bria!" she heard her mother call. "Ben is here!"

For some reason, when it was really time to go,

she felt her heart beating harder in her chest. And when her sisters ran downstairs to greet Knox, she opened her nightstand drawer and lifted up her old journal. She used the little key she kept inside of the bottom drawer to release the lock on the edge of the book, and flipped to the middle where she found just what she was looking for: a single condom that a drunken Mari had given her at a party one night. Bria had laughed it off like it was a joke at the time, but it didn't stop her from keeping it.

She wasn't sure why she was bringing it. But she stuffed it into the bottom of her duffle bag and walked downstairs.

"Hey, baby cakes," Knox said, reaching for her bag, "you ready?"

"Yeah!" she said, leaning into the kiss that was waiting for her from her mother.

"Okay guys, be safe!" her dad said, kissing her forehead and shaking Knox's hand.

"Have a good time, and let us know the minute you get there, okay?" her mom said.

As they got in the car, she was surprised to see that it was just the two of them.

"Just us?"

"Yeah, Teddy and the rest are meeting us up there," he said, throwing her bag into the trunk.

The drive was fun and relaxing. They listened to music, chowed down on chips and soda, and talked about the first day they met.

"Oh my gosh, I was such a dork," she said, instinctively touching her forehead, as if the knot from the football was still there.

"Stop it," he said with a chuckle, "you were a supermodel." She rolled her eyes, but she could feel her cheeks flush again.

After about two-and-a-half hours, they pulled up to a bridge, and passed a big wooden sign that read "Meade Lake."

"Finally here," he said, turning down a street and down a long, gravel driveway. Everything was covered in a thick layer of snow that didn't look like it would be going anywhere soon.

The house was huge; it was meant to look like a log cabin, but it was anything but cabin-like in size. Large windows poked out from all sides, and tall evergreens formed a shield around it, making the home look like it had been tucked in with a green blanket.

"So this is the famous Knoxville lake house?" Bria asked, pulling her bag up onto her shoulder.

"I don't know about 'famous,'" he said, "but this is it. This is probably my favorite place in the world."

Bria could see why.

Inside was even more breathtaking. The kitchen, complete with cherry cabinets and a center island of gleaming granite, opened up to a vast, but cozy great room furnished with two soft leather couches and a huge, two-story fireplace in the center. Floor-to-ceiling windows lined the back of the house, allowing for an unobstructed view of the massive, frozen lake in the distance. Bria's eyes bugged out of her head as she took it in, mesmerized by the contrast of the flat, solid ice next to the piles of fluffy snow gathered on the edge, untouched except for the footprints of a few woodland creatures.

"I see you found my favorite view, huh?" he asked from behind her, startling her a bit.

"Yeah, I could stare out there all day," she said.

"Well, we only have about a half-hour or so left of sunlight. You wanna go for a walk down to the water?"

"Sure."

The layers of snow and ice hanging off everything shimmered in the last bit of sunlight, making everything around them shine bright. Bria was surprised at how far the walk down to the water actually was; from the house it had seemed so close.

Knox led her down the path through the trees.

"I can't believe you've never been up here," he said, holding back a branch for her to walk through.

"Me either. It's so nice."

"So, heard anything more from Mr. Dreamy Eyes?" he asked. She scrunched her nose and gave him a sarcastic smile. 'Mr Dreamy Eyes' was Matt Thomas, who had been texting Bria incessantly for the last two weeks. He was sweet and her friends had gushed about his "dreamy blue eyes," but for whatever reason, she just wasn't feeling it.

"Yeah, he texted me this morning, actually," she said, trying to get a gauge on Knox's reaction.

"Oh? And what did he want?"

"I think to marry me. And for me to have his babies. Casual," she said. Now he gave her a snarky smile.

"He should be so lucky," he said quietly. Just then, as she took a step, she planted her foot smackdab in the middle of a patch of ice. She felt herself going down, and reached for the nearest branch, bringing with her what seemed like a hundred pounds of snow onto her head. Knox froze, waiting for her reaction. She quickly rolled herself around, pulling her fist up under her chin and kicking her feet up behind her, posing glamorously with a pile of snow on top of her head. Knox couldn't control it anymore. He burst out into a fit of laughter.

"Wait, wait," he said, as she was about to get up, "this has to be captured." He whipped out his phone, snapping what felt like a million pictures as she rolled around, switching poses, pursing her lips, raising her eyebrows. "Oh yeah, work it!" he said.

She held her belly as she laughed uncontrollably like a little kid. Finally, he reached out a hand to pull her up, and when he did, she slipped, again. But this time, he was there to catch her. And she couldn't help but notice how close their noses were. She could smell his breath, and the smiles quickly faded from both of their faces.

Beep, beeeeeep. The rest of the crew had arrived. Bria

felt Knox's shoulders drop just before he set her back on her feet.

"Let's go, Clumsy," he said, "they're here."

"Let the festivities begin!" Teddy shouted, as he opened the trunk, unloading what looked like an endless supply of alcohol.

"Jesus, Ted, did you rob a bar on your way up here?" Knox asked, helping him unpack the car.

"Hey, hon!" Becca Shin called out in her obnoxious, shrill voice. She threw a horridly fake hug around Bria before trotting off toward the house, leaving all of her bags for Teddy. They had been dating for about a month now, and Teddy was head over heels.

Darren Downs, the full-back, hopped out of the passenger seat, and, to Bria's surprise, Courtney Blake rolled out from around the back, totally stopping Bria in her tracks. Knox likely didn't mention that Courtney was coming because he knew how Bria felt about her. She shot him a look that could kill as Courtney followed Becca inside.

"Hey, Bria," Darren said, giving her a warm hug, "glad to see you could make it." She smiled back at him.

That first night was actually fun. Judging by the rest of the company, Bria thought for sure that it would be a miserable weekend. But after a few drinks, she felt herself letting loose. Until she saw Courtney, legs draped over Knox on the couch, running her finger up and down his ear. Fucking Courtney.

"So, how's good old Dalesville High?" Darren asked, pulling up his chair weirdly close to Bria's. Out of the group, only she and Courtney were still in high school.

"Ah, you know," she said, "same old. How's college?"

"So much better than high school," he said with a grin, throwing his head back to suck the last few drops of beer from his bottle. "So, do you know what you're gonna do after high school?"

"Um, not positive. I mean, go to school somewhere, but not sure where," she said.

"Do you know what you want to be?" he asked, making nauseating slurping sounds as he licked the bottle clean. Seriously, she thought the label might come off in his mouth. But she thought for a moment, then answered him.

"A mom," she said. He snorted.

"A mom? That's it?" he asked, a stupid grin on his face again.

"Not *just* a mom. I want to be a mom. I want a career, too. But I want kids," she said. He nodded, the sarcastic smile still across his lips.

"Geez," he said. "I don't even know if I can handle a dog. You've got it all planned out, huh?"

She nodded. Knox had always had the same reaction, whenever the subject of the future came up, which was rare for the two of them. He thought he might want to try to be a cop, or maybe a teacher. He wanted to move around the country a bit. That was all he knew, and his mind changed a lot. But for Bria, she knew she wanted a family. And he'd always laugh and shake his head at a concept that was so foreign to him.

Just then, a shriek of excitement came from the living room, as the bass of an Usher song blasted through a speaker. Becca was in the middle of the floor, getting down with her bad self.

"Court, come on!" she waved. Courtney hopped off Knox, as if it were choreographed, and leapt across the room to Becca, swaying her butt back and forth, running her fingers through her hair. She occasionally looked up at Knox seductively, and Bria actually had to stifle a laugh.

"You don't want to join the girls?" Darren asked, scooting even closer to her.

"I'm good," she laughed. Suddenly, she felt his hand on her leg.

"I'd like to see you do that," he said to Bria,

pointing to them again. "I have a feeling you know what you're doing on the dance floor." He was sort of whispering now, his lips just inches from her ear, his breath smelling heavily of whatever cheap beer Teddy had brought. Out of the corner of her eye, she felt Knox glaring at the two of them. Ever since she'd dated Brett and learned that she could get a rise out of Knox, she liked playing these kinds of games with him. But right now, she kind of just wanted Darren to get the fuck off of her.

"I'm good," she said, gently pushing his hand off her thigh. Not wanting to make a scene, she stood and walked to the kitchen, dumping a few empty bottles into the trash can. She didn't want to be the lame high schooler that brought the party down. She could handle Darren. She'd just avoid him. But to her dismay, there he was again, popping out from behind the kitchen wall.

"Hey, you wanna go downstairs, maybe watch some T.V. or somethin'?" he asked her.

"I think I'm gonna just hang up here," she said, refusing to make eye contact with him. She hated how anxious he made her; after all, she was in a house full of people. What could happen? But as she washed out a cup in the sink, she felt him press up against her.

"Aw, come on, Bria," he said. She could feel specific parts of him. And they weren't soft.

"Stop, Darren. I'm good up here." But he didn't budge. "Darren," she said, sternly now, raising her voice.

Out of nowhere, Knox seemed to fly across the room, ramming his fists into Darren's chest, and pushing him up against the wall behind her.

"Did you not fucking hear her, Downs?" he asked.

"Jesus, Knox, what the fuck?" Darren said, shrugging Knox off of him. The music stopped as the rest of them looked on.

"Knox," Bria whispered, grabbing on tight to his arm. "It's okay."

"No, it's not," Knox said. He kept his eyes laser focused on Darren's. She'd never seen such seriousness in him; such anger. "Leave her the fuck alone."

Darren backed a few steps away from them, and looked at Bria.

"I'm sorry," he said, holding his hands up. "I'm sorry." He disappeared downstairs to the basement.

"Well, now that *that's* over," Becca said, reaching for Teddy's collar, "I think you and me have some business of our own to tend to upstairs." Teddy smiled, leaning in for a kiss.

"Night, ya'll," he said.

"Yeah, I'm a little tired, myself," Courtney said. "Knox, did you want to come up, or. . .?" Bria looked down at the ground. Sometimes, she actually felt a little sorry for Courtney. She played it off as if the whole no-strings-attached thing didn't bother her; that she was mature enough to handle a purely sex-based relationship with no other feelings. But Bria could see right through it, anytime that Knox wasn't feeling it, or was hanging on somebody else.

"You know what, you go ahead, I'm not super tired, yet," Knox said. Bria raised her eyebrows. She'd never known Knox to turn down a hook-up, especially from a hot blonde. Courtney looked like she had been slapped in the face.

"Oh, okay. Night," she said, turning on her heels and running up the stairs.

"Night," Knox responded, softly.

Bria stood over the sink again, washing the dishes that were left.

"You don't have to do all those," he said, walking toward her.

"Oh, I don't mind. You're letting us stay here for free. It's the least I can do."

"You ok, B?" he asked, leaning across the counter toward her. "I'm really sorry about that. He's so drunk. I know that's not an excuse, but. . ."

"I'm fine," she said, "thank you."

"Look," he said, visibly nervous, "do you wanna crash with me tonight? I'm gonna stay in the master down here, and I just want to keep an eye on ya. Not sure where Darren went, and I just don't want him bothering you anymore."

She felt her heart beating excessively fast again.

"Um, sure, yeah, okay," she said.

"Can't have Mrs. K mad at me," he said, smiling. She smiled back.

Bria walked into the bathroom, digging through her bag and staring into the mirror. Holy shit. She was about to sleep with Knox. Well, not *sleep* with him. Actually sleep. Or. . .maybe? No. He said so himself. It was just to keep an eye on her and make sure Darren didn't mess with her anymore.

But that didn't stop her from brushing her hair, pulling on her extra-short pajama shorts, and even dabbing on a tiny bit of perfume behind her ears before she walked back into the room. Knox was propped up in bed, flipping through the channels. He was wearing a Dalesville football t-shirt and his baggiest sweatpants, but he looked sort of delicious.

"Hey," he said, "will the T.V. keep you up?"

"No, I'm good," she said, "thanks for letting me stay in here."

"Hey, it won't be the first time we slept together," he said with a wink.

She slipped under the covers, laying close enough to him to show him that she was comfortable being next to him, but not close enough that he would think she was making a move. A re-run of *Friends* was on the television, but Knox barely seemed to be watching.

"B?" he asked, scooting his hand immeasurably close to hers on top of the covers.

"Hmm?"

"Despite what Dickhead Darren tried to pull tonight, I'm really glad you're here. And I hope you know that I wouldn't ever let anything happen to ya."

She smiled, looking deep into his eyes. She knew with her whole being, she could believe him.

"I'm really glad I'm here, too. And thank you for saving me from him today." And she reached her hand over, letting it gently graze the top of his. But she was careful not to rest it there too long or let their fingers interlock.

And neither rolled over toward the other, pulling the other into them, kissing their lips, and cheeks, and neck. Neither let their hands explore the other.

Neither told the other how much they meant, how long they'd waited for this.

Instead, they laid there with their hands barely touching, while Ross told Rachel that it had always been her on the television.

THIRTEEN

Now

"So, do you wanna go?" Sam asked, dropping a box of Spongebob macaroni and cheese into the cart.

"I guess," Bria shrugged, crossing granola bars off of her list. "I haven't been to a Dalesville football game in years."

When Friday rolled around, Bria dug through Sam and Katie's closets, trying to find some old Dalesville gear to wear. She pulled on a pair of her old track sweatpants, and one of Katie's new hooded sweatshirts. As she pulled her hair up into a messy bun, she couldn't help but smile at herself in the mirror. If someone didn't know any better, they'd probably think she was still a high schooler.

She climbed the bleacher steps, following her dad's whistle as she pushed her way through crowds of familiar faces, waving, hugging, and patting her on the shoulder. There was still a half-hour till the game started, but people got to the school early for home games. After all, if you weren't there to save your seat, you might be left standing on the track the whole game. Dalesville rules.

"Hi, hon," her mom said, patting the bench next to her. "How was work?"

"Oh, it was fine," she said.

Bria looked out over the field. She hadn't sat here in such a long time, but the landscape had barely changed. The water tower sat perched on the hill, with "Dalesville" painted across it in big, green letters, the church steeple rose up from the other side, poking through the trees. The bright lights bordering the track made everyone under them look just the slightest bit fluorescent. For all her jokes about the sleepy cow town, Bria had actually missed this.

As she took stock of all the parents who hadn't changed in years and the kids that had grown into young adults, she saw him walking across the bottom of the bleachers. Knox pointed up to a different person with every step he took, waving, winking, yelling back to them with his deadly smile.

"Oh, hey, there's Ben!" Louise said.

"Yep," Bria said, keeping her eye on him as he strutted the whole way across the bleachers, never even thinking to look up in the crowd for her.

At halftime, she made her way down to the busy snackbar. As she stood patiently in line, someone sneaked their hand around her and snatched the five dollar bill she was holding right from her hand.

Knox.

"Hey!" she said, snatching it back.

"I see your reflexes have improved greatly since your teen years," he snickered, letting her take it back. She playfully shoved him.

"Very funny," she said.

"Enjoying the game?"

"Oh, of course," she said. "It's actually good to be back. It would be more fun if you were still out there, though."

"Yeah," he said with a thoughtful smile. "You

going to the afterparty after this?"

"Wow, they still have those?" she asked. All through their teen years, after every home game, a different family in town hosted a massive afterparty. Players, coaches, cheerleaders, seemingly *everyone* in town showed up to these things. The adults often stayed inside, drank, and gossiped, while the kids hung outside, taking advantage of their parents' inebriated states.

"Yeah," he laughed, "I think tonight it's at the Hardens'," he said. The Hardens lived two houses down from her parents.

"Oh, well, I guess I could make that. You going?"

"If you are."

After the game, she parked her car in her parents' driveway and ran up to her room. She changed out of her baggy sweat clothes and into some tight yoga pants. She dabbed a little bit of perfume behind her ears and fluffed her hair.

As she made her way to the Hardens' backyard, she spotted him, already claiming his spot by the bonfire, his feet up on stump and a beer in his hand.

"Hey," he said, holding his hand out to the empty chair next to him. Teddy sat next to Knox, standing up to give her a hug as she walked toward them.

"Bria Kreery!" he said, bending down and picking her up for a big hug. Sweet Teddy. He tried so hard when they were in high school, to be liked, to be the ladies' man that Knox was, but it never quite worked for him. It was surprisingly nice to see him. Teddy was a friendly guy, but he was also a little too comfortable being in Knox's shadow. He hadn't played sports, and was kind of a loner in high school. It was a surprise to many people that Knox and Teddy were actually friends; their social lives were very different. But they had been buds since grade school, and despite Knox's rise to Dalesville High fame, he had never left Teddy behind. That was one thing Bria loved about

Knox. He was unapologetically loyal. Didn't matter who was watching.

"Mr. Teddy Bill!" she said, squeezing him back. "It is so good to see you! How have you been?"

"Ah, you know, same old. Stuck here in cow-town with this guy here," he said, playfully rubbing Knox's dark hair. Knox swatted his hand away.

"You two haven't changed a bit," she giggled.

"So, Knox finally convinced you to come back to Dalesville?" Teddy asked. Knox didn't say anything, but he glared at Teddy so viciously that Teddy actually got up and walked into the house.

"What did he mean?" she asked.

"Nah, nothing. He's just messing around," Knox said, opening another beer. "You enjoying your time home?"

"Yeah, I'm surprised how good it feels to be back," she said, leaning back in the chair. She looked across the yard at a teenage couple laying together in a hammock, staring at their interlocked fingers as if they were a painting on a wall. And as the young lovers turned to look into each other's eyes, Bria remembered the fire that burned through her when she was their age. That feeling of absolute assuredness, that the guy she was with was her soulmate. She had been wrong, of course, a number of times, but in those exact moments, it felt so right. And that feeling was real, if fleeting.

"I remember those days," Knox said, also looking at the hammock couple. "The good old days. You were around a lot more, then."

She turned to look at him. She could tell he was slipping across the line between buzzed and drunk.

"Well, I'm here now," she said. He let his head sink down toward her, resting it ever so gently on her shoulder. Her stomach flipped.

"I miss you, Bria," he said.

"Miss me? I'm right here," she said with a nervous

giggle, her chest throbbing.

"No, no no," he said, waving his hand in the air, "I miss you a lot. All the time."

She didn't say a word. She wasn't exactly sure what to say to that. She knew what she *wanted* to say. But not what she was supposed to say. Instead, she let her fingers pet his hair once, before bringing her hands back toward her lap. All these years, she had missed him, too. And she knew he was drunk, but she also knew that his drunk words were sober thoughts. At least that's what that mug at the Hallmark store said.

Another hour or so passed, and people started packing up their things. Bria knew if she let her guard down some, she could sit here with Knox around this fire for hours. But she knew it was time to go.

"Come on," she said, nudging his head gently, "I'll drive you home."

"I'm actually staying at my parents' this weekend. I'm watching the dog while they are away," he said. She nodded, standing up.

When they got to the Knoxvilles' house, a wave of nostalgia came over her. She hadn't pulled into this driveway in so long. As she put the car in park, he stumbled a bit getting out.

"Do you need help?" she asked.

"No, no," he said, waving her off. But as she watched him wobble, she took the keys out of the ignition and walked around to the other side, throwing his arm over her shoulders. As they walked around to the back of the house, he laughed. She hadn't noticed quite how much he'd had to drink at the party.

"What's so funny?" she asked.

"I'm just thinking about all the times you've helped me get into bed," he said with a goofy smile. She smiled back.

"Yeah, I'm a pro at it, now," she said, pushing open the sliding glass door and leading him down the hall.

She couldn't believe how drunk he was. In fact, she was actually wondering how much of it might be an act. "Okay, there ya go," she said, flopping him down on the bed. Just as she went to stand up, he grabbed her arms, and they both froze, their faces inches apart.

"I miss you, Bria," he said again. She swiveled his legs up onto the bed, and brushed through his hair with her fingers once more.

"Shh, goodnight, Knox," she said.

The next morning, she woke up to a text from him.

Hey. Thx for driving me home last nite. Also, sry if I said anything weird. I haven't drank that much in a while lol

She looked up at the ceiling, as if the perfect response would be written there. She sighed.

Oh, no worries. You didn't say anything weird at all.

FOURTEEN

Then, Bria's Senior Prom

"I can't believe my little baby is going to her senior *prom!*" Mari said over Skype. Bria laughed and rolled her eyes.

"Yeah, about that. I don't know if I want to go," she said. Ever since Mari and Knox and the rest of the friends she had grown so close with had graduated, high school hadn't really been the same for Bria. She had a group of friends her own grade, but they didn't have the same connection. Actually, Bria had been feeling pretty lonely at school. She was glad Knox was still around town.

"What? Why?" Mari asked, looking genuinely concerned. "Oh, B. You have to go. It's your senior prom! You never get that back. Who cares if you don't have a date? Go with the girls. It's just a night where you get to dress up, and look gorgeous, and dance. Who doesn't love that?"

Mari had a point. Bria did like dressing up

occasionally, and she did *love* to dance. But, with her friends gone, it felt like she had no one worth sharing it with. It felt easier, and probably more fun, to skip it.

"It's next week. I don't even have a dress," she said.

"Well, promise me you'll think about it," Mari said.

"Okay, I promise."

But, she didn't. She had made up her mind. No prom for her.

The next Saturday rolled around, and as expected, *everyone* in town was going nuts over the dance. The parents in the PTA were planting signs all over the place, the local junkyard delivered a beat-up old car to the front of the school to show kids what happens when you drink and drive. You know, cheerful things.

"Aw, sweetie. I wish you would have gone," Louise said, washing a pan in the sink.

"Yeah. After all, your mother was my prom date," Joe said, putting his arms around her waist. Her parents were so adorably disgusting.

"Sorry to disappoint ya, guys," Bria said, standing up from the table, when all of a sudden, there was a knock at her front door.

"I'll get it," Sam said, running toward the door. "Oh, my gosh!" she exclaimed when she opened it.

"We're here to get this prom party started," Bria heard Mari say, and her knees buckled.

"Mari!" she cried, running to the door and jumping on her. Mari had an armful of dresses in one hand, and a curling iron in the other. Behind her stood Johnny Ridges, football stud from Centerville, dressed in a tux and holding out a corsage.

"We weren't sure which dress you were going to go with," Johnny said, "so we picked out a white corsage. Should go with any of them."

"Wha. . . what?" she asked, utterly confused.

"I brought over some of my old dresses, and I brought you a date," she said, holding her hand out to Johnny and smiling. "Johnny's sister goes to UCLA, and funnily enough, we met during freshman year. We were talking about people we know from back home. She said her brother went to Centerville and knew a bunch of Dalesville people. I said my best friend needed a date, and bingo."

Johnny gave her a sweet smile. He was really, very dreamy.

"Guys. . ."

"I couldn't let you miss this, B," Mari said.

"Are you sure you want to do this?" she asked him. "I mean, you've been graduated for two years."

"Of course," he said, a kind smile on his lips. "I'm happy to be the lucky guy that gets to take you to prom." Bria felt herself blush, and she couldn't help but smile back..

"Oh, this is just the sweetest thing," she heard her mother say.

"Okay, let's get this going," Mari said, shoving Bria toward the steps.

"I can't believe you convinced him to do this," Bria said, holding her eyebrows up while Mari applied purple eyeshadow to match the dress that Bria had chosen.

"Convinced him?" Mari said. "Psh, there was no convincing. I just called him and said I had this idea, and he said he loved it. I mean, Johnny was Mr. Social Butterfly. He's like Knox. He has a ton of friends at Dalesville. Plus, I was signing him up to spend four hours with you, which I'm sure he didn't mind."

"Why? He doesn't even know me." Bria said.

"Doesn't matter. He said he met you once, and he's thought you were cute ever since. He's apparently a frequent flyer of your Facebook page," Mari said. Johnny had friended her shortly after Knox's accident. But she hadn't really given it a second thought.

"Now hold still."

Marisol added the final touches, and one more thick layer of hairspray before they made their way downstairs. And when she got to the bottom, she saw Johnny perk up.

"Well," he said, "looks like everyone's going to be jealous of me."

Bria expected the ride to the dance to be excruciatingly awkward. But it wasn't. Johnny was a perfect gentleman, telling her over and over again how amazing she looked. And when they got to the dance, she couldn't help but enjoy how everybody's eyes were drawn to them as Johnny held her hand.

"Hey, Bria," Courtney Blake said, taking her ticket. Aside from being the soccer star, and seemingly, a supermodel, she was also student council president. Because of course she was.

"Hey, Courtney. You look great," Fake Bria said, with an ultra-fake smile.

"Oh, stop, you're sweet," she said, "you, too. Hey, Johnny," she said, wiggling her fingers at him like an idiot. "What are you doing in our neck of the woods?"

"Oh, ya know, just came to escort this pretty lady to her senior prom," he said, placing his hand on the small of Bria's back. She smiled back at him.

"Oh, nice," Courtney said. Just then, hands snuck around Courtney's waist. "There you are," she said to Knox, as he gave her a little squeeze. Bria felt her heart sink.

"Knox?"

"B," he said, in a shocked whisper, looking from her to Johnny. "I thought you said you didn't want to go to prom." He stepped back ever so slightly from Courtney.

"What are you doing here?" She wanted to play it casual. She wanted to keep it easy. She didn't want to show how absolutely devastated she was, knowing that he was at *her* senior prom, with someone else.

"I uh—"

"Well, since I went with him to his senior prom, we thought it would be fitting if he came with me to mine," Courtney said, slipping her arm around his back and smiling up at him. He smiled back briefly, but never took his eyes off Bria. *We. We* thought it was fitting. And she had to go and remind Bria about the fact that he took another sophomore to *his* senior prom, instead of her.

"What are you doing here, Ridges?" Knox finally managed to ask.

"He's with me," Bria said, staring back at Knox with fire in her eyes.

"Well, my shift at the table is done. Let's go inside. You guys have fun!" Courtney said, walking toward the dance hall, and tugging Knox along behind her. Bria watched as Knox turned back to look at her once more, remorse all over his face.

Bria was surprised at how many people knew Johnny at Dalesville High. Everywhere she turned, someone else was coming up to hug him, or shake his hand. But she liked that through it all he stayed there, with her.

Some of Bria's friends waved them over to the dance floor as they walked in, and Johnny happily stepped in behind her Bria, rubbing up on her quite a bit as the song got faster. Finally, a slow song came on, and she spun around to wrap her arms around his neck.

"I know I've already said this," he said, whispering, "but you really do look beautiful tonight."

She blushed, grateful the lights were out in the dance hall.

"Thank you, Johnny," she said. "And thank you so much for agreeing to come." He smirked.

"You kidding me? When I found out that *you* were the friend Mari was talking about, it was no questions asked." She raised an eyebrow.

"Why is that?"

"Well, I guess I've sort of had a little crush on you ever since I met you that time at the hospital." Blushed again. Thank God for darkness.

After a few more dances, Johnny excused himself to get them drinks.

Bria sat down at a table by herself, putting her feet up on the chair across from her. Suddenly, the song came on.

"Now, I've had the time of my life," Bill Medley sang over the speakers. She couldn't help but look around aimlessly. This was *their* song. When her mother introduced her to *Dirty Dancing* in eighth grade, she fell in love. She memorized parts of the final dance, and she was pretty sure she had a sexual awakening the first time she saw Patrick Swayze without a shirt. Her obsession with the movie lasted years.

Bria had made Knox do the lift with her so many times, that she could probably give Baby a run for her money. Just as the music got going, she saw him, making a b-line for her through the crowded dance floor. He stopped when he reached her, sticking his hand out.

"What are you doing?" she asked, arms crossed. He wasn't getting off that easy.

"It's our song."

"Well, I have a date. And so do you," she said, trying desperately to stand her ground, although she could feel it slipping out from her under her when she saw him smile.

"Come on," he said, leaning in. "Nobody puts Baby in a corner."

Oh my God. She almost couldn't take that level of corny. But part of her was desperate to take his hand. So she did. And just as Johnny was returning with their drinks, Knox pulled her onto the dance floor, twirling her around and pulling her into him without missing a beat. She was still mad, and she knew he could feel it.

"Are we going to attempt the lift?" he asked her.

"In this dress? Probably not a good idea," she said, without cracking a smile. He twirled her out, then twirled her back in to him as the crowd cheered them on.

"I should have asked you," he said.

And she looked up at him, just as the part of the song comes on where Patrick Swayze lip syncs to Jennifer Grey. Bria had rewound and rewatched that part a hundred times. And just like in the movie, he guided her arms around his neck, singing the words to her perfectly. And she couldn't help but smile like an idiot. Damn it, he was too good.

"Mind if I cut in?" Johnny asked, awkwardly. She jumped back.

"Oh, no, of course not," she said, letting go of Knox and stepping closer to him.

"Here's your drink," he said, handing her a cup of punch. She screwed her face all up and pursed her lips.

"Did you spike this?" she asked. Knox took a step toward them.

"I thought we could make it a little more fun," Johnny said.

"Dude," Knox said, giving Johnny a disgusted look. "Bria, you don't have to drink that."

She looked over at him. She hated when he made her feel like a child. And she could feel Johnny seething as he glared at Knox. The rivalry was still strong with these two. She looked at Knox, tilted her head back, and downed the glass in one gulp. She handed the cup back to Johnny.

"Fill 'er up," she said. Johnny smiled, pulling out a silver canteen from his suit pocket. Knox tilted his head back, and slowly slipped away to find Courtney, who was sulking at their table with her band of faithful followers crowded around her.

As the night came to a close, droves of people were leaving the building.

"Hey," Kayla Krauss said as she passed them,

"you guys coming to post-prom?"

Bria's head was pounding.

"If Bria's up to it," Johnny said, slipping his arm around her waist again. "I should have gone a little easier on the punch."

"Aww, try not to miss it," Courtney said, with Knox on her tail, "it's going to be a blast." Knox paused as he walked by their table, but said nothing. He held his tux jacket over his shoulder, and hung his head as he walked by.

The room was spinning slowly and Bria had a pounding headache, but she could see that she and Johnny were one of just a few couples left.

"Wanna get out of here? I just gotta grab my suit coat," Johnny said. Bria nodded.

As they made their way out of the dance hall and toward the coat closet, Johnny held her up. To be honest, she didn't really *need* him to hold her, but she kind of liked the attention; she liked being taken care of.

"Come on, Bria, just a little closer," he said, leading her to the coat closet.

"Thanks," she said, as he practically carried her across the floor.

"Don't thank me," he said, "I'm so sorry that you're trashed at your senior prom. I shouldn't have added so much vodka." She smiled.

"Aren't you *supposed* to get trashed at your senior prom?" she asked. He smiled at her. And then, out of nowhere, she felt herself push him up against the wall inside the coat closet. Then she felt herself kissing him hard, her tongue exploring his, her fingers running through his hair. He stopped her, pulling her off for a moment.

"Bria, we don't have to. . ."

But she shot down his attempt at being a gentleman as she threw herself back onto him, closing the closet door with her foot. Johnny reached over and turned the lock. The temperature in the closet was rising, but she didn't care. She felt him tugging at her hair and her dress, and she could tell how badly he wanted it. She reached down, pulling up her dress, above her knees—*knock, knock, knock*.

"Occupied," Johnny said, holding the door shut.

"It's a fucking coat closet," she could hear Knox say from the other side. "You can't occupy a coat closet. Open the fucking door."

"Fuck off, Knox," Johnny said.

"B?" Knox called. "Ridges, open the fucking door! She's drunk."

Johnny looked at her, waiting for her to intervene. She let him pound for a few moments, just as her heart was. Finally, she spoke.

"I'm fine, Knox," she said. "Leave us alone." Then there was nothing but silence on the other side of the door. Her heart sank, but she didn't dwell. She leapt back onto Johnny, pulling up her dress again. He lay her down on the floor, fumbling with the condom he had kept in his suit pocket all night.

Her first time lasted two minutes and twelve seconds. She only knew because she actually counted every single second that went by, Johnny moving on top of her, Bria wincing in uncomfortable, foreign pain. As Johnny moaned and groaned and grunted, she made noises that she deemed appropriate to convince him that the pleasure was mutual. But the truth was, when he was done and finally rolled off of her, she felt an overwhelming sense of relief. And then, an uncontrollable wave of sadness. This was not how her first time was supposed to be. On her back in a coat closet, giving it up to a guy she barely knew. It should have been with someone who cared about her. Someone she cared about. It should have been with . . . no, never mind.

As she dusted herself off, Johnny could sense her mood change.

"I'm sorry, Bria," he said, looking down at the

ground. "We shouldn't have done that. I shouldn't have let it . . ."

"No, no," she said, laying a kiss on his cheek, "it was great. Really." He smiled weakly, reaching for her hand as they exited the closet.

As they pulled into post-prom at the arcade nearby, Bria was dreading it. Inside, Johnny, naturally had a blast, killing the basketball games, beating some of the other guys in some hunting video game. She smiled as she watched. He was the life of the party. Sort of like someone else she knew.

"He's so much fun!" Courtney said from behind her. She did a double-take. If Courtney was there, so was Knox. When she looked up at him, he looked away from her. As if he couldn't bear to look her in the eye. He snuck off, walking toward the ski ball lanes.

"Mind if I join you?" Bria asked.

"No, go ahead, you can play," he said, setting his ball down and getting ready to walk away.

"What is your problem?" she asked.

"You don't need me around. You're fine. You're with Johnny, and we don't want to piss him off," he said. He hung his head, shaking it and walking back toward Courtney.

What an asshole. As if she didn't hate herself enough already for losing her virginity to some football player in a fucking coat closet, she didn't need Knox to hate her for it, too.

She wanted to yell at him, scream, tell him how unfair he was being. But her emotions got crossed, and all she could do was burst into tears. So she ran to the doors, leaving Johnny to entertain the crowd.

"B," she heard Knox call after her, but she ignored him. Finally, he caught up to her, standing underneath the awning at the end of the entrance. "I shouldn't have said that. I'm sorry." She wiped her eyes and looked up at him.

"Why is it okay for you to sleep with everything that moves, but when I do it, you can't even look at me?" she asked. He was taken aback by her question.

"I'm sorry, Bria," he said after a few moments of silence. "It's not my place. And you're right. I guess I just wish it was someone, *anyone* but Ridges."

She had remembered that in high school, and even after, the rivalry between Knox and Johnny was a strong one. Knox despised Johnny, and she was starting to feel a little guilty about being here with him now. Johnny got to be everything that Knox wasn't, a high school football star, a college player. And she wondered if that's what made Johnny so much more alluring to her—he was the version of Knox that wanted her.

"And I don't know, I mean, I'm not mad," Knox went on. "And even if I was, I don't have the right to be. I guess I just never thought of you as someone who would. . . Someone like me. I guess I thought you deserved better. I mean, Jesus, even Balkner treated you well, and took you out, and waited around for you to be ready."

She looked down at the ground, feeling a little lower about herself than she already did.

"Yeah, well, I never slept with Brett," she said. He looked shocked. "That, just now, was my first time. And it's a little late now. I can't take it back."

Knox nodded.

"I didn't know. . . I always thought you and Brett. . . It doesn't matter. I'm sorry I made you feel shitty about it. You just. . .you just deserve so much, B." She smiled. "So, you going back in there?"

She shook her head."Nah. I think I'm gonna call a cab." He held up his keys, jiggling them.

"Knoxville Taxi Cab at your service," he said.

"What about Courtney?" she asked. He smiled his devilish, dangerous smile.

"She told me if I followed you out here, not to

bother coming back in." She smiled back at him. "Let's go home."

FIFTEEN

Now

Louise shuffled around the kitchen, moving things from place to place, a classic sign that something was on her mind.

"Man, what is the big deal?" Bria asked, skinning potatoes over the sink.

"I just hate that we never did anything to celebrate Sam. The big deal is that she worked extremely hard, and we totally missed out on giving her the recognition for it. It's bad enough that she didn't walk at her graduation, but we didn't have a party, not even so much as a lunch for her," Louise ranted, sliding the sugar canister out from the back of the counter, wiping it down, and moving it back.

Bria rolled her eyes. Her mother tended to have a hard time letting things go. Sam had graduated from college a few months before, and the fact that she refused any sort of celebration still haunted Louise.

"But she didn't *want* to walk," Bria said. "She walked at her high school ceremony. You know she absolutely hates being in front of a crowd, and she thinks stuff like that is lame. If she didn't want to do it, we couldn't make her."

Louise looked defeated, and suddenly Bria felt for her. The family had been so consumed by Katie's medical woes for weeks. Having something to celebrate would be refreshing. Bria caved. "I know it's been a few months since she graduated, but maybe we can convince her to let us throw a party here. Just a small thing," she offered.

Louise visibly perked up.

"Yeah, a party!" Katie called from the other room as she made her way into the kitchen.

"Nothing too crazy, just family maybe. That way we can celebrate, but she doesn't have to be the center of attention in front of too many people," Bria suggested. Louise seemed appeased.

"I'll call her and ask," Katie said, whipping out her phone.

Katie was always up for a party or get-together, anything that meant that she could socialize with someone other than her parents or sisters. Katie walked out of the room, and re-entered about ninety seconds later. "She said yes!"

Louise beamed. "Great! Let's start planning. I wonder who from the family could make it next weekend."

"That's awfully short notice, hon," Joe said, leaning over the sink to see what Bria was cooking.

"Well, the only person who might not be able to make it is your mother," Louise said, shooting him a look. He rolled his eyes. Thirty years they'd been married, and Louise still couldn't resist a good dig at Joe's mother.

"Well, I'll call her and find out," he said, spanking Louise's tush lightly and kissing the top of her head. Ugh. So gross and cute at the same time.

"Okay, come on girls, we have a lot to do," Louise said, grabbing a pen and paper from a kitchen drawer and sitting down at the head of to the table. Katie and Bria shot each other a look. If Louise had her pad out, she meant business.

That weekend came quickly, as they normally do when you feel like you don't have enough time to prepare for something. But the Kreery girls knew how to get their shit together on short notice thanks to years of practice under their mother.

Sam finally made her way downstairs, looking extremely uncomfortable in the black dress and heels their mother insisted she wear.

"You look great, Sam," Bria said, careful not to gush.

"Thanks," Sam said, smoothing out the bottom of the dress.

"I'm so excited for tonight!" Katie said, filling a bowl with a bag of chips and moving it to the center of the table. Bria and Sam smiled. If nothing else, at least Katie would have some fun this evening.

"Yeah, yeah," Sam said, "let's just get this over with."

"I just can't wait to meet Abby," Katie said, putting a spoon in the ranch dip. Bria and Sam froze, standing straight up.

"What?" Sam asked, raising one eyebrow.

"A-Abby," Katie stuttered, "I found her name in your contacts. I figured you'd want your girlfriend at your graduation party."

Bria's head sunk. Oh, Katie. Sometimes, she was still so naive.

"Oh, Katie," Louise whispered.

"You decided to invite my new girlfriend to the house to meet our *entire* family at once? Including those family members in particular who still don't know I'm *gay?*" Sam asked.

Now Katie was staring down at the ground. Bria's heart was wrenched for both of her sisters. For Katie, because she meant no harm by it. For Sam, because she was so private about her dating life. When she had come out to their parents, she told them she didn't want to make a big deal of it to the rest of the family. She wanted it to just "happen," that someday she'd be living with another woman, or show up to an event with another woman, or be married to another woman, and the rest of the family would just find out. Joe and Louise had agreed; it was Sam's life and her decision. Over the years, a few of the family members did find out, a few aunts and uncles, Grandma Gayle. When Grandma had heard the news, she had sent Sam a card, which Sam and Bria thought was the funniest thing. It was a "Congratulations" card, which made it even better.

"'Hey, granddaughter, congrats on being gay,'" Bria had said to Sam before they both hunched over in a fit of laughter.

The one person who absolutely did not know yet was Uncle Tom, Louise's oldest brother. He was in his late fifties, single, and generally clueless when it came to women. He was also the most old-fashioned of the entire group, and the most opinionated.

"Okay, this is okay, we can just play it off. We can say she's a friend," Bria said, her fix-it instincts kicking in.

"No," Sam said. "I'm not going to have her think I'm ashamed of her." Bria nodded.

"I'm so sorry, Sam," Katie said.

"It's fine," Sam said, crossing her arms. It was clearly *not* fine. But before Bria could fix anything further, the front door opened, and the family began filing in, Aunt Sarah's loud voice carrying throughout the whole house, a few of their young cousins already running through the living room, Grandma Gayle setting down her bowl of fruit salad on the island, Uncle Tom in his best Lynyrd Skynyrd concert tee and high-top trucker hat.

Behind a load of her unruly but endearing relatives came Drew, looking as sharp as ever in a tight blue sweater, his cologne hitting her before anything else did.

"Hey, you," he said with a smile as he wrapped his arms around Bria's waist, kissing her softly.

"Hi, hon," she said, trying to sound extra excited to see him while simultaneously attempting to devise an escape plan for Sam.

"Hey, Sam," Drew said, nodding in her direction, "congrats."

"Thanks," she said back. There was always something a little off between the two of them. Drew was pretty progressive, but it was like he wasn't exactly sure how to talk to Sam once he learned she was gay. With Katie, it was no problem. She adored everyone, and usually it was mutual. But with Drew and Sam, there were some sort of invisible blockade, and Bria hated that.

Drew helped himself to some snacks, then made his way through the Kreeries before plopping down on a recliner in the back of the living room.

"Do you want to call Abby, maybe give her a heads-up?" Bria whispered to Sam by the back door as they both stepped out of the crowd for a glass of punch. Sam shook her head.

"No. I don't want to make her nervous," she said. Just then, a bouquet of flowers flew over top of their heads, landing in Sam's hands.

"Congrats, kid," they heard him say, as he rested his chin on Sam's shoulder.

"Knox!" Sam said, turning to hug him. Bria felt her heart do a little jump. "I didn't know you were coming."

"Kates invited me, and I couldn't miss it," he said, kissing Sam's cheek and looking back at Bria. Bria smiled.

"Hey," she said, giving him a painfully short hug. She would have held onto him a little longer, given him a little squeeze, if she didn't feel Drew's eyes burning through them from across the room.

A half a second later, there was a knock on the door. Sam and Bria looked at each other. No one else would knock; their relatives were famous for simply walking through each other's doors. It had to be Abby.

"Well, let's get this over with," Sam sighed, making her way toward the foyer.

"What's going on?" Knox asked.

"Katie invited Sam's new girlfriend," Bria explained. Knox raised his eyebrows.

"Yikes. Not everyone knows, right?" he asked. Bria almost smiled. She couldn't believe how in touch he still was with her whole family.

"Right. Poor Sam," she said, watching her sister protectively. But as Sam opened the door, her pained expression melted away, making way for the widest smile Bria had ever seen on her sister's face. Without hesitation, Sam took Abby into the biggest, warmest embrace, and Bria was sure it was the most affection she had ever seen Sam show. Bria felt her heart swell. She watched as Sam snuck a peck on Abby's cheek, grabbed her hand, and took a deep breath.

"So," Sam said to Abby, "you ready?"

Abby smiled and nodded. "Of course."

Sam led her into the center of the living room where the family was running wild. Bria swallowed hard.

"Everyone," Sam said, but it wasn't anywhere near loud enough to grab the attention of the insanity that was their family. She cleared her throat. "Guys!" she shouted.

The room went silent. Sam looked at Bria, then to Katie, then down at the ground. Then she looked at her own hand, intertwined with Abby's, and suddenly, she looked steady, peaceful.

"I want to introduce you all to Abby," she said, "my girlfriend."

A few of the aunts who hadn't been told gasped. The younger cousins looked around, trying to gauge the adults' reactions. Grandma Gayle put her hand on her heart, proud that she was in on the big secret. All eyes found Uncle Tom who shifted uncomfortably in his seat.

The room was deafeningly silent, and Bria felt herself growing panicky. She wanted to say something, *anything* to draw the attention from her sister. But she was frozen.

"Well," Knox said, taking a step forward to Sam, "I, for one, am devastated by this news." Everyone's eyes grew wide, including Sam's. "Now I'll never have a chance with you," he said, pointing to her.

Everyone froze for a moment longer, until Sam burst out in uncontrollable laughter. Bria felt herself take a breath. Knox was a genius. She watched as he sauntered across the room, kissing Sam on the cheek again and shaking Abby's hand.

Now, everyone in the room was laughing, smiling, and practically standing in line to meet Abby, including Uncle Tom. All because of Knox.

"Why's he here, again?" she heard Drew whisper into her ear as he stood next to her, marking his territory.

"Katie invited him," she said.

"Why?"

"Why not?"

"Well, I think that went pretty well," Knox said, making his way toward them. He stuck his hand out to Drew. "Hey, man," he said. Drew took it hesitantly.

"Yeah, that wasn't bad at all," Bria said, uncomfortably moving under Drew's arm.

"Yeah, good thing you saved the day with that line," Drew said, taking a sip of his drink.

Knox looked to the ground and shrugged. "Just wanted to take the pressure off of Sam," he said.

"It was great, what you did," Bria said, fighting back the urge to reach out and grab his arm. Knox gave her a faint smile.

"Ben, you remember Grandma Gayle?" Louise asked him, as she and Grandma came in at just the right moment.

"How could I forget Grandma Gayle? I knew you were here when I saw that fruit salad in the kitchen!" he said, wrapping her in a big hug.

"Oh, I just can't believe how grown up you are! It seems like just yesterday you two were just a couple of kids!" Grandma Gayle said, pinching his cheek.

"Well, B and I might have grown up, but you haven't aged a year, I swear," Knox said, his arm around her shoulders. Grandma Gayle let out a silly, bashful giggle as she patted his cheek again. Then she led him to the dining room where he was enveloped by hugs from the rest of Bria's aunts and cousins.

"Jesus," Drew said, throwing back whatever was left in his cup. "This guy's just full of the lines."

"Lay off it, Drew," Bria said, just above a whisper. Drew turned to her.

"Gosh," Aunt Jamie said, walking back to the kitchen island and pouring herself another glass of wine, "I forgot how cute that Ben was! He was so freaking adorable when you two were kids, but *now?* He's a *man!*"

Bria's jaw dropped. Come *on*, Kreeries, get it together.

It was as if they couldn't see Drew standing right next to her, already seething over the subject of Knox. She probably should have put her arms around Drew, whispered something in his ear about him being the hottest guy she'd ever seen, given him that little bump in self-confidence that Knox was unknowingly stomping on. But a part of her worried Knox might see, and she didn't want that, either. So instead, she said nothing, and took a much-needed sip, no, gulp, of her sangria.

"Hey," Knox said, after a few more minutes with her family, "I think I'm gonna head out. It was great to see you guys. Good to see you, man," he said, sticking his hand out to Drew again.

"You leavin'?" Bria asked, trying not to sound as disappointed as she felt.

"Yeah, don't want to stay and see how many more of the Kreery women you can win over?" Drew asked.

Bria glared at him—if looks could kill, Drew would have been dead, buried, dug up, and buried again. Knox smiled and looked down at the ground, then back up to Bria.

"I'll see ya," he said, making his way out of the side door.

Bria didn't say anything, she just shot Drew one more deadly glance before following Knox outside.

"Knox," she called. He spun around toward her as he pulled his keys out of his pocket. "I'm really sorry about him. He's just. . . I don't know. Protective, I guess."

Knox didn't look shaken. They'd been through this before.

"No worries," he said, holding his hands up. "I don't want to cause any problems."

"You sure you have to leave?" she asked him.

"Yeah, I have to get going, anyways. I told my mom I'd meet her for a late dinner. I just wanted to congratulate Sam, see the family. See you," he said, looking up at her. She felt her heartbeat quickening, and she instinctively took a step closer to him. "Funny, I was just thinking, I've now been to one of Sam's grad parties, and none of yours," he said with a sly smile.

Bria smiled back, leaning up against his car.

"Wow," she said. "I haven't thought about that night in years."

SIXTEEN

Then, Bria's Graduation

Bria looked at herself in the mirror one last time, staring at herself up and down. This wasn't exactly what she thought she'd look like on her graduation day. Her hair was frizzing up under her cap, and she couldn't get the foundation that her mom had lent her to blend. She felt overdone, fake. But, as she took a deep breath, she realized this was all she had to work with.

"Come on, Bria!" Joe called up the stairs. "Jeesh, that girl will be late to her own funeral."

"I heard that," she called back, making her way down the stairs. Louise was already crying while taking pictures. Sam and Katie were already complaining about the heat, and Bria was already dreading the next few hours of her life. It was tradition in Dalesville for the graduation ceremony to be held on the football field, fresh smell of manure and all. She actually liked the idea of the tradition, but the heat was going to make it unbearable.

As they pulled into the school parking lot, she felt her phone buzz in her hand.

Congrats baby cakes. Knock em dead. And plz don't trip on stage.

Bria felt her face relax into a smile. Always there when she needed him. With the commotion of her final exams and getting ready for graduation, she hadn't seen Knox in a few days, and suddenly, realizing that now, she missed him terribly. She had to get through a few hours of scorching heat and laughing at the principal's attempts at pleasing his teenage crowd, but then, he'd be there. She kissed her parents before running down from the car, as fast as she could in her three-inch wedges, to the field.

As soon as the ceremony was over, Courtney and the other members of the student council walked around handing out yearbooks, and Courtney stopped Bria.

"Congrats on your superlative win!" she said. Bria raised an eyebrow. She hadn't even realized she was nominated.

"What did you win?" Sam asked as Bria fumbled through the pages. There, at the back of the book under the Senior Superlatives, was a picture of her, running the cross country course. Her face was fierce, the muscles in her arms bulging out, the next girl just a blur in the background behind her. Above it read: "Most Likely to Leave Dalesville." Beneath it, the caption read: "We all know Bria is a runner. And we bet she will be running for the hills. . . or *away* from them. . . the second she graduates!"

She smiled. She hadn't realized that she had been so vocal about wanting to leave. And then, as her parents both faked a smile, Bria realized they had no idea how badly she wanted to get out. And she immediately felt like the lowest branch on her family tree.

Ever since things had gone downhill so quickly with Katie's diagnosis and never-ending treatment, taking her family's financial security with them, Bria found herself in dire need of some new scenery. She wasn't exactly sure how, but she felt like if she went away to school, and maybe even *stayed* away after college, she had a chance to avoid the same problems she had at home. She could get a good job, make money, and escape the bad luck that seemed to be attached to her last name. She was holding onto the notion that those problems would stay in Dalesville, unable to follow her.

She closed the book, and her parents dutifully went to task snapping pictures of Bria with every one of her friends and her favorite teachers. As Bria posed with a few people, even Courtney Blake, she realized that she had checked out of high school long before she had actually graduated.

After a few more minutes of painfully forced hugs, congratulations, and explaining her future plans to parents of classmates she hadn't seen since elementary school, Bria was saved by her mother, who put a hand on her shoulder. Finally, Louise had snapped into party mode, and began rushing them all toward the parking lot.

"Come on, guys, we have a *lot* to do before the party starts." Joe, Bria, Katie, and Sam took turns making faces and rolling their eyes behind Louise's head.

When she got home, Bria changed into the lacy green party dress her mother had bought her for her party, and tried desperately to fix the mess that was her hair. She looked down at her phone.

What time will you be here? she sent to him. No response.

A few hours went by, and a few people had already started showing up. Her family, some of her friends from the team, Coach Boone. Mari and her family, Courtney and her followers.

But still no Knox.

Bria played hostess well; it was one of the skills each of the Kreery girls had inherited from their mother. She spent time with every single guest, asking them about their parents, or kids, or their plans for college next year, depending on who it was. Teddy appeared from around the side of the house. She ran to him, giving him a Knox-like hug.

"Hey," she said.

"Hey, congratulations!" he said, handing her a card that his mother probably bought.

"Thanks. Is Knox on his way?" she asked. Teddy shrugged.

"I thought maybe he was already here. I haven't heard from him all week," he said. She nodded, pulling out her phone again.

Hello? she sent. Still nothing.

Bria felt a ball of nerves forming in the pit of her stomach, but she wasn't quite sure why.

After an hour, Joe pulled her away from some of her friends.

"Hon, your mom and I would like to say a few words about you," he said. She nodded.

"Okay, can I have five minutes?" she asked.

"Sure."

She made her way to the front of the house and pulled out her phone, dialing him frivolously. *Ring, ring, ring.* No answer. Dammit, Knox.

"Hey, you comin' around back?" Sam appeared on the front porch. Bria was quiet for a moment, staring down at her phone. She slowly shook her head.

"Sam, I have to go."

"Go? Go where? It's *your* party," she said.

"Can you cover for me? Just try to stall?" Bria said, walking toward her car.

"Bria? Bria!" Sam called out to her.

"Please, Sam. I need to. . . I just have to run out. I'll be back."

She knew she was going at least fifteen over the speed limit the entire way to the Knoxvilles' but she didn't give a damn. When she pulled in, the only car in the driveway was Knox's. She hopped out of her car, running around to the back of the house in her party dress. She let herself in, quietly tip-toeing toward his bedroom. She knocked lightly, but there was no answer.

"Knox?" she whispered. She froze for a moment. God, what was she about to see? What was she about to witness?

She opened the door slowly, the hall light sending a stream of light cascading through his room. She saw him, balled up in his bed, covers pulled up to his chin. He rolled over slowly to look at her. She silently sighed in relief.

"B, what are you doing here?" he asked, his voice scratchy, as if he hadn't spoken in days. Her heart sunk. Here he was, her best friend, all alone. He needed her. He needed her bad. She slipped her shoes off and climbed up the bed, settling in next to him.

"B, what are you doing here?" he asked again, his eyes wide in the dark now. "You're missing your own party."

She smiled at him, reaching out slowly to stroke his face. She propped herself up on the pillow next to him, lifting his head lightly and resting it on her chest.

"This is the only party I want to be at," she whispered. She felt his hand reach up, squeezing her arm.

"B, I can't let you miss it," he whispered, and she wasn't sure if he was crying.

"Shh," she said. "I'm not going anywhere without you."

For a while, they sat in complete silence, their heads resting on one another as they watched T.V. Bria made popcorn, knowing that he likely hadn't eaten anything substantial for a few days. A few hours passed, and she awoke to him stirring in the bed next to her. She reached around for her phone. Shit. It was past midnight, and she had fourteen missed calls from her parents. Shit, shit, shit.

She scooted to the edge of the bed, pulling her shoes back on.

"Hey," he said, sitting up sleepily.

"Hey," she said. "I gotta go. My parents are looking for me."

"Oh, God, B, you missed the whole thing," he said, putting his hands to his head.

"Hey, look at me," she said, reaching out and pulling them down. "I was right where I was supposed to be. Now, hang out tomorrow?"

It took him a moment, but a faint smile appeared on his face. He nodded.

"B?" he asked before she reached for the doorknob. "I'd be lost without you."

She couldn't respond with anything but a bashful smile and a wink before slipping out. She pulled into her driveway and climbed out of her car as quietly as she possibly could. All the cars that had been parked in front of their house were gone, and only a few empty cups remained outside. She hopped up the porch steps, quietly turning the doorknob, and tiptoeing inside, until she saw her parents, seated at the kitchen table waiting for her. Her shoulders dropped.

"Hi," she muttered.

"Sit down," Louise said. It took Bria aback. She wasn't used to this tone, despite the fact that she totally deserved it. She did what she was told.

"Where were you?" her father asked.

"I was. . . I was at Knox's," she said. Her father hung his head, rubbing his eyes.

"What? At Ben's? Why?" Louise asked. But before Bria could answer, Louise popped up from the table, pacing the kitchen. "Do you understand you missed almost your entire party? You missed the Grants, the Peters, The Hardens, the whole damn neighborhood. You missed your *grandparents,* and Nellie Goldstein."

"You missed *everything,*" her dad said. "We didn't even get to give you our toast."

Bria stared down at her folded hands on the table.

"I'm so sorry," she finally muttered, failing

miserably to stop the tears from streaming down her face.

"Just tell us *why,*" her mother said, making her way back to the table. "Why did you go to Ben's? Why wasn't he here?"

Bria swallowed hard, wiping her tears on the back of her hand. She had never talked about Knox's problem to anyone. She'd never told a soul about his moods, his bad spells. Not even Mari or Sam. She felt like she would be betraying him, sharing a secret that wasn't hers to tell.

But the truth was, Bria was scared. She wasn't sure how to help him. She knew lying in bed with him for hours, or even days at a time wasn't healthy. It wasn't a solution. But she didn't know what else to do. So she just laid there and held him until he smiled again.

"Knox has this . . .this problem," she finally said.

"What kind of problem?" Joe asked, leaning in. Her mother sat back down in the chair next to her. "B? What kind of problem?" Bria sniffed and wiped her face again, the damn foundation rubbing off everywhere.

"I guess he's sort of. . . depressed."

Both of her parents raised their eyebrows. Bria went on. "He has these days, well, sometimes weeks, where he's just really sad. He won't leave his room. And so usually we just lay there, and we watch T.V., and we just wait for it to pass. And tonight was one of those nights."

Louise scooted her chair in closer to Bria, putting an arm around her shoulder.

"Oh, honey. How long has this been going on?" she asked. Bria shrugged.

"A few years now," she said, "ever since his accident." Louise looked to Joe, and back to Bria.

"Do his parents know?" Joe asked, reaching out for Bria's hand. Bria nodded.

"They know he gets sad, but they say he'll get over it. I don't think they know how to help him, either."

Joe sat back in his chair. "So that's where you went tonight. To be with him." he said.

Bria nodded. "I'm so sorry I missed the party. I just, I just got scared. Teddy hadn't heard from him either, and I was just so scared that I was going to find him. . . I don't know," she said, actually sobbing now, unable to put her worst fear into words. Her mother pulled her in for a long hug, the kind only a mother can give.

"Oh, sweet Bria," she whispered, "shh, it's okay sweetheart."

"That's a lot of weight for you to bear, B," Joe said, patting her hand.

"It really is, hon," her mother said. "You love him." Bria's eyes flashed to her mother. "He's your best friend. It's okay for you to be there for him. But he might need more help that you can't give him."

"Have you thought about suggesting therapy to him?" Joe asked.

Bria shrugged. Despite everything she knew about Knox, there was something that felt too pushy about suggesting medical intervention.

"It could really help him, hon. He could learn some good techniques, maybe start some medication. I can help you look up a few therapists around here. He could go, and his parents don't even have to know."

"Yeah, honey. And you won't always be able to be there for him. I mean, what will he do when you're at college? Or when you start dating someone again?" Joe asked.

Bria hadn't thought about any of this. She had stupidly just assumed that she'd always be able to hop in bed next to him whenever he needed. But they were right.

"Okay," Bria said, accepting reality. Eventually, lying next to him wouldn't work anymore. Although, sometimes for her, lying with him seemed to be the solution to all of life's problems.

Louise and Joe stood up, surrounding Bria on either side with a joint hug, kissing her forehead and squeezing her tight.

"Guys?" Bria said when the moment was over.

"Hmm?"

"Is it too late to hear my toast?" she asked. Joe and Louise smiled at each other.

"We thought you'd never ask," Joe said, reaching into his pocket for his reading glasses as Louise pulled a piece of paper off the island.

The next morning, Bria pulled back into the Knoxvilles' driveway. Knox was out of bed, showered, and dressed when she got there.

As she drove him to the park, she felt the nerves swirling around in her stomach again. She shouldn't be so worried about talking to her best friend, but she was. She felt like she was going to cross some invisible line.

"How are you feeling?" she asked as they each took a swing. He shrugged.

"Better today, I guess," he said. "I feel so awful about your party. Were your parents upset?"

"They weren't happy," she said.

"What did you tell them?" he asked. She looked down.

"Well, I wasn't exactly sure what to say. . ." she said, swallowing nervously. He nodded. "But listen, Knox, I want to talk to you about this." She could feel him tensing up next to her.

"Okay."

"Do you think it might help you to . . . maybe, see someone?"

"Someone?" he asked, raising an eyebrow. "Like a shrink?"

Bria nodded.

He barely paused to think, then shook his head. "No."

"Do you think maybe you should?"

"No."

"Why not?" she asked. He stood up from the swing.

"I don't know. Because it's not that big of a deal. I get over it. I'm fine."

"But, it happens a lot. And you don't *have* to feel like this."

"I don't feel like that all the time. I'm fine."

"Knox. . ."

"Bria, I'm not seeing a shrink. I don't need it being written down on paper somewhere that my head's fucked up. I already know that. I'm good. I'm fine."

She stood up, walking to him and throwing her arms around his waist. She rested her head on his chest and breathed him in.

"Promise me that you'll think about it. But in the meantime, promise you'll let me be there, when you need."

She felt him let out a long breath, letting her arms coil a little tighter around his middle.

"I promise."

SEVENTEEN

Now

"Hey, hon," her dad said over the speakerphone in her car. "On your way home today, do you think you could stop at the pharmacy and grab Katie's prescriptions? The doctor called in a few more today."

"Yeah, of course," Bria said. "I'll be home within the hour."

She walked through the drugstore while she waited for the prescriptions to be filled, smelling all the fancy lotions and half-painting her nails with a million different colors.

"Ms. Kreery," the pharmacist called to her, "your prescriptions are ready."

As she made her way to the back, she tripped over a display of umbrellas, sending about ten of them flying across the floor.

"Of course," she said to herself, bending over to pick them up. She heard a laugh and looked up.

"So you haven't grown out of that," Knox said, crouching down to help her. She chuckled back at him, quickly brushing herself off and standing back up.

"Thanks. How are you?" she asked.

"I'm good," he said. He was holding a white pharmacy bag, and he saw her eyeing it. "Happy pills," he said with a nervous smile, jiggling the bag in front of her.

"Oh, wow," she said, "good for you, Knox. That's great."

"Yeah," he said looking down at the ground. "I couldn't depend on you to come get me out of bed forever," he said with a chuckle.

"Well, I would have done it for as long as you needed," she said, quite seriously. "But I'm glad that you took things into your own hands. Are you doing better?"

"Yeah, I think so. You know how it is. Some days are harder than others, but the bad spells aren't as bad." She smiled and nodded.

"Knox?" she said.

"Yeah?"

"Jimmie Cone?"

As she took the cones from the window, Bria moved one toward him, then paused. Something in her gut was telling her not to, but she did it anyway. She licked his cone, and handed it to him with a chocolate-and-vanilla-covered smile. His eyes widened with delight.

"Hey," he said, taking a lick right where her tongue had been, "that's my move." She shrugged and led him to a table.

"So, are you seeing someone?" she asked. He looked up at her. "A therapist, I mean."

"Oh. Yeah, I've been seeing one for about four years or so, now."

"And it's helped?"

"Yeah, I think so. It got really bad right around the time. . . right around the time you went away to college."

"Oh. Why then?" she asked. He looked at her.

"I don't know," he said finally.

"I wish you would have told me," she said.

"Well, there was one night I almost did. Actually, Teddy almost did."

"What? When?"

"The night you got engaged."

She suddenly wasn't hungry, anymore.

"What?"

"Yeah, I think I drank the whole night. Teddy found me in my own puke. Not one of my best nights," he said with a smile.

"Knox, what happened?"

He shrugged. "I had just been having a tough couple of months. Then I saw the announcement on Facebook."

"What about it?" He shrugged again and held his hand up.

"Eh, it really doesn't matter. Point is, I started seeing a therapist, and I've really been doing a lot better. Those bad spells, they don't come around near as much."

She so badly wanted to pry for more information. Why that night? But that was a line she no longer had a right to cross. That was information she no longer had a right to know.

"Well, I'm really glad you're doing well," she said, grabbing his hand for a brief second. "And I hope you know that if you ever do have one of those times, I'm still going to answer when you call."

He smiled at her. She hated that there was so much about his life over the last few years that she didn't know about.

"Thanks," he said, "but I don't know if Drew would like that. I know I wouldn't, if you were my fiancée."

Suddenly, she felt a pang of guilt.

"Well, I should get going," she said. "See ya around."

Later that night, she lay in Sam's bed, scrolling through Facebook on her phone. Across the room was a tall bookshelf, and out of the corner of her eye, she spotted her old yearbooks. She pulled them out, lugging the big pile to the bed and began to flip through.

She turned all the way to the back, where he had signed each year.

Baby cakes -

Thanks for being the sun in my sky, the rose to my thorn, the . . . yeah, I'm all out of clever lines. Thanks for being you, and for being mine. Your Baby Cakes, Knox

It was funny, but all these years later, the note still gave her a little tingle, just as it had the night he wrote it.

As she traced his handwriting with her fingers, her phone buzzed on the bed.

Ya know how I said the bad spells weren't as bad? his text read.

Yeah. . .

I guess I sort of lied. They still suck.

Do you want to talk?

If thats ok. Im outside.

She jumped up from the bed and ran to her window. Sure enough, there he was, in her parents' driveway. She snuck down the stairs as if she were a teenager, and quietly unlocked the back door, hushing the dog.

As she stepped out onto the back patio, she shivered. She had underestimated how cold it was. She rubbed her arms as she walked down the driveway.

"Hey," she whispered. "You wanna go out back?"

"Sure," he said. She quietly dragged two chairs to the back corner of the patio, where she knew they couldn't be seen through any of the windows in the house. She knew this from experience—it's where she and Brett went to make out when her family was home.

"Thanks," he said. "Sorry it's so late."

"So what's going on?" she asked, her voice quivering in the cold. He smiled and shook his head, pulling his hoodie up over his head and holding it out for her.

"Here, ya nut." She hesitated for a moment, but took it, pulling it quickly over her own head. His scent almost knocked her out. It had been so long since she had smelled him, and she had forgotten how musky and sweet it was.

"Thank you," she said, giving him a quick smile. "Talk to me." She looked at her friend, begging him with her eyes to open up, and to let her be that person again.

"I don't know, I just. . . I feel like ever since. . . When I saw you and Drew at the bar, I just kinda. . ."

"What?" she asked, trying not to sound as impatient as she was.

He looked down at the ground again. The silence was deafening.

"Remember that first party at my house you came to?" he said with a faint smile.

"Yeah," she said, wondering what this had to do with the night at the bar, or the demons he was dealing with.

"God, and that day the ball hit you! I almost forgot about that," he said, and she realized he was avoiding the question.

"Knox," she said.

He looked up at her, and suddenly, leaned in closer to her. His eyes were moving from side to side as he stared into hers, as if he were looking for some sort of answer. He lifted his hand, lowering it just above hers, but quickly stopped.

"I'm sorry," he said, standing up. "I shouldn't have texted you."

"What? No, Knox, don't apologize. You can talk

to me. It's still me," she said, standing up and grabbing his arm. He looked down at her hand on him, then into her eyes. For the shortest second, he placed his hand on top of hers, squeezing it.

"No. I'm fine, really. I'm sorry. I really shouldn't have texted you, or shown up like an idiot. I'm gonna head home."

"Knox," she said, reaching for his arm and spinning him around. For a moment, their foreheads touched, and they both stood perfectly still. He closed his eyes, taking in a few slow breaths. Finally, he stepped back.

"Sorry again," he said.

She wondered how hard she could beg him to stay before it sounded desperate. Then she decided not to at all.

"Wait, your sweatshirt," she said, pulling it off over her head. In high school, he'd put his hand up, and say, "keep it." But tonight, he just took it back slowly, and got back in his car.

She snuck back into her house, climbing the stairs quietly, skipping the creaky ones, and plopped back into bed. After a moment, her phone buzzed again, and she practically fell off the bed to get it.

So sorry I didn't call after work. Got off late. Had another surgery today! I'll call you in the a.m. Love you!

She sighed, her shoulders sinking in disappointment.

Awesome! Can't wait to hear all about it. She sent it. Then, as she set her phone down on her end table, she jumped back up.

Love you, too! she added.

EIGHTEEN

Then, Summer Before College

"I'm not sure what else we can do," Bria heard her mother say. She and Sam sat in the hallway, as they had so many times as kids, eavesdropping on their parents' kitchen table conversation. She never really understood why her parents had these so-called private discussions in the kitchen; it was an open floor plan, and their voices carried perfectly. But she and Sam would never dare point that out for fear of losing out on their vantage point.

"I'm not either, hon," Joe said. "I guess we can try and sell your car. We can carpool to work, you can drop me off."

"We can also cancel cable, for now," her mother said.

Bria heard her mother blow her nose, and knew she was crying. Earlier that day, she had seen her mother open a piece of mail, and as she read the contents, her hands started to shake. Louise seemed to be in a hurry during dinner for the girls to finish up and get ready for bed. So Bria and Sam knew it was probably a bill collector, or the bank.

"I can't believe this is happening. Jesus, Joe, what if we lose the damn house?" her mother whispered. Just then, Bria heard another little sob from next to her. Sam had tears streaming down her face, and she was clutching her stomach. Bria held her finger to her lips, telling Sam to hush, and led her into their shared bedroom. When Katie got sick, her parents had moved Sam in with Bria so Katie wouldn't wake Sam when she needed to take pills, or was uncomfortable during the night.

"Sam, it's gonna be just fine. You heard them, they'll just get rid of one of the cars. That will help a ton. Plus, I have savings. Don't worry, okay?" she said, stroking Sam's hair.

"I'm scared, Bria," Sam said, sniffling.

"Shhh. . ." Bria said, rubbing her back until she finally dozed off to sleep.

That night, Bria lay in bed, her stomach in a thousand knots, knowing she wouldn't drift off to sleep. She had no idea what to do. Or if she could even do anything. She was supposed to be leaving for college in less than two weeks. But how could she leave her family like this? She looked at the clock. 2:43 a.m. There was only one person who *might* be up right now.

Bria snuck down the stairs and out to her car, driving the backroads to his house. Bria snuck around the back of the house, careful not to set off the motion sensor lights. She paused at the back door for a moment. What if he didn't want to see her? Or, worse, what if he already had someone in there? But, it was too late. She was already here, and she was desperate.

She tapped lightly on the glass at first, then a little harder. Finally, a light shone from the back hallway, and a sleepy Knox came out in nothing but a pair of basketball shorts. He rubbed his eyes as he unlatched the door.

"B?" he whispered, opening it wider. "What's

going on, you okay?"

Instead of answering him, she stepped inside, wrapping her arms around him and burying her face into his bare chest. And then she cried. And cried. And cried. He led her into his bedroom to muffle the sounds from waking his parents. He got her a cup of water from the bathroom, and sat down next to her on his bed. When she finally calmed down, he propped the pillows up on his bed and patted them for her to lie back next to him.

"What's going on?" Knox asked again, once fluids had stopped pouring from every orifice on her face.

"I think my parents are going to lose the house," she whispered. He pulled the covers up around her. "And I don't even know if they will be able to finish paying for Katie's treatment. And I'm supposed to be leaving, and now I don't know if I can go. It's too late to apply for financial aid, and they will need the money. . ." she felt the tears welling up again, and the lump in her throat was back.

"Shh," he whispered, wrapping one arm around her and pulling her into him again. "B, your family is going to be fine, okay? I promise. And so is Katie. There are definitely some programs they can look into, or loans they can get. . .I promise, they will be fine. You have to go, B. You need to go." She didn't say anything, she just lay her cheek on his chest, and let his steady breathing lift her head up and down. It had been looming all summer, but this was the first time they had talked about the fact that she'd be leaving. UMD was only an hour away. But she was still *going away*. She wouldn't be commuting to school like he was. She'd be a full-fledged college student. She finally looked up at him.

"You need to go," he said again. But just before she drifted to sleep, she heard him whisper, "but I don't want you to."

The next morning, they woke to a knocking. She

was curled up in a mix of sheets and him, his long arms wrapped around her. She squinted as she slowly opened her eyes. *Knock. Knock. Knock.* Holy shit. She was still in his bed. And it was light out.

"Knox! Wake up," she whispered, shaking his shoulder. He quickly jumped up. "We fell asleep!"

"Shit!" he said, jumping up and pulling a t-shirt on that he had grabbed off the floor.

"Knox? I'm coming in," Mrs. Knoxville said.

"Hold on, Ma, I'm—" *bam.* The door burst open. Mrs. Knoxville stood there, her hand on the doorknob, her jaw at the floor.

"Oh, good morning, Bria," she said, looking flushed.

"Hi, Mrs. Knoxville," Bria said, her voice shaky. Fuck.

"Mom, this isn't—she just came over to hang out and we fell asleep. . ." Knox started to say.

"Well, whatever *this* is," she said, motioning to the two of them, "the Kreeries just called. They are looking for you, Bria."

"Oh, my God!" Bria said, scurrying out of the bed. "I'm so sorry," she said, pulling on her shoes. "Knox, I'll call you later!"

Luckily, Louise and Joe hadn't changed their approach to parenting overnight, so there was nothing in the way of punishment. Just a quick "tell us from now on when you'll be out," was all she got. She supposed that if it was Knox she was with, they weren't worried; they never suspected that their relationship was anything but platonic. And ever since she had told them about his depression, they were even more lenient when she was spending time with him. She knew she wouldn't be in trouble, she just hated to cause them any more worry or anxiety than they were already dealing with.

Later that evening, as she helped her mom clean up from dinner, she pulled out her phone.

I'm so sorry I fell asleep. But thank you, she texted.

Don't be sorry. I like sleeping with u ;) it's all gonna be ok, he sent back, almost immediately.

She smiled and clutched the phone to her chest. She didn't know if he was right, but it felt good to have him in her corner.

The rest of the short week passed, and before she knew it, it was her last night at home before leaving for College Park. Her parents and sisters were helping her load up both of their cars with all the new things they had bought before Katie started treatment, for her dorm. It had been two weeks since Bria heard her parents discussing their possible foreclosure, but nothing had come of it. It was too late for her to apply for loans, and Bria wondered if she would get to school and get kicked out right away because her tuition wasn't paid. But she shook her head. Her parents wouldn't do that to her.

Louise had been crying off and on all day.

"I can't believe my biggest baby is leaving," she said, laying a long kiss on Bria's forehead as she shoved one more box in the back of the car. Bria swallowed hard, her anxiety levels peaking. Tomorrow was the day she'd leave for college, but she'd be leaving behind her family on the brink of a financial crumbling. She couldn't help but wonder about what they'd do, or if Katie would ever get better. The knot in her stomach grew ten sizes as she tried to control her breathing. But she couldn't hide it from her mother.

"Sweetie," Louise whispered, pulling in her for another hug, "stop worrying. We are going to be just fine." Just as Joe slid the last of Bria's boxes into the back of the car, his phone rang.

"Be right back," he said, exiting to the kitchen. After no more than five minutes, he came bursting out the front door.

"Lou, Lou! Great news, we're all caught up with the mortgage, *and* have six months paid in advance!" Her mother's eyes grew wide.

"Wha—what? How?" Louise asked, bringing her clenched fists to her face.

"I. . . I'll tell you later. But it's all taken care of, baby!" he said, laughing, and pulling her in for a long kiss. The girls laughed and clapped their hands. Knox was right. It would all be okay. And just as Bria imagined sharing the news with him, down the cul-de-sac came Mr. Knoxville's beat-up old pickup truck, the one he let Knox drive after his accident. Knox pulled up in front of her house and hopped out.

"Knox!" Katie said, running to him for a hug. He scooped her up and made his way to the car, giving Sam a hug.

"Hey, Kreery clan," he said, turning to Bria. "I couldn't let ya go without stopping in to say goodbye."

She looked up at him, eyes watery.

"Somehow . . . my parents got caught up with their bills," she said quietly. He flashed a devilish grin and pulled her into his chest.

"Told ya everything would be okay," he whispered back.

"Girls, come on in and help me grab these last boxes," Louise called. Sam and Katie scurried inside.

"I'm glad you came by," she said.

"Of course. I couldn't not say goodbye, baby cakes," he said. She smiled and squeezed him again, tight.

"Will you come visit?" she asked.

"Parties and free booze? You know I'm there," he said, giving her that knee-weakening grin again. "I'll see you soon, baby cakes."

NINETEEN

Now

It had been a little over a month since Bria's promotion, and work was going absolutely perfect. She enjoyed the people on her new team, and she got a lot more freedom with the projects she was working on. The extra money wasn't half-bad either, and it had helped tremendously with the Kreeries' expenses. The commute from Dalesville really wasn't much worse than her commute from D.C., and she could beat traffic if she left early enough.

As she pulled into the driveway, Louise was walking down the porch steps, with her purse on her shoulder.

"Where you going, ma?" she asked.

"Oh, just to the grocery store. I've been so busy with your sister this week, that I haven't had a second to go."

"Well, you want some company?"

As they strolled the aisles, they talked about just about everything, from Katie's treatment, to the bills, to the wedding, to Sam's new girlfriend.

"I really couldn't stand that last girl she was with, that Rebecca," Louise said, placing a jar of pasta sauce into the cart.

"Yeah, me either. She was so spoiled and uptight," Bria agreed. Samantha was definitely the quietest out of the three of them, but for whatever reason, she tended to pick loud, high-maintenance girlfriends. And Bria tended to be extra-overprotective when it came to Sam.

"She seems to really like Abby, though. She was really sweet at the party. I liked her a lot," Louise said. Bria nodded. She had actually liked Abby, too.

As they turned down the dairy aisle, Louise stopped the cart.

"Hi, Tonya!" she said, pulling the cart up next to Mrs. Knoxville's to give her a long hug. Bria followed.

"Hello, Kreery gals," Mrs. Knoxville said. "How are you guys?"

"We're doing well! Just enjoying having my big girl home," Louise said, looking at Bria lovingly. She was really enjoying her time with her family, too. More than she had expected to.

"That's great! I think Ben mentioned you were home," Mrs. Knoxville. Bria felt her stomach do a small flip. "Now, you're getting married, right?"

"Yep, in just a few months, actually," Bria said. "We're just finalizing the last details now."

"We are all so excited," Louise said.

"I bet! That's so exciting. We're going out to dinner tomorrow night with Ben and his new girl."

"Oh, Ben has a *girlfriend?*" Louise asked, her eyes wide. It was pretty well-known around Dalesville that Ben Knoxville was never tied down, even now, as he was pushing thirty. "How exciting! Did you know that, Bria?" Bria put on a closed-mouth smile and shook her head.

"He's still not saying she's his *girlfriend,* per se, but they've been out a few times, and he seems to really like her. A mother can hope, right?"

"Hey, fingers crossed! You never know! Bria and Drew only went on a few dates, and look where they are now!" Louise said.

Ugh. Bria wished her mother would stop talking. She didn't know why, but she felt like she'd been punched in the gut, and she just wanted to go home. As they said good-bye, Bria grew quiet.

"Well, that's exciting," Louise said again. "He never had a girlfriend all through high school, right?"

"Nope," Bria said, grabbing a bag of shredded cheese off the shelf and dropping it into the cart.

"I always thought it was funny that the two of you never. . ." Louise started to say. "Nah. I guess that would have been too weird."

"*Way* too weird," Bria said. "We were never like that. So Drew talked to his parents again last night," she said, desperate to switch gears, "and they are putting the final payment down on the food this week. We should be all set."

"Oh, wonderful," Louise responded, but Bria could tell from the look on her mother's face that she felt it was anything *but* wonderful.

"What's wrong?"

"Oh, nothing. I just wish we could do more. I wish I could be taking care of my daughter's wedding, instead of my daughter having to take care of me."

The words struck Bria to her core. She hated that her parents struggled so much with money. But she mostly hated that they felt like failures because of it.

"Mom," she said, grabbing Louise's arm, "I would get married in a freaking barn, if you wanted me to. I really don't give a shit about stuff like that, you know that. And I wish you'd stop saying that, about me taking care of you. You and dad have taken care of us for our whole lives. There's nothing I'd rather do than return the favor. Okay?"

Louise smiled sadly, squeezing Bria's hand.

"You are such a wonderful daughter," she whispered. Just then, they heard someone calling their names from the checkout line.

"Bye Louise, bye Bria!" Mrs. Knoxville called, as she finished checking out.

"Oh, bye, Tonya!" Louise said, as they waved back. "I wonder if whoever he's dating has money," Louise wondered out loud.

Whoever he's dating.

That night, Bria sat with Katie on the couch, screaming at *The Voice* on television when the young, one-armed songbird from Texas chose Blake over Adam.

"What is *wrong* with her?" Katie asked, shaking her head. But Bria wasn't really listening. Instead, she was spinning her phone around and around between her fingers.

"Dude, just call him," Katie said, never taking her eyes of the screen.

"What? Call who?" Bria asked, as if she had been caught.

"Drew. You've been spinning that thing around for like, an hour."

"Oh, yeah. I want to, but he's working late tonight," Bria said. But she didn't really want to call Drew. She finally stopped spinning, and opened up a new text message.

Saw your mom at the store tonight. It was great to see her. It's been years. She sent it. She waited anxiously for a few moments until she felt her phone vibrate on her leg.

I heard. That's awesome. I'm sure she missed u.

Bria paused for a moment, contemplating her next message.

Heard they're meeting your new girl tomorrow. She paused again before sending it. She couldn't decide if it was too nosy, if she should even bring it up. But, she was compulsive. Off it went. After three agonizing minutes, her phone vibrated again.

Something like that.

She sat back on the couch. So it was true. She needed to see him. She needed to evaluate just how serious this was. And figure out why he hadn't mentioned a thing about this purported "girl" of his over the last few weeks.

Well, that's awesome. Hey are you around to run tomorrow evening?

Well, we're going to dinner.

Shit. Duh. Then her phone buzzed again.

But, I could run before that.

Bria smiled.

Perfect. I'll meet ya at the path around 4?

I can pick u up, if u want.

Sounds good. See ya tomorrow.

The next day, she chose her running outfit carefully—a tight pair of leggings and a sleek tank. In high school, she could eat three helpings of pasta for breakfast, lunch, and dinner, and not gain a pound. But now, it took a little bit more than that. She had worked her ass off for this body. And now was her chance to show him. She waited around the front door for him to pull up, careful not to stand too close, so that he wouldn't see her waiting. Finally, her phone buzzed.

Here. She waited a moment before going out, so it didn't seem like she had been staring out the window for the last fifteen minutes.

"Hey," she said, getting in the passenger side.

"Howdy," he said, moving whatever crap was on the front seat to the back.

"Well, some things never change," she said with a laugh. He wore a t-shirt with the sleeves cut off, and she couldn't help but notice how defined his arm muscles were.

"Man, it's been a while since we've done this," he said, parking his car in the lot at the beginning of the path.

"It really has. Remember when we used to finish

our runs early so we could swing over there for a while?" she asked, pointing to the park that stood a few yards away.

"Yeah," he chuckled. "If it had been up to me, we never would have gotten started running. We just would have swung the whole time." She laughed and shook her head.

"Yeah, you always did hate it," she said.

"Yeah. But you loved it. So I did it," he said, matter-of-factly. She swallowed.

As they started down the path, Bria let a few moments of necessary small talk go on before she finally brought it up.

"So," she said.

"So," he said, knowing it was coming.

"Tell me about her." He laughed.

"Talk about things not changing," he said.

"What do you mean?"

"You used to have to know *everything* about any girl that I was remotely interested in," he said with a half-smile.

"That's not true," she said, giggling. He shot her a look. "Okay, it is. But it was only because I needed to check up on them and make sure they were good enough for you. You weren't so good at deciding that yourself." That brought out a laugh from deep from in his belly. Wow. She had missed that.

"Okay, I'll give you that. This one's a little different, though," he said, growing a bit more serious.

"Oh? How so?" she asked, but she didn't know if she actually wanted to hear the answer.

"She's really. . .grown-up. I know, shocking for me," he said. "But it's refreshing."

"Wow. How did you meet her?"

"We actually went to high school with her. Do you remember Karly Shepherd?"

Bria stopped in her tracks for a moment, then

nodded. Karly Shepherd. *That's* why he didn't mention it. Of course she remembered Karly. She was the only girl at Dalesville High that came close to breaking Knox's heart, so Bria sort of, well, totally hated her. Last Bria had heard, Karly was finishing up dentistry school.

"Yeah, of course. Wow, Karly. How did you two reconnect?"

"I actually ran into her at a bar a few weeks ago. I know, classy," he laughed again. "We just started talking, and we've gone out a few times."

Bria didn't say anything, just nodded.

"Aww, come on Bria," he said, nudging her playfully. "That was then, this is now."

"Oh, I know. I guess I never really got past what she did to you."

"Aww, come on. If I can, you can. That was so long ago, we were all just kids."

His flippant words struck her, as though one of the big trees they were running under had fallen and hit her. It wasn't *that* long ago. Karly had still broken him. And Bria couldn't help but wonder if the "just kids" comment was what he thought whenever, if ever, he thought about the two of them, Bria and Knox. She wondered if everything they had was just a "good old days" kind of memory for Knox. Something to be left in the past.

TWENTY

Then, Freshman Year of College

After three or four weeks in College Park, Bria felt like she was finally getting the hang of the college life. It had taken some getting used to, but she was starting to have a little bit of fun. She'd made a few friends and gone to a few parties. She'd even had a moment of rebellion and gotten a tattoo. She'd always fiddled with the idea, but she couldn't commit to a design she really wanted. But as she stood in the tattoo shop with her roommate, Miranda, she spontaneously decided on a branch of dogwood flowers, for no particular reason, down the side of her shoulder. She had a moment of panic as she admired her ink in the mirror that night, where she realized the permanence. But it wore off the more she stared at the bright pink petals on her arm. Her life had been so conventional. This made her feel a little unorthodox, edgy.

She was starting to figure things out, like which professors and classes she wanted to take the next semester, and that she definitely wanted to change her major from psychology to marketing. Things were going okay. But she missed home. She missed her sisters. And she missed Knox.

They talked almost every day, him checking in on her, seeing how classes were going, casually asking about the guys she was meeting on campus.

She'd laugh and tell him not to worry about it; she liked being a little sneaky, hoping that he'd want to put a stop to any hanky-panky that she might be getting into. But in reality, it was none. Zero. Zilch.

In her short eighteen years, sex hadn't come to mean much to Bria. She supposed that was because she hadn't had much of it; losing her virginity in a coat closet sort of set her out for a lifetime of underwhelming sexual experiences, she assumed. So after a few awkward hookups on campus, she had thrown in the towel for a while. Unless, of course, she could do it with someone that actually *meant* something to her. Just as she was adding names to her list of prospects, which included Jeremy, the hot graduate assistant that taught her English 101 class, and both of the Hemsworth brothers, her phone buzzed in her bag. She dug it out just in time.

"Hey, you," she said, smiling as she kicked a pebble in front of her.

"You comin' home this weekend?" Knox said, crunching on something on the other end.

"Yeah, I think I will," she said. "What are we doing?"

She wanted him to know that she just assumed he'd be spending most of the weekend with her. She wanted him to know that it was important for her to see him.

"Well, I want you to meet somebody," he said. Her heart starting beating inexplicably faster.

"Oh? Who?"

"Okay, well it's not really *meeting* someone, per se, it's more like re-meeting them."

"Who is it?"

"Remember Karly Shepherd?" he asked. There was an unfamiliar tone in his voice; one that was light, and airy, and almost dreamy.

"Yeah," she said.

"Well, I think we are sort of, together."

"What? When did this happen?" Bria asked. She played it off like she was just offended that he hadn't mentioned it to his best friend. But in reality, she was panicking. This was so weird, so foreign to her. His place in her life till now had always been so clear. But what would hers be in his, if there was someone else?

"Well, we've been talking for the last few weeks, and we're actually going to meet up at Dalesville Day. But I wanted to have a group of people over afterward." Bria stayed silent. "So, I was thinking that you could join us."

Bria thought for a moment, perplexed.

"I guess. But won't that be weird?"

"No. You know me. You know this whole thing is awkward for me, actually *talking* to a girl. It would be more weird if we were by ourselves. "

For a second, Bria actually felt bad for him. His normal "connection" with a female consisted of laying his smooth moves on her, and then sleeping with her, and promptly ending it. It was clear he had no idea how to have a relationship. She suspected it was because of his parents; she knew they weren't the happiest. They weren't miserable, but she didn't see them hugging, or kissing, or showing any affection. They'd often take trips without each other, and they both seemed to be okay with that. To be fair, though. Bria didn't really know them. Despite how close she and Knox were, she really hadn't spent a lot of time with his parents because they were never around. They had a lot of money, and they liked to spend it. Knox was their youngest, and they were waiting for him to be out of the house before they enjoyed the fruits of all their years of labor. He was on his own a lot.

"Yeah, okay. I'll be there," Bria responded.

"Yes, thank you, baby cakes."

For the past few days, Knox had been talking incessantly about Karly, but Bria had just assumed she was his catch of the week. Karly Shepherd was a year older than her and one year younger than Knox, and was possibly one of the most beautiful humans Dalesville had ever seen. She was tall and tan, but had naturally blonde hair that fell to the middle of her back. She had electric blue eyes, and she was incredibly smart. Everyone knew Karly Shepherd. She was one of the girls that you wanted to hate, but you also wanted to be friends with. She had recently broken up with her long-time boyfriend since high school, Tony Welsh. The rumor was that he had broken up with her for another girl in town, but it hadn't yet been proven true. Karly was reportedly struggling with the break-up big time, until Knox started giving her some attention.

That Friday, Bria and Knox grabbed some ice cream before they went to his house. She was only home for two days, so she wanted to soak in as much Knox as she could get. Even if it meant she had to share him.

"So," he said, snagging a lick of her cone, "at Karly's soccer game last week, she introduced me to some of her friends. I think I might go down and stay with her at school in a few weeks." Bria nodded.

"You went down to watch her play?"

Karly went to school on the eastern shore of Maryland. And though it was only a few hours away, Bria was surprised by Knox's commitment level.

"Yeah. She's so good," he said. "What's up with you?" he asked, detecting that her usual spark seemed to be zapped away.

"Oh, nothing. I guess I'm just worried she's using you as a rebound," Bria told him. Even though he was a player, she felt defensive of him when it came to his actual feelings. She didn't see them getting used very often, after all.

"Nah, I don't think it's like that. She's over Tony. Besides, he's already moving on with Franny Leibowitz."

"Franny? Franny was the other girl?" she asked. Franny was Karly's best friend all through school. They were roommates together in college. "Damn. That's cold."

The next morning was Dalesville Day, the annual parade and fair that happened every fall. As a teenager, Bria found it so painfully lame; most of the parade "floats" were just her neighbors on their newest John Deere tractors, broken up by the small herds of farm animals, and the streets were always filled with animal feces after the parade was over. But, for the first time in her life, Bria was actually missing home. And she couldn't wait for Dalesville Day. Maybe because she missed her hometown, or maybe because she was going with Knox.

When he picked her up, he was on the phone. He didn't come to the door like he normally did, asking for her sisters or her mother. Today, he seemed to be in a bit of a rush.

"Yeah, that sounds good. We'll meet you in front of Jimmie Cone." he said, hanging up. "Karly should be there soon."

"Cool," she said. "By the way, hi."

"Oh, yeah, hey!" he said, patting her leg once. "Welcome home!"

Parking at Dalesville Day was a always nightmare, and everyone and their mother knew to wear good walking shoes. It didn't matter where you parked, you'd likely have to walk to get a good view of the festivities.

When Knox and Bria finally came upon the perfect spot, a single patch of unoccupied grass in front of Jimmie Cone, he snagged it, standing in it as if he were protecting his own property.

"So, how is school going?" he asked, obviously preoccupied with finding Karly.

"It's school. Classes are alright. Parties are better,"

she said, hoping to muster up some more interest from him.

"Good, good," he said, standing on his tip-toes now to look over the people next to them. Finally, out of the clearing, stood Karly. The crowd seemed to part for her like the freaking Red Sea, and Bria couldn't help but roll her eyes. Shit like this *never* happened for her. She'd be the one lost behind the masses, quietly muttering "excuse mes" and "oops, sorries" until the end of freaking time. But not Karly. Apparently the universe was more in-tune with Karly. And she guessed, so was Knox.

"Hey, you," Knox said, wrapping Karly in a weirdly long hug. It wasn't the same kind of hug he normally gave to Bria. It was more. . . intense.

"Hey, yourself," she said, her sing-song voice reverberating through Bria's temples.

"You remember Bria?" Knox said, holding his hand out toward his friend when he finally remembered that she was there.

"Of course," Karly said, reaching out to give Bria an unexpected hug. "It's so good to see you!"

"Oh, hey, you too!" Fake Bria said. "Knox says you've been killing it in soccer this season."

Karly visibly blushed. "Oh, he's too kind," she said, reaching out and stroking his arm.

As the parade started, Bria couldn't help but notice how many times Knox took the opportunity to touch Karly, placing his hand on the small of her back, holding her hand. And when Knox offered to grab them ice cream, and snuck a lick of Karly's before giving it to her, Bria felt her heart crunch up like a leaf on the sidewalk.

Out of the corner of her eye, she saw a bleach-blonde figure making its way across the street, and it was calling out, no, *screaming* out Knox's name. Courtney Blake and her band of followers. *This should be interesting,* Bria thought, as she watched Karly stand up in heightened awareness.

"Knox!" Courtney called again, dramatically draping herself around his neck. Bria watched as Karly cleared her throat, finishing off her ice cream cone. The other girls took turns hugging Knox and kissing his cheeks. For a second, Bria actually felt sorry for Karly. Lord knew that Bria knew just what it felt like to fall to the background of Knox's love life.

"Hey," Knox said. And as Bria braced herself for him to get distracted, losing himself in their embraces, Knox took a step back, un-hooking Courtney's arm from his. "You guys remember Karly, right?"

Without missing a beat, Knox hooked his arm around Karly's waist and pulled her in to him. She looked up at him and smiled, nodding to Courtney. Of course they knew each other; they had played soccer together all through high school, and there was a definite rivalry between them. Courtney sunk back on her hip, looking them up and down.

"Oh. Yeah, hey, Karly," she said.

"We're just here with Bria, watching the parade," Knox said. It sort of made Bria cringe. It made it seem like she was the third-wheel. Which, apparently, she was. She'd never seen Knox turn down any sort of female attention before. And as much as she had wished for Knox to blow off Courtney in high school, in this particular situation, Bria didn't think she liked it. As he pulled Karly in again, this time, leaning down for what she could only assume to be the wettest kiss in history, Bria texted her mom.

You and dad still here? I might ride home with you.

Yup, getting ready to leave. Meet us in the pharmacy parking lot.

"Hey, guys, I'm gonna head out and meet up with my parents," she said. Knox turned to her.

"You sure?"

"Yup, I'm sure."

"Okay," he said, with an ounce of concern in his

eyes, "but we're still on for tonight, right?" Jesus, did he really still need her? She sighed to herself.

"Yeah, still on for tonight."

As the sun started to descend that evening, Bria found herself a bit uncomfortable thinking about the night ahead. She wasn't exactly sure how to act. She and Karly had been friendly, but didn't know each other all that well. And she knew Teddy would likely be there. After high school, Teddy was living it up as the sole member left in Knox's posse. And he was constantly hanging on Bria, as if she and Teddy were as close as she and Knox were. But she resolved to deal with it for one night, for Knox.

When she got to Knox's house, Karly hadn't arrived yet. Bria made herself comfortable on the basement couch next to Teddy, asking him about his community college classes. Knox paced around the basement nervously, tidying up the bar, checking the back door. An hour passed.

"Think you've been stiffed, dude," Teddy said, taking a swig of his beer.

"Nah, nah, she's coming. Just said she was running a little late."

Finally, after two hours, Karly knocked on the back door. Knox practically flew from the couch to open it.

"Hey!" he said, leaning in for a kiss.

"Hey," she said, offering him a quick peck. "Hey, Teddy, hey, Bria."

"Hey."

"Hey."

For a few hours, Bria sat with Teddy on the couch, laughing at the TV and picking through a bowl of Chex Mix. She watched as Knox and Karly sat on the other couch, his arm around her. He would whisper in her ear, and she'd smile. But Bria couldn't help but notice how distant Karly seemed. After a little while longer, Karly stepped outside to take a call. Bria waited a few minutes, then snuck out back, too, hoping to have a quick word with little Miss Shepherd.

Karly quickly ended the call when she saw Bria.

"Hey," Bria said. "Everything okay?"

"Huh? Oh, yeah, just fine."

"Cool. Listen, I know things are getting pretty serious with you and Knox."

Karly looked down at her phone, flipping it around in her hands. Bria continued her speech.

"I just wanted to talk to you, okay? As his best friend. . . you just have to know that sometimes he has these moments, and—"

"I actually need to talk to him." Karly cut her off. Suddenly, Bria felt the nerves come alive in every inch of her being.

"Wha-about what?"

Karly shook her head. "I just don't think this is going to work." She looked back down at the ground again before slipping back in through the back door. Bria knew just where this was going and her stomach turned. She would have expected to feel somewhat happy; God knows there was a part of her selfishly hoping Knox would stay single forever.

But right now, her heart was aching. Because she knew that his was about to be broken. So Bria followed Karly back into the basement, preparing herself to pick up the pieces.

"Hey, listen," Karly said to him, with a stern look on her face, her voice barely above a whisper, "can we, um, talk outside for a minute?" Knox's face dropped.

"Yeah, sure," he said, leaning over to grab his coat off of one of the barstools.

Bria sat back on the couch with Teddy while she waited anxiously for the back door to open again. Finally, after eight minutes, Knox came back in. He didn't say anything, just shut the back door and walked down the hallway to his bedroom. Bria and Teddy looked at each other.

"Damn," Teddy said. "Doesn't sound like that went well."

Bria got up and walked down the hall. She tapped lightly on the bedroom door.

"Knox?" No answer. She tapped again.

"Now's not a great time, Bria. I'm sorry."

She could practically hear the heartbreak in his voice. Nope. She wasn't leaving him like this. She pushed the door open to find him sitting on the edge of his bed, head in his hands. She sat down next to him.

"You were right, okay?" he said. "I was the rebound. She and Tony are already back together. She said I'm not 'exactly the boyfriend type.'"

Fucking Karly. Stupid, perfect Karly.

"Oh Knox, I'm so sorry. Ugh. I just had a bad feeling from the start—"

"Yeah, I know, you said. Guess I'm not as good as picking them as you are." He seemed more than a little irritated.

"Well, I'm really sorry it's not working out. But Knox, you need to know something. She's an idiot, okay? She is. She has no idea what she's losing out on by choosing someone else over you."

He scoffed. "No one does. Because there's nothing to offer."

Her heart broke for him again into tiny little pieces. Knox had been such a crowd-pleaser in high school. He was popular, he had no shortage of female companions, he was well-liked by all his teachers and coaches. But she knew there was one thing missing, and that was the fact that he didn't actually like himself. And to Bria, that was unfathomable.

"Benjamin Knoxville," she said, lifting his chin with her finger, "I hope you don't mean that. I hope you know that when I've been at my lowest, *you* are the person I want. You are the person I need around. You make *my* life better. Even if you never touched another person again, you've touched me. You have *so* much to offer. Screw her if she can't see that."

He flashed her the saddest, yet the most sincere smile, and she could have sworn she saw a tear twinkling in his eye.

He reached out and hugged her. And when he let go, he held her face in his hands for a moment, stroking her cheeks with his thumbs.

"I don't know what I did to deserve you," he whispered, "but I hope I never screw it up."

She remembered the very first time he had said that to her, after his accident. She had tried to take it as a friend-to-friend comment. He was still delirious from his medications; there's no way he meant anything more by it. But this time, she almost forgot to breathe. This conversation, what they were saying to each other, or at least what she was saying to him, this was heavy. Part of her worried she had said too much, and the other part worried she had said too little.

The truth was, she'd be lying if she didn't say she thought about Knox often, especially since she'd been away at college. She hadn't made a lot of friends yet, and she certainly hadn't met any other guys of interest. Throughout their whole friendship, whenever she pictured a future with any of the guys she had been with—yes, during her most naive times, she even thought she'd marry Brett Balkner—Knox was always a part of her future. She just wasn't sure how, exactly, he fit. He was always there, but he was always separate from the love story being written at the time. It was like she pictured a double-life, where she could live in perpetual teen bliss with Knox, but also have the family and future she always wanted. Knox wasn't her future. He was always her "now." She turned back to him. She had to know.

"Knox?"

"Hmm?"

"What. . . what are we?" She felt his whole body stiffen uncomfortably.

"What do you mean?"

"What is this? What. . . what am I, to you?" She could hear her own heartbeat in her ears.

"You're Bria. I'm Knox. You're my best friend. And you're probably the only person in the world who really gives a damn about me."

She felt her body grow heavy. This didn't quite go along with the reel that played in her head so many times, and that was the moment she realized what had happened.

She had finally fallen for the charm of Benjamin Knoxville. She lasted longer than any other girl had, but she still fell for it. Even after everything they had been through. Even after all the times he was her shoulder to cry on. Even after she pulled him from the car. They were still just Bria and Knox.

Never again. Never again would she fantasize of some romantic revelation where he confessed that he always wanted more. She wished so desperately she could go back in time thirty-five seconds and un-ask the damn question. She didn't want to know the answer. But it was too late. She had asked it. She so badly wanted to go back to him being her person, and she being his. No strings attached, no saying anything out loud; just him and her. Just letting everything go without saying. But she knew after tonight, she lost something. And Bria and Knox as she knew it, was no more.

She left his house with a smile plastered on her face, pretending his answer didn't crush her to her soul. She had said, "see ya soon," as she got into her car, knowing that it was probably a lie.

She drove back to UMD in complete and utter silence. Normally, she'd take advantage of an empty car by dance-driving to some Pitbull song, or belting out "My Heart Will Go On" while no one was there to hear it. But not today. When she finally found a parking spot on campus, she grabbed her big duffle bag from the backseat, along with the trays of food her mother had sent back with her. She piled them on top of the bag, and as she made her way to the dorm, she realized she didn't have her key card out. Shit. She fumbled around, shifting the trays to one arm and swinging her bag over the other. But the weight of the bag sent the trays—and her—flying to the ground. Mortified, she hopped to her feet. But the evidence—her mom's homemade spaghetti—was all over the sidewalk, and all over her.

"Here, let me help you with that," she heard a voice say. She looked up to see a dazzling man leaning down to help her collect whatever was salvageable of the food.

"Thank you," she said, breathless. He was tall and trim, but with strong, defined shoulders. His blonde hair was trimmed into a neat cut, and he had striking blue eyes that smiled with his mouth. "I'm such a klutz," she added, with a nervous laugh. He smiled, amused by her statement of the obvious.

"Do you need help getting all that up?" he asked.

"Oh, no, I should be fine. Thank you so much for stopping to help, though," she said. Her heart was racing. He was gorgeous, and apparently, sweet as pie.

"Are you a freshman?" he asked, apparently not ready for their conversation to end.

"Yeah, I am. How about you?" she asked, still fumbling to get her stupid key card out of her purse.

"I'm actually a med student at the Baltimore campus. I'm just here catching a lecture."

"Oh," she said, feeling dumb. Of course he wasn't a freshman. Or even an undergrad. "Impressive."

He smiled again, and her knees went weak.

"How are you liking Maryland?"

"I'm still getting used to how huge it is, but I love it, honestly. Plus, it's close to home," she said, trying desperately not to show just how difficult it was to hold up the increasingly heavy trays of spaghetti.

"So you're from around here?" he asked.

"Yeah. Dalesville. It's about forty-five minutes or so away. What about you?"

"Yeah, I grew up in Alexandria. So not too far," he said. "I like being close to my family."

Bria nodded, not wanting to stop looking at his beautiful blue eyes, but also feeling awkward as she balanced piles of food in her shaky arm. Apparently noticing, he cut to the chase.

"Listen, I know this is a bit pushy, seeing as how we just met and I don't even know your name," he said.

"It's Bria."

"Bria," he said with a smile, "I'm Drew. Would you like to go out sometime?"

She smiled back at him, blissfully forgetting the smeared spaghetti sauce all over the front of her shirt.

"Yeah, I'd like that." They exchanged numbers, and afterward, she changed her tune and let him help her get her things upstairs. She felt a bit childish letting him into her dorm, seeing as he was an older, sophisticated med student, but she reminded herself that at some point, he had been and undergrad with a dorm room.

They set a date for the following Friday, and as soon as he left, Bria started freaking out.

"Mari, I have *nothing* to wear," Bria told her a few days later.

"That's not true," Mari said, audibly eating something crunchy on the other end of the line. "I gave you that little black dress like two years ago. I know you still have it. You put a picture up on Facebook of you in it like three weeks ago."

Oh, bless her! Mari always had the answer.

"Oh, yeah! You're right. Okay. What shoes?"

"Those black strappy ones. Not the ones with the high heel. We don't need you breaking an ankle in front of this guy on your first date."

Bria laughed. Mari knew her so well.

"Hey, by the way," Mari said, still chomping, "have you heard from Knox lately?"

No, Bria hadn't, actually. And she hadn't thought about him much since she met Drew.

"Not since last week," Bria answered. "Why?"

"I don't know, he randomly texted me the other day asking me if I knew which building you lived in on campus. I thought it was weird that he didn't just ask you himself. Has he not been there yet?"

Bria sat on her bed, puzzled. That was weird.

"No, actually, he hasn't. I saw him last weekend when I went home. Haven't talked since."

"Oh, did something. . .happen?"

"Something? Like what?"

"I don't know, I just had this weird feeling when he texted me."

"Oh, nope. Nothing. Just same old Knox."

"Got it. Wonder if he will ever get his shit together. Well, I have to go, love. But don't forget to call me immediately after you get home tonight and tell me everything!"

"You know it. Love you!"

Mari was a junior now at UCLA, but she and Bria hadn't skipped a beat since high school, despite the 3,000 miles between them.

Bria took one final look at herself in the mirror before she headed down to the lobby. She had told Drew to meet her in the parking lot, since there wasn't anywhere near her building to park. As she made her way across campus, she couldn't help but feel like she was killing it. She hadn't put this much effort into her looks in a while, but she felt amazing. Just as she reached the parking lot, she stopped dead in her tracks when she saw Knox, walking across the lot, headed directly toward her.

"Knox?" she said.

"Hey, baby cakes," he said, pulling her in for a hug.

"What are you doing here?" she asked, feeling herself pull away from him faster than normal.

"Well, first of all, where are *you* going dressed like that?"

"Oh," she said, forgetting that she didn't have her hair in the loose ponytail that he was so used to. "I'm actually going on a date."

Knox's eyes grew wide for a moment, but he quickly smiled.

"A date, whoa," he said. "Well, you look awesome. Who's the lucky fella?"

"This guy I met on campus last week. You never answered me. What are you doing here?"

"Oh, yeah, I, uh, Grady and his roommates are having a big party tonight, so I told them I'd come down. I was gonna actually call you while I was here, to see if you wanted to get breakfast or something."

She nodded. It was true that Knox and Grady were still good friends, but they definitely weren't as close as she and Knox were. And she was actually a little irritated that he had made the trip, but hadn't called her ahead of time to make sure she was around. Was he avoiding her? Well, whatever. It didn't matter now. She had a date to get to. A hot, sexy, almost-doctor date.

"Got it. Well, yeah, maybe if I have time. Just let me know. I gotta run," she said.

"Yeah, yeah, go ahead. I'll text you."

Barely a moment later, Drew pulled up in his black Lexus. He got out and walked around the front of the car, opening the passenger door like a gentleman. He took her hand.

"You look amazing," he said. She felt her heart flutter at a million beats a minute.

Dinner was delectable, and the company wasn't bad either. Drew took her to a fancy steakhouse a few miles from campus, where they talked about their families, their hometowns, and their academic pursuits.

"I've always wanted to be a pediatrician, ever since I was a kid," he said, signing the receipt and handing the bill back to the waiter.

"Really? Even when you were a kid?"

"Yeah. When I was a kid, my sister, Natalie, got really sick. She had some crazy infection, and our pediatrician figured it out before it was too late. Ever since then, I knew that's what I wanted to do. I wanted to help kids. Plus, it will make it a little easier to make sure my own kids are healthy, one day."

Whoa. Kids. Out of all the dates she'd been on, and all the friends she'd had, all the guys she'd met, Drew was the first one to bring up having a family before Bria. Man, she couldn't wait to be a mom. Even at fifteen, sixteen years old, she knew that's the main thing she wanted out of life. She wanted a career, and a good job, and a marriage. And she wanted kids.

She thought about all the times Knox freaked out about it. "I don't even know what I want to do tomorrow, and you're already planning to create some tiny humans, and take care of them. Crazy," he'd say. She had laughed. She knew most people their age felt the same way he did. She was supposed to be concerned with how she could sneak some booze for the next party, or whether she would pass the AP History exam. . .not planning how she would pay off her student loan debt so that she could save for a house.

"So, you want kids?" Bria asked Drew, taking a sip of her water with feigned nonchalance. Earlier, when the waiter had asked if either of them wanted a sample of wine, she had tried to change the subject so that it wouldn't occur to him that she still couldn't legally drink.

"I can't wait to be a dad," he responded. "I mean, I can wait. I have to, just because of school, and my residency and stuff. But I can't wait."

"Yeah, me either." Bria responded, a grin sneaking across her lips.

The ride home was quiet, but pleasant. Jack Johnson played low on the radio. She wasn't the biggest fan, but it was good listening music. She bobbed her head back and forth to the music, letting her fingers drum on her legs. She kept her head turned out the window so that she wouldn't be tempted to keep staring at him. He really was gorgeous. The contrast of his icy blue eyes and tan skin made him look like some sort of cologne model. He was so put-together, and he smelled *so* damn good. His hair was short, but thick. . . there was definitely enough there to run her fingers through, to tug on gently while they. . .she cleared her throat and tugged at the hem of her dress, as if it had inched up in response to her dirty thoughts. When she finally succumbed to her desire to look at him, she was surprised to see that he was doing the same, with a melt-worthy grin on his face.

"Well," he said, pulling up to the lot. "Let's get you back to your place." He unbuckled his seatbelt.

"Oh, no, you don't have to walk me in."

"Nonsense. It's dark now. Can't have you walking across campus by yourself."

She thought about protesting him again, but decided against it. She wasn't quite ready for the date to be over.

"So, listen, I had a great time tonight," he said, as they strolled up to the door of her dorm. "Would you want to do this again, sometime?"

She looked up at him, his eyebrows raised slightly in anticipation. How could he possibly think her answer would be anything but yes?

"Definitely," she said. He leaned down, landing a soft kiss on her lips.

"I definitely need to hear more about this Dalesville place," he said with a smile. "Does this weekend work?"

"Yeah, sure! Thank you again. Tonight was great." She kissed him again, letting her hand slide up his neck and into his hair.

That night, as she was shaking her shoes off and unzipping her dress, still in a haze from the date, her phone buzzed on her bed.

Breakfast tmrw? Knox. She stared down at it. But as she thought about the kiss, and pictured a few more of them, she totally forgot to respond.

TWENTY-ONE

Now

As she got in her car after work, her phone rang.

"Hello?"

"Hey, babe," Drew said, sounding extra chipper.

"You're calling early," she said.

"I know. I got off early today, and I was thinking I could come up there for the night."

"You want to come up to Dalesville?" she said. It wasn't often that Drew came to Dalesville, and when he did, it was never his own idea.

"Yeah. I haven't seen your family in a few weeks. And I thought it would be nice for you to not have to drive into the city."

"That would be wonderful," she said without hesitation. "You know I'm down with any chance to see you."

"Great. I'll see you in a little bit. I love you."

"Love you, too, babe. See you soon."

Drew got to the Kreeries' right before dinner.

"Come on in, sweetie, you're just in time," Louise said, kissing his cheek as she carried a platter full of chicken to the table.

"Yum, it smells delicious," he said.

"Hi, babe," Bria said, making her way toward him and wrapping her arms around his neck. He kissed her hard and long, long enough to make her feel uncomfortable in front of her mom. She cleared her throat as she pushed him away gently. "Was traffic bad?"

"Nope, not at all."

Dinner was fine. Her father made small talk with Drew about golf, and Katie gave them the scoop on her "hot new science teacher." Sam was happy to be back home, still on the job hunt. Bria smiled as she watched everyone interact. For so long, she thought she wanted someone to get her away from all of this. She didn't want a reminder of the constant struggle. She wanted to be away from all things Dalesville. But lately, Dalesville didn't seem so bad.

Shortly after dinner, the rest of her family called it a night.

"So," Drew said, sneaking in behind her to kiss the back of her neck as she washed the last of the dishes, "what's there to do around here after 9 p.m.?" Bria laughed.

"Not much. We could go cow tipping, or rearrange the crop signs on Mr. Jacob's farm." Drew stared at her blankly. "I'm kidding."

"Oh, thank God. It's hard to tell around here sometimes." She rolled her eyes.

"Well, Andy's is still open. We could go for a drink?" He smiled as he kissed her neck again and playfully tapped her butt.

"Let's go."

When they walked in, the lighting was dim as always. They seated themselves at a back booth, leaning across the table and holding hands. Out of the corner of her eye, Bria saw two people, also stretched across a booth table, making out like two teens in the back of a movie theatre.

"Jesus, get a load of that," Drew said, taking a sip of his beer.

"Knox," she gasped. Knox. With his tongue down Karly's throat.

"Knox?" Drew asked, just a *little* too loudly. She glared at him. They stopped kissing and looked over. Knox looked down at the table and cleared his throat before standing up to walk over. He held out his hand to Karly, leading her to them.

"Hey, guys," Knox said. "Good to see you. Ah, Bria, you remember Karly, right?"

Bria nodded, smiling. "Of course, how are you, Karly?" Ugh. Bria wanted to hate her so much. She wanted to point out all things wrong with Karly. But that was easier said than done. Karly was still as flawless as ever, long legs and all. And honestly, she'd probably be good for Knox. She'd probably be good *to* him. It really had been years since she had broken his heart. Good for him. Bria was happy for him. Really. Well, sort of. Mostly, she was happy for him. But she was also sort of panicking, and she wasn't sure why.

"I'm doing well. It's so nice to see you, Bria," Karly said.

"And this is. . ." Knox said, holding his hand out to Drew.

"Drew," Drew said, obviously perturbed. Bria glared at Knox. He knew Drew's name.

"Yes, this is Drew, my fiancé."

"Nice to meet you," Karly said. "When's the big day?"

"In April," Bria said. "We're getting there. We can't wait," she said, squeezing Drew's hand. She heard herself saying the words, but it was like a record playing. They were involuntary, rehearsed.

"So exciting," Karly said, seeming as genuine as ever. Ugh. Stupid Karly.

"Hey, you know what would be fun?" Bria heard herself saying it, and hated the idea as it poured of out of her mouth, but she couldn't stop herself. "We should go on a double-date sometime this week."

Drew and Knox both looked at her quizzically. What on earth made that sound fun?

"Uh, yeah," Knox said, hesitantly.

"That would be great," Karly added.

"Great," Drew said, taking another swig of beer.

Bria didn't know why she had suggested it. She didn't really want to see them together. But she also felt that if she could be with the two of them, she'd have more control over the situation.

"Great! Maybe Tuesday? We could go out in Bethesda?"

"Sounds great," Knox said, looking at her with not so much as a smile on his face.

"Why would you do that?" Drew whispered, once he was sure they were out of earshot.

"Why not?"

"Because. . . it's weird. You guys aren't even friends anymore. She *clearly* is not looking forward to it. Maybe more than I'm not."

"Oh, stop. We were good friends. It'll be good to catch up." Bria spoke as if she thought it wouldn't be the most awkward social situation she had been in since high school. But as she took a nervous gulp of her drink, she knew it totally would be.

Bria sped back to the apartment from her office Tuesday, anxious to pick out just the right outfit. One that was nice enough for dinner, but also one that showed off her shape for Knox. Oops. Drew, not Knox. She wanted to look good for *Drew*.

She found a sleek pink dress in her closet that was probably Samantha's, not that she would ever wear it.

Since she had come out, Sam's style had become much more lax, maybe because she felt like she didn't have to pretend to enjoy getting gussied up anymore. The dress had a high neckline, but it was skin-tight. The perfect amount of sexy.

Bria added a pair of black pumps, and straightened her long brown hair. Like clockwork, Drew walked in the door.

"Babe, I'm home," he called from the kitchen.

"Let's get this over with." She rolled her eyes as she walked out from the bedroom. Drew's jaw dropped. "Damn."

"What?"

"We should go out with Knox more often, if you're gonna look this good," he said, pulling her into him and laying a long kiss on her. She played it up, pressing her body against his, running her fingers through his hair, but her mind was on the door. They were going to be late.

"Let's go," she whispered, finishing off the long, drawn-out kiss with a peck. He followed her like a puppy out the front door.

They waited fifteen minutes for Knox and Karly, leaving Drew to bitch about the fact that they couldn't be seated until the whole party was there. Finally, she heard a familiar sound—Knox's hearty laugh. Although, it didn't lift her up like it normally did; instead, it broke her a little bit. Because he wasn't laughing with Bria. He was laughing with Karly. They walked in, his arm around her waist. She looked perfect, as always. And she probably didn't even try. Stupid fucking Karly.

"Sorry we're late," Knox said, looking down at Karly, "we forgot how far away from the rest of the world Dalesville is."

They both laughed like it was the funniest damn thing anyone had ever said.

"It's fine," Bria said, "let's just get our table."

To her surprise, dinner started off well. Probably

because Karly and Drew actually hit it off, talking about their med school experiences for a solid twenty minutes, while Knox and Bria sat quietly. When there was a break in the med school chatter, Bria seized the opportunity to bring up stories of her and Knox. She reminisced about the times they drove around Dalesville at all hours of the night eating pizza and ice cream. As she spoke, she knew that not a single person at the table wanted to hear her mundane tales, but she couldn't stop. She wasn't sure who she was telling them for, honestly. If it was for Drew, or Karly, or maybe a reminder to Knox, of their deep, true friendship. Finally, Drew changed subjects.

"So, you two dated in high school, and then got back together?" Drew asked. The table went silent. "Something like that, right?"

Knox cleared his throat. Karly looked extremely uncomfortable, tracing the edge of her wine glass with her finger.

"Yeah, something like that," Knox said, pulling her in close to him, as if to reassure her that it was all in the past. "Karly here was the only girl who really tied me down." He smiled at her, looking straight into her dumb, beautiful blue eyes.

"Yeah, then Karly here completely broke Knox's heart," Bria heard herself say. She choked on the sip of wine she tried to take, not fully believing she actually spoke the words out loud. But judging by the look on Knox's face, she definitely had.

"We were kids," Knox said, glaring at her wide-eyed. "It wasn't a big deal."

"Yeah, tell that to sixteen-year-old-me, who had to take care of ya after," she said. *Jesus, Bria, tone it down a notch.* She tried giggling, as if that made the conversation a little lighter.

"Excuse me for a moment, I'm just going to run to the restroom," Karly said quietly, scooting out from the booth.

Drew looked from Bria to Knox, unaware of the heaviness of the conversation the two were having without speaking a single word. Just then, Drew's cell phone rang on the table, that horrible, circus-like song that Bria hated so much.

"Oh, this is the hospital. I need to take this," he said. When he walked away, Knox glared up at her again. They sat in silence for a moment, until he broke it.

"What the hell are you doing?"

"I—"

Drew cut in, jogging back toward the table, "Bria, I'm really sorry, but they need me back at the hospital." He grabbed his coat, leaned down and kissed her. "Do you want me to run you home real quick?"

"No, I'll take a cab."

"Okay," he said. "Sorry about this, man. Rain check?"

"Sure thing," Knox said, standing and shaking his hand. Karly came around the corner, looking like someone had told her that her nail polish was chipped.

"Knox, I'm actually not feeling great. . ."

"No problem. We're heading out anyway."

"Bye, Bria," Karly said, walking to the front door of the front restaurant. She didn't stick around long enough for Bria to say goodbye back. Knox still sat across from her in the booth, the glare cutting through her like a laser beam.

"What are you doing, Bria?"

"I don't know, I guess I'm just overprotective. You know how I am."

"Ya know what, Bria," he said, shaking his head, "that's bullshit. I don't come in, causing issues with you and your fiancé. Why do you need to do this? Ya know, all those years, you had someone else. It was fine for you to have a boyfriend. And now, when I *finally* have someone else, it's a problem?"

She didn't know what to say. She just stared at him.

"I'm serious. Don't mess things up for me. More than you already have. There's always a Drew, or a Brett, with you. Let me have a Karly."

She watched him walk away, sitting alone in the booth. She had never thought about it that way, before. For most of their friendship, she had recognized that Knox sometimes used her, then had no problem dropping her in public when a dazzling blonde came along. But she never considered the fact that she had used him, too. He was her backup, her go-to when another guy had broken her heart or pissed her off. But she lived for Knox to be her hero. She wanted to him to be the one that saved her every time.

"Is the party leaving?" the waitress asked, startling her.

"Oh," she jumped, "um, no, not leaving. Just, dwindled down to one, I guess."

"No problem. I'll be right back with another glass of wine."

Later that night, as she lay on the expensive leather couch Drew had insisted they buy, watching *Fresh Prince of Bel Air* reruns, Bria couldn't ignore the huge knot growing in the pit of her stomach. She replayed each part of the brief, but biting speech Knox had given.

First of all, why did he need to point out that she was rarely without a boyfriend when they were young? Was he saying that he would have liked a chance? Or was he just saying that she was hardly single?

And why did he mention not messing things up with her and Drew? Was he saying that he *wanted* to? Or was he just saying she should be respectful of his new relationship?

God dammit. This resurfacing frustration was familiar, but one she hadn't felt in years. It was the same frustration she felt the night she asked Knox if what they were. It was the same frustration she felt each time he held her hand in a playful way, but for a little longer than a friend would. It was the same frustration she felt when he would hug her—no, when he would hold her—and then make out with her friend in the hallway the next day. Suddenly, Bria was fifteen again, wondering if Ben Knoxville could ever want her, and she hated that. She was so angry, so pissed off, she didn't notice the tears streaming down her face until the front door opened. She quickly jumped up, wiping the black mascara streaks from her cheeks.

"Hi, hon," she said.

"Hey," he said.

"How was your night?"

"Ah, fine. Sorry I had to leave dinner. Although, it was kinda awkward, so maybe I'm not so sorry," he said with a chuckle as he cracked open a can of seltzer water from the fridge.

"I thought it was fine. I'd like to try and reschedule," she said.

"Ugh, seriously?"

"Yes, seriously. Why is it such a problem?" To be honest, she wasn't even sure if Knox would agree to it again. Or if he would even talk to her.

"Why are you pushing it so hard? It's awkward. And you clearly have nothing to talk about except for how much you two were into each other ten years ago."

"That is *not* true. We were friends."

"Yeah, okay," Drew said, plopping down on the couch.

"I'm serious," she said, stepping directly in front of the television. He looked up at her.

"Look, maybe he wasn't into you, but you were *definitely* into him. Who remembers that kind of shit about someone like you do, unless you're into them?"

She wasn't sure if it was the fact that he wouldn't

agree to going out again, or if it was the fact that he was insinuating that she had feelings for Knox, but she was seeing red. The idea that she might feel differently, feel more, for Knox than he did for her was something she had been terrified of since her sophomore year of high school. And now, her fiancé was bringing it to light.

"I don't have feelings for him," she said, glaring down at him.

"Well, I would hope not *now*."

"I didn't have them then, either."

"Okay Bria, whatever you say. Can you step like an inch to your right, please?"

"I did *not* have feelings for him then."

Why *was* she pushing this so much? Drew didn't seem to care that she liked him then, so she could have easily dropped it. But she wasn't trying to convince Drew. She was trying to convince herself.

"Okay, fine," he said. She knew he was just saying whatever magic words would make her move an inch to her right.

"I want to go out with them again."

"Well, I don't. It's not fun for me."

"You don't even know him."

"Yeah? Well neither do you, anymore. Why is it so important to hang out with them again? If you want to go out with people, we can go out with Tara and Cody."

Bria genuinely liked Tara; she was a sweet girl, one of those people who asked you a question about yourself, thoroughly listened to what you said, and then remembered the answer. Tara actually gave a shit about people. It was refreshing. She was just so different from Bria. She grew up with money, and lots of it. And clearly, she would never know anything different. Drew had grown up with money, too. His parents had sent him to the most expensive private high school in the city, and he graduated from Maryland without a single dime of student loan debt. And he had always seen her debt as a bit of an inconvenience.

"Well, hopefully we can pay that off early, so it doesn't affect your credit scores too bad," he would casually drop in a conversation. "I'm sure my parents will help us get rid of it faster." Bria had rolled her eyes at that. She got along fine with her future in-laws. They lived in Virginia, just outside of D.C., in a house big enough for three families. They had welcomed her in, her mother-in-law taking her shopping all the time, her father-in-law treating them to dinner a few times a month. They were wonderful. They were just different. Their lives were different, and their stress was so different. Drew's parents had graciously offered to pay for the alcohol, rehearsal dinner, and the upgrade from buffet to seated meals at their wedding, because his mother said buffets were "just a little tacky."

Drew knew Bria's family struggled financially, but she knew he didn't really *understand* it. In fact, he didn't really understand a lot of what her family went through. And it was because he didn't care to. She just couldn't talk about her family's stressors with him, because he had nothing to offer. He wasn't Knox.

And as her mind wandered from Tara and Cody to Drew and Knox, Bria suddenly realized she had left her fiancé hanging in conversation.

"I just want to," she finally answered.

"You know," Drew said, suddenly losing interest in the television, "you keep stressing that you don't have feelings for him. But you fighting to see him again doesn't really back that up."

"I'm not fighting anything. If I want to see them again, I will," she said, arms crossed now.

"Them? Give me a break. You have no interest in seeing that Karly chick again. It's not 'them.' It's 'him.' Just tell me, Bria, what is so special about that guy? I mean, I get that when you were younger, he was the older guy, probably paid attention to you to try and get into your pants. But now? I mean, look at you, and look at him. You have a good job. You're getting married. We're gonna be doing great in a few years once I'm in a private practice. He's still stuck in cow town."

And now, Bria was seething. How dare he belittle what she and Knox shared. And joking about "cow town" was only okay when she did it. And how dare he humiliate her, making assumptions on what she felt for Knox. And how dare he assume that Knox didn't feel something, too. And worst of all, how dare he assume that Knox didn't measure up to her, just as Knox himself had done all those years ago. She walked across the room and grabbed her bag off the counter.

"Aw, come on, Bria. Enough with the dramatics," Drew said, still lounging on the couch. She slammed the door as hard as she possibly could behind her. He didn't catch up to her until she was downstairs, clutching the handle of her car door.

"Come on, Bria."

"Fuck off, Drew. Leave me alone."

"You know what? Go. I'm sick of this petty shit. Ever since you went back there, it's like you forgot how to be a grown-up. You call me when you're over your little crush."

She didn't say anything. She just stared at him as she ducked down into her car. On the way back to her parents, she was shaking. What was she doing? If she was trying to sabotage her own engagement, it seemed to be working. But that was crazy talk. She and Drew would be fine. Right? And what about Knox? How angry was he? When she crossed over the town lines, she passed through the quiet Main Street, all lights out.

But instead of turning down her parents' street, she made a left into the development where Knox lived. She paused to look for his car, and when she spotted it, she double-parked behind it. She looked around the lot for a car expensive enough to be Karly's, but unless she drove a beat-up Honda with a missing hubcap, there was no such vehicle to be seen. Bria took a breath and walked up the front steps of the townhouse, and knocked.

She held her breath, half-expecting him to see her through the peephole and wait till she gave up. But, to her surprise, the door opened.

"Jimmie Cone?" she asked. "It might be our last chance before they close for winter."

He hesitated for a moment, then closed the door. She stood on the stoop, dumbfounded. Suddenly, the door opened back up, as Knox pulled a sweatshirt over his head, leading her to the car. She sighed in relief.

They didn't say much until they got their ice cream. She treated, since she felt like it was the least she could do. She was tempted to lick his cone before she handed it to him, but she wouldn't dare. Not tonight.

"Look, I'm really sorry about earlier. It was wrong of me," she said, when they were settled at a picnic table.

"Yeah, it was," he said, licking his cone. "But it's okay. You know I'll always forgive ya." A pained half-smile crept across her face.

"Where is Karly, anyway?"

"Well, I'd guess that by now she's off with someone else. Probably someone more like Drew."

Bria's eyes grew wide. Oh no. She had ruined it for him. Karly had ended it because of her. His heart. . .it would be broken all over again. Only this time, she couldn't be there for him every day until it healed.

"Oh, no, Knox," she said, "I'm so—"

"No, don't go beating yourself up," he said, holding up his hand. "I ended it, not her."

"W-why?" she asked. He shrugged.

"I don't really have a solid reason. I just, I don't know. After tonight, I just wasn't feeling it. I'm ready for something that makes me. . .I don't know. Something that feels more than what it felt like with her. I guess like what you have with Drew."

Bria looked up at him at the mention of Drew's name, for the second time. She nodded.

"Speaking of the doc, where is he?" Knox asked. She clapped the crumbs off of her hands and wiped her them on her jeans.

"In D.C.," she said. "Mad at me." She felt a little dirty getting into it. She didn't want to betray Drew, but in the same breath, this might be her chance to cross that bridge with Knox again.

"Got ya. Well, whatever it is, I'm sure you two will work it out and be hunky-dory tomorrow." She nodded. Okay, guess not. "You want to know something?" he asked.

"Hmm?"

"I don't really like Jimmie Cone," he said, matter-of-factly. She felt her eyes grow wide, as if he had just told her he killed someone.

"You *what?*" she asked. He smiled at her and shook his head.

"It's true. I'm not a big soft-serve fan."

"But. . . but we've been coming here for over a *decade,*" she said, in utter disbelief. She knew it was silly, but for some reason this revelation bothered her. Maybe because Jimmie Cone was *their* spot.

"I know," he said with a chuckle. "I mean, the ice cream is okay, but I more so came for the company."

She felt her cheeks flush, and she held the back of her hand to the side of her face.

"So, does that mean we can still come?" she asked. He laughed again.

"As long as you want to," he said.

As they pulled back into his neighborhood, and he got out of the car, she reached for his sleeve.

"Knox?" she asked, her heart pounding. He stopped and turned to her. "I know tonight kind of sucked. But I hope you know that I really do want you to be happy. Whatever that means."

He smiled at her, and squeezed her hand for a moment.

"You too, baby cakes," he said, closing the car door. She was pretty sure the butterflies in her stomach could have flown the whole car home.

That night as she lay in bed, she replayed Knox's words again. *You know I'll always forgive ya.* It was the "always" part that kept sticking to her brain. As if he thought he'd be around for always.

And just as she was about to close her eyes, she realized something: she hadn't spoken to Drew since she took off. He never texted her to see if she made it home. She never texted him to apologize. They never even said goodnight.

TWENTY-TWO

Now

On her way back into town the next day, Bria stopped in at Tucker's to get some gas. Tucker's was great on chilly days like this, because they were the only place in town that still pumped your gas for you.

"Hey, Carl," she called out her barely-cracked window, "can you fill it up? Regular, please." Carl had graduated with Knox, and had been working here since they were in high school. She hadn't known him well in high school; only as the first boy of many that broke Christa's heart. He tipped up the brim of his hat and Bria smiled. Some things really never changed in Dalesville, and lately, she was feeling like that wasn't such a bad thing.

"Oh, my, God!" she heard someone shriek from the other side of the pump, "Bria Kreery?"

Bria turned to see Courtney Blake, Soccer Captain-Student Council President- Extraordinaire, jumping out from her gunmetal gray Beamer. Of course she had a Beamer.

"Oh, my gosh, Courtney!" Fake Bria shouted, her fakeness hitting maximum levels. She hopped out of her car, running into Courtney's embrace.

"How the *hell* are you?" Courtney asked, holding onto Bria a little longer than Bria would have liked. "I saw on Facebook you're engaged, right? Let's see the ring!"

Bria smiled, sticking out her hand. When she had first gotten engaged, she practically walked into rooms with her hand sticking straight out, waiting for people to "ohh" and "ahh" over it. She posted one too many pictures to Instagram where she happened to be holding a mug in her left hand, ring pointed toward the lens, or a picture of her hand on Drew's face, the rock gleaming in the light. She lived for it. It felt a little different today, though. She showed it off, but quickly stuck the hand back in her pocket.

"Yep, wedding's in April, actually," she said. Saying those words out loud made her realize just how soon she was going to be Mrs. Drew Baker. Or maybe Mrs. Kreery-Baker. She hadn't decided.

"*So* exciting! I saw the pics. He's cute!" Courtney said. "So listen, I have to run for dinner, but tomorrow night a bunch of us are meeting up at the Music Café for drinks, since so many of us are in town for the Thanksgiving. You should definitely come! Knox will be there," she said, "but I'm sure you knew that already."

Bria smiled. On one hand, she liked that people still associated her with Knox. But on the other, it made her realize how sad she was about the connection she had lost with him. They weren't the same Bria and Knox that everyone knew from high school. She just nodded.

"Yeah, definitely, I'll try to make it up there."

The next day, she waited until nine o'clock to head out the door. She wanted to be fashionably late, so she could scan the room once she arrived and see who might be there. But she also didn't want to be too late, and miss out on time with Knox.

When she walked in, she saw a group of Courtney's old friends gathered by the dance floor. A DJ was on the stage, already playing dance music.

"Bria!" Courtney waved her over, causing an influx of ex-cheerleader and ex-soccer player hugs to come at her at an overwhelming volume.

"Hey, guys! Oh my gosh, it's been *years!"* Fake Bria said. They laughed and she listened to stories about how each of them graduated and got exactly the job she had always wanted. Some of them were living it up in Baltimore or D.C., a few of them were back home in Dalesville.

Bria smiled and nodded, but her eyes were scanning the back door, waiting for Knox to arrive.

After an hour and three margarita swirls, she was feeling pretty good. But alcohol doesn't disguise disappointment, in fact, in her case, it was magnifying it, and she was actually pretty concerned with how sad she was that Knox wasn't there.

"Come on, Bria!" Courtney said, pulling her up from her chair. "I *love* this song!"

Actually, Bria loved it, too. And since it seemed that Knox was a no-show, she figured she may as well let loose. Just as they reached the floor, the back door swung open, and she laid eyes on him. She watched him scan the room, making his way toward their tables.

And when he saw her, he stopped walking, staring right at her.

So she started shaking it. What else was she supposed to do? She spun around, ran her fingers through her hair, danced up on Courtney. And the whole time, she kept her eyes on his, knowing exactly what she was doing every single time she wiggled her butt. He shifted uncomfortably as he stood, and she gave him a dazzling smile. Finally, the song was over, and she stepped off the dance floor. He handed her a glass.

"Look like you could use a drink after that," he said with a smile.

"Thanks," she said.

"So you two are still best friends, after all these years?" Courtney said, plopping down on the chair next to them. "That is *so* cute."

Bria looked at Knox. She was thankful that the answer was just assumed, because honestly, she didn't know if it was still true.

"So Bria," Angie Carp, Co-Soccer Captain, said, "let's see that ring!"

"Yeah!" the other female voices echoed. Bria's eyes flashed to Knox quickly as she slowly stuck her hand out. But when she looked down, the ring was gone.

"Oh, I'm sorry, I didn't put it back on after I ran today," she said. Holy shit. She hadn't gone a day without wearing her ring since the day Drew proposed. Today, she'd totally forgotten to put it on. "There's pictures on my Instagram, though," she said, as if Drew were there to hear her.

She heard herself going into detail about Drew, and what he did, and where he worked, and how they met. Then came the questions on the proposal story. And as she told it, she wondered about what Knox's face looked like. But she couldn't bear to look at him. When she finally turned back, he was in a deep conversation with Teddy.

Just then, a familiar song came over the loudspeakers, as Courtney made her way back to the table from the DJ booth.

"Now, I've had the time of my life," Bill Medley started to sing. Bria's eyes darted to Courtney.

"Come on, guys, re-do of prom!" she shrieked.

"Yeah!" cried the ex-soccer player army. Bria felt an entire flock of butterflies migrating in her stomach, first flying north, then flying south, as her eyes slowly found Knox. He was looking at her with a half-smile, eyebrows up, waiting for her to make the next move.

"What? No, come on, guys," she said, sheepishly. And then she watched as his shoulders sunk. She stood up, sticking her hand out to him.

"Alright, Johnny Castle," she said, "let's do this."

He looked at her for a moment, before smiling and taking her hand.

She followed him to the dance floor, a little warily at first. But as he slid his fingertips down her arm and she felt the hairs on the back of her neck rise, she knew it was go-time. Seriously, *nobody* puts Baby in a corner.

He reached around her body and took her hand, flinging her out and back into him. Each time she brushed against his chest, she felt her breath catch in her throat. He smelled *so* damn good. He was warm, and his smile made her a bit wobbly on her dancin' feet.

He pulled her in for the last spin, his chest to her back, and suddenly, neither of them were smiling. Instead, it felt like they were fighting something off. Some sort of pull.

"Ready?" he whispered in her ear, and she felt those damn hairs rise again. She breathed him in, not wanting the moment to end quite yet. But they had an audience. And she was an engaged woman, after all. No time for soaking it in. She nodded, and he swung her back out and away from him, letting go of her hand.

"Let's do it," he said, holding his hands out to her. She cocked her neck in play, and pretended to stretch briefly before running full-speed ahead. He caught her, and they held the lift for about three seconds, the longest they had ever done. And as the rest of the group clapped and cheered, she couldn't help but notice how tightly he held onto her as he spun her back into him each time. And how much she liked it.

But as he pulled her back in and she put her arms around his neck, she realized just how tightly she was holding on to him, too. And she realized just how dangerous this was getting.

A few songs later as the crowd slowly dwindled, Bria realized she better call it a night. Thanksgiving was the next day, and she shouldn't really be out this late, drinking, with Knox. As she stood to grab her purse and say her goodbyes, she felt a little unsteady.

"Hang on there, killer," Knox said, reaching for his own coat. "You'd better let me take you home." Before she could protest, a massive headache was already starting to form in her temples. She nodded.

"Man, that was fun," he said after a few minutes of silence. "We haven't done that in so long."

"Yeah," she smiled, her head rested back against the seat. "I can't believe we still remembered it all."

When he pulled into her parents' driveway, he put the car in park. She paused for a moment before unbuckling herself.

She turned to him, her body completely facing his.

"It was really nice to see everyone tonight," she said.

"Yeah, that was cool."

"And I'm really glad we got to catch up more. Me and you, I mean."

"Me, too," he said.

"I've missed you, Knox," she said, looking down at her hands.

"I missed you, too," he said, shifting in his seat so that he was facing her, too. And she felt herself slide across her seat, closer to him. She leaned over, covering his hand with hers for a moment. She knew she was a little tipsy still, but this wasn't the alcohol making the moves. This was all Bria. His whole car smelled good, like that musky, manly, delicious scent that Knox always seemed to carry, whether he was dressed in a suit, or finishing up a pick-up basketball game. His bright green eyes shone even in the dark, and she stared at his long lashes, the ones she'd always been jealous of. She watched his Adam's apple bob as he swallowed hard. She pulled herself a little bit closer, stretching across the center console. She reached a hand up slowly, and he swallowed again. She gently stroked his perfectly-pointed chin, pulling herself even closer, their noses inches apart. She leaned her head in, letting her forehead rest on his. She closed her eyes, soaking in what she couldn't at the Café.

But then she sighed, opened the door, and got out.

TWENTY-THREE

Now

Three days passed, and the only communication between Bria and Drew were a few text messages here and there, letting each other know that they got everywhere safely, checking to see if the cable bill had been paid. He worked on Thanksgiving, so it was easy to explain to her parents why he wasn't coming to dinner.

One of the things they had in common was that they were both insanely stubborn. Fights, even smaller, petty ones, took days to clear up because neither of them could be the first one to apologize. But this time, it felt a little different. There wasn't that reassurance that was usually on the other side, that confidence that told her they would get over it and be fine. Instead, the future was a little blurry for her.

She felt herself growing a little groggy, like she was just going through the motions of her daily life, but it wasn't because she couldn't sleep without Drew, or that it broke her heart not to talk to him. It wasn't because she missed him. It was because she didn't.

"What's up with you?" Sam asked, handing her a cup of soda as she sat next to her on the couch. Her parents were off with Katie at her appointment, and probably wouldn't be back for hours.

"Ah. . . I don't know. Just a lot of stuff." Bria sometimes had trouble opening up to her sisters. Since she was the oldest, she felt like she needed to be their go-to for advice, their secret-keeper, but that they shouldn't have to bear the weight of hers in return.

"Uh-huh," Sam said. "Trouble in paradise?" Bria shot her a look. There it was again, that overwhelming feeling that Sam wasn't particularly fond of Drew. But she wouldn't dare ask her about it. She didn't really want to know.

"We're. . . fine." Now, Sam shot *her* a look.

"Ya know, I'm not a kid anymore. You can actually talk to me, if you want," she said, picking through a bowl of Chex Mix for the chocolate pieces. Bria smiled at her. Honestly, she'd been feeling sort of alone the last few days. She guessed she could give her sister a shot.

"We got into a fight, and we haven't talked for a few days," Bria told her, reaching across the couch to snag a chocolate piece before Sam could grab it.

"Oh. Is the wedding still on?" Sam asked, matter-of-factly. Bria laughed and shook her head.

"Of course. We will be fine," she said, but the words were actually hard to say.

"Well, what was it about?" Sam asked. But before Bria could speak, Sam asked, "Was it about Knox?"

Bria almost choked on the Chex Mix. That's what she got for eating only the chocolate. "Why would you ask me that?" she asked.

Sam shrugged. "I don't know."

"Well, what made you think of Knox?"

"I don't know," Sam said.

"Sam, something had to make you think of him."

"I guess it's just. . . I don't know, you've been, like, a different person since you've been home. Since you've been hanging with him. And mom said you guys were going on a double-date, and I just put two and two together. Drew seems like he could be the jealous type."

"Well, he's . . .I . . . I don't know. Knox definitely bothers him. He doesn't get that we're just friends." Sam accidentally snorted, then quickly covered her nose. "What?"

"You and Knox have not been 'just friends' since before you had boobs. Anyone can see that there was something a little more goin' on there. The sexual tension between you two is intense."

"Sam! Ew! He's like my—"

"*Don't* say he's like your brother. We both know that's not true. And sisters don't get all googley-eyed over their brothers shirtless like you used to do with Knox when you were in high school."

"I did not!" Bria said, grabbing the pillow from behind her and whacking Sam in the face with it, until they were both on the floor in a fit of laughter.

"But seriously, dude," Sam said, "I know you probably don't want to hear this, because it's confusing as hell. You and Knox, you're *not* just friends."

Bria sat back, resting her head against the arm of the couch. Jesus, she knew that that was a possibility, but having someone else say it out loud made it so much more terrifying.

A few hours later, they heard the door open, Katie running through the front room and leaping onto the couch, laying on top of Sam and Bria.

"Hey, Kates," Bria said.

"Get off me, brat," Sam said, playfully shoving her off.

"How was your appointment?" Bria asked. Her parents made their way into the living room, both with huge smiles on their faces.

"Tell them, Kates," her dad said.

"Well, they think everything looks good. They think I'll be done with treatment in just a few *weeks!*" she said, standing up on the couch and jumping around it like a lunatic.

"What? How can that be? It's only been a few months!" Bria said, so excited she felt like she might cry.

"They said my treatment worked faster than they thought!"

"Well, we still have to go back in a few weeks so they can just do a few more scans and some final bloodwork. But if all of that is clear, the doc thinks she's good to go," her mother said, stroking Katie's long, golden locks.

Sam and Bria clapped their hands as Katie jumped off the couch and onto the floor, dancing around in happy circles.

"I can go back to a normal schedule next semester!" Katie said, squeezing her mom's hand.

"That's right. And Bria, you can finally move back to D.C. And back to your wonderful life," Louise said. Sam shot Bria a look. "But I don't want you to ever forget how grateful we are for everything you've done for your family. We are so lucky to have you," her mother added, pulling her oldest daughter in for a long hug.

Louise had tears running down her cheeks, and Bria felt them welling in her own eyes, but for a totally different reason. She felt's Sam's eyes on her, as if she thought Bria might make some sort of drastic life declaration.

"But, mom, are you guys sure you're okay with money?" she whispered to her mother.

"Yes, honey, we are totally fine."

"God Bless the Knoxvilles!" her dad called out, then cowered, quickly realizing what he'd said.

"Joe!" her mother scolded him.

"What?" Bria asked, turning to her father. "What about the Knoxvilles?"

"Dammit, Joe. You know he didn't want her to know," she heard her mother whisper.

"Know what? What about the Knoxvilles?" Bria pressed. Her mother sighed.

"Well, I guess we have to tell you now," Louise said, glaring at Joe.

"It's been so long anyway," he mumbled, consoling himself for his slip-up.

"When your sister was really bad off the first time, we were in really bad shape, financially. Really bad. You know that," Louise started. Bria nodded. "Well, after you went to see Ben that night before you left, he talked to his parents. You know they have some money. Well, Ben called up his dad and told him what was going on. That day, they called us up and gave us enough to pay of all of her medical bills so we could keep the house. But he made us swear," she said, "that we wouldn't tell you. Ben didn't want you to know."

Bria jumped back to that day, that moment when her father burst out of the house with the news that they wouldn't be losing it. There were only a few moments in her life when she felt as purely happy, as relieved as she did then. And Knox had given it to her. The tears in the back of her eyes were now surging toward the front.

"Why didn't he want me to know?" she asked, wiping them before they could roll down her cheeks.

"Well, when the Knoxville boys were each born, their parents set up trust funds for them. The money came out of Ben's," she said. "And he thought if you knew, that you'd refuse to take it and you wouldn't go to school. He was probably right. Such a sweetie. So, we've been paying him back ever since. That is, until Kates got sick again. Ben called up your dad after you told him and he told us that we were square. We still owed him over ten thousand dollars."

Bria nodded, but she didn't speak. She knew her voice would crack. She stood back against the doorway, resting her head against it. She breathed in and out, but it felt labored. Her sweet Knox.

That night, she offered to run to the store for her mother, knowing she would be making a pitstop on the way. When he opened the door, he smiled.

"Hey," he said. "I'd ask if you wanted Jimmie Cone, but a thirty-degree night might not be the best night for ice cream."

She nodded, but when she tried to smile, she was overcome by the emotion she was feeling. She leapt onto him, wrapping her arms around him and burying her face in his neck.

"Hey, hey, what's wrong?" he asked, rubbing her back, holding her a few inches off the ground.

"I can't believe you gave them the money," she whispered.

"Oh, they told you?" he asked, lowering her back down to her feet. She nodded. He sighed and looked down at the ground. He sat down on the top stoop step, and she sat down next to him. "Bria, I would have. . .I would have done anything for you," he said. "Still would."

Oh, God. He still would.

"I want to pay you back what my parents still owe you," she said. He shook his head and held up his hand.

"Stop, B," he said. "Don't."

"No, please, I'm serious."

"Bria, I didn't do it so that you'd owe me. I never wanted you to find out because I knew you'd lose your mind over it. Please, just let it go. Just let me hold on to the fact that I was able to help you. Please."

She looked over at him, and a warm smile came over her face. For half a second, she let her head rest on his shoulder.

"So, since we're not getting ice cream, how about some hot chocolate?" he asked, standing up and offering her his hand. She grabbed it tight and followed him to his car.

The weekend rolled around, and Bria, Sam, and Katie had decided to have a girls' day, watching a chick flick and eating chocolate ice cream right from the tub. Their parents had gone away for the weekend, finally taking a much-needed breather after Katie's good news. Bria and Drew had been talking a little bit more; he'd finally called a few days before and they talked for an hour, Drew catching her up on all his stories from the hospital. Bria had sounded cheery and asked all the questions she knew he so badly wanted to answer, but her heart wasn't in it.

And while he spoke, she felt herself drifting in and out of focus. He was on-call this weekend, so she'd stayed back in Dalesville. She told him she loved him when she hung up, but something about the conversations lately felt rehearsed, stale. And she couldn't quite put her finger on it.

Bria watched as the couple on the screen ran to each other, in a simultaneous, unrealistic realization that they were perfect for each other, and simply could not make it without the other. She made a mocking puke sound, but in reality, her heart was beating just as fast as any other girl's would. Just then, Katie piped up.

"I'm not gonna lie," she said, "I'm a little sad you won't be living here anymore."

Bria swallowed. So was she, kid. So was she.

"Me too, Kates. But I'm not far away. And soon, you'll be away at school again. You won't even be here to miss me. But, I don't know if I'll be leaving just yet." Sam looked up at her.

"Why?" she asked.

"Yeah, doesn't Drew want you to move back in? I mean the wedding is only a few months away," Katie said.

Bria swallowed nervously. They were set to have an April wedding. Drew really wanted to get married after his residency ended in July, but Bria hated the idea of being a sweaty bride. The only other option was to wait until fall, but Bria couldn't bear the thought of putting off marrying Drew any longer. Now, though, the thought of a fall wedding seemed better, smarter. And there was a small part of her that wished they'd agreed to push it off a little longer.

"Yeah, but Kates, you *just* got the news and we still have to wait for the results. . ." Bria said, knowing that her hesitation had nothing to do with Katie.

"Bria, I'm fine," Katie said. "Don't use me as your crutch. And don't worry yourself sick about us. You have your own life." Then, Katie looked up at her big sister with a mischievous look in her eye. "Unless there's another reason you want to stay."

Sam stared at Bria, waiting for a response. But as they sat in silence, Bria realized that she hadn't seen Drew in almost three weeks. And she hardly missed him.

As if he heard her thoughts, there was a knock on the front door.

"I'll get it," Katie said, hopping up from the couch.

"No, you won't." Katie may have been an adult, but she was still Bria's baby sister, and Bria took every opportunity she could to keep her safe. When she opened the front door, her stomach dropped.

"Hi, baby," Drew said, his sad eyes looking down at her. She let him dramatically wrap his arms around her, holding her tight, just like the nauseating couple in the movie. She wrapped her arms around him, but didn't bury her face in his neck. "I wanted to surprise you," he said. "I got the night off. I missed you so much," he whispered.

"Shhh," she said, squeezing him tight, letting him kiss her face all over.

"I'm so sorry I couldn't come sooner. And I'm

sorry about all that shit before, with Knox. I know I was being overdramatic. And I was acting like an ass, and you didn't deserve it, and I'm just. . . I'm so sorry," he said. Her eyebrows shot up. This was so out of character for Drew. Stubborn, steadfast Drew, who was almost *never* in the wrong.

"It's okay, babe. I'm sorry, too." He leaned down again, kissing her hard. She closed her eyes, trying desperately to feel like she couldn't go on without him.

"Look," he said, pulling himself back, "can I. . . can I take you somewhere?" She looked back at him, lifting an eyebrow.

"Okay," she said, taking his hand.

She got in his car hesitantly, a little afraid of where they were going. Not because she thought it would turn into some sort of slasher, killer-fiancé scenario; she was actually afraid it would turn into the exact opposite. Something sweet and endearing. Something that would make it harder for her to blow their fight out of proportion and drag out the anger she was feeling toward him a little more. And she hated herself for that. Why did she want to be mad at him? Why did she want him to be wrong? They drove for twenty minutes or so, then Drew pulled into a neighborhood. Where the hell was he taking her?

The houses were huge, with big windows and three-car garages. They all had massive, perfectly mowed lawns, and as Bria noticed the ultra-straight lines, she realized no one who lived in this neighborhood mowed the lawn themselves.

"Where are we?" she asked, just as he pulled up to one of the houses. It had two huge stone pillars in front, with a wide porch and a maroon door. As Drew parked the car and took off his seatbelt, she saw the FOR SALE sign in front of it. She swallowed. "Drew, where are we? What is this?"

He didn't answer her. He just got out of the car,

walked around, and opened her door. He reached for her hand, and she took his, knowing that hers was clammy and gross.

He held his hand out, as if he were presenting the house to her.

"I've been an ass about this whole thing with Katie, and your family," he said, his voice shaky, "and Knox."

Bria was uncomfortable. She still wasn't used to shaky Drew. She was used to overconfident Drew. Drew who always knew he was getting exactly what he wanted. Drew that was a little easier to argue with, or disappoint.

"And I know that all you've been trying to do is take care of them. And instead of supporting you, I acted like a child. I wanted you to myself. I wanted to stick to the plan. But I see now," he said, pulling her toward the driveway, "that sometimes plans have to change. And I want you to know that I'm okay with it. And I support it, and I want to do whatever you need to make our life exactly what you want. And I thought we could start here," he said, holding out his hand toward the house again.

"What. . . what do you mean?" she asked, desperately not wanting to know the answer.

"Well, this house is only twenty minutes from your parents," he said, "and I spoke to a mortgage lender, and my parents offered to cosign. Bria, if you want this house, we can buy it. Right now. You'll be closer to your family, and we can start the life you've always wanted. Or if you don't like it, we can look somewhere else. We can live in Dalesville. I'll make the drive every day. I don't care. I just want you to be happy, whatever that means."

She felt tears welling up in her eyes, and the nerves churning in her stomach. A shiver went down her spine, and it wasn't the chilly December air. Dammit, Drew.

"This house is beautiful," she managed to choke out, her eyes overflowing like damn waterfalls. Drew smiled, mistaking the tears of confusion for ones of overwhelming joy. He wrapped her in a long hug.

"Oh, B, I'm so glad you like it," he said, kissing her. "I'll call my dad and the lender tomorrow."

She forced a smile, but couldn't manage another word.

Bria was quiet on the way back to Dalesville, as she tried to hide the panic inside that was rising to the surface. *Poor freaking Bria,* she thought. Her McDreamy fiancé wanted to buy her a massive house a few minutes from every other person she loved. Life was so tough.

But if things were so perfect, why did she want to hurl all down the side of his car?

"I know it's a little overwhelming," he said as he pulled back into her parents' driveway, "but once we put in the offer, we will need to think about a few possible closing dates. And then obviously we can officially move in once things are all settled with Katie."

She swallowed hard as he wrapped his arms around her shoulders, walking her up the porch steps. In the midst of their endless argument, she hadn't mentioned that her sickly sister was no longer sick.

"Drew!" Katie said, running up to him, ending their kiss abruptly.

"Hi, Katie," he said, giving her a one-armed side hug.

"Guess you're a happy guy, huh?" Katie said, putting her dishes in the sink. "We don't have to keep her hostage anymore!" Bria's eyes grew wide, frantically searching for some rational excuse as to why she would be avoiding moving back in with her fiancé.

"Katie. . ." Sam whispered, picking up on the hint that her sister had so clearly missed.

"Oh?" Drew said, looking from Katie to Bria. "Why is that?"

"I'm all clear," Katie said, a bit less enthusiastically now, as she was finally becoming aware of the shitstorm she was about to cause.

"Oh, when did you find that out?" Drew asked, his eyes still on Bria.

"Uh. . . a few days ago."

"When were you going to tell me?" Drew asked Bria, just above a whisper. Bria wanted to clap back with some legitimate reason, but she had nothing. He looked down at the ground for a moment, then back up. "So, you can come home?" She looked at him, then back at her sisters, then at the ground.

Then, as if the gods of love hadn't tested Bria's sanity enough, Knox's car rolled up into her parents' driveway. One part of her was so excited to see him. And the other just thought, oh, Jesus, not right now. Drew followed her gaze to Knox, his whole body stiffening immediately. Knox hopped out of his car with a smile on his face, carrying a bouquet of roses. He almost tripped up the porch step when he saw Drew.

"H-hey, guys," he said, looking back and forth from Bria to Drew. He held up the bouquet. "Katie called the other day and told me the news. I just wanted to drop these off for her," he said, sweetly making clear that the roses were most definitely *not* for Bria.

Drew turned back to Bria slowly, looking down at her with so much hurt, so much disappointment in his eyes, that she actually had to look away. He hung his head, shook it, and walked down the steps to his car.

"Drew, hold on," Bria called. But it was like he didn't even hear her. She looked at Knox. "I have to go."

He nodded and followed Katie inside. As Bria made her way down the steps after Drew, she felt a tug on her hand.

"Sam, let go, I need to talk to him," Bria said, shaking her off.

"Bria, you know I don't believe in fate, or God, or any of that stuff. But please open your eyes for a minute, and realize there is a reason that Knox just showed up at the exact time Drew did. Please open your eyes and realize that these things don't just happen."

Bria's head was spinning. And in the background, she heard Drew starting up his car.

"Please, B. I just want you to be happy," Sam said. Her eyes were pleading. Bria felt a storm surging inside of her, and she wanted to scream.

"Sam, Drew wants to make me happy. He wants to buy me a fucking house, okay? He wants to get me out of here so my life isn't consumed by an endless pit of money issues and sick sisters. He wants me to have my own fucking life, away from the madness that is this family."

Sam's eyes grew wide as she stepped back on the porch, and Bria hated herself the second the words came out. "I'm sorry, Sam. I'm so sorry. I didn't mean that. I'm just. . . I'm so confused."

"Then you should probably go talk to your fiancé. And you might want to tell him you're in love with someone else." Sam said, matter-of-factly. She turned on her heel and slammed the front door shut.

Bria felt like she might throw up as Sam's words reverberated in her head. She sighed and ran down the steps to Drew's car.

"Can we go somewhere and talk, please?" she asked. He didn't say anything, just waited for her to get in.

Shit. She had no idea what to actually say to him. She just knew she needed to be alone with him. She would figure it out. Or, at least, she hoped she would. She directed him past town, to the old farm that had been vacant for decades. In high school, this is where the kids would come to smoke weed and make out. Bria never did—she just came here once with Knox when he was running away from some girl he had made out with under the bleachers, who wouldn't leave him alone. But that warm nostalgia was quickly melting away as Drew put the car in park. They sat in silence for a moment. Her heart pounded. The next move she made, the next thing either of them said. . . so much rode on it.

Her future was planned. And it was going to be a good one. It was the one she wanted. But lately, she felt like she was talking about someone else's life when she was discussing the wedding, or her life with Drew. She felt like she was misplaced; like she had stumbled upon such an amazing guy, such an amazing future, by mistake. Like she was about to live out some other girl's dream life.

For most of her life, Bria had done everything by the book. She got the diploma. She got the acceptance letter, she got the degree. She got the job. She played by the rules. She got the guy, she got the ring. She could have the marriage, she could have the kids she had always dreamed of having. She had a golden ticket to the life she thought she always wanted, the life that would be just far enough from Dalesville, far enough from all the pain and struggles of her own family.

But, as the lump rose in her throat, she knew that she didn't want to leave Dalesville. It was her home. Her family was her home. Knox. . . he was her home. Well, Knox was a truly different story. She had no idea what they were, or what they might be. But she couldn't think about him in this moment. She took one more breath, and turned to speak, but Drew beat her to it.

"Are you in love with him?" he asked quietly, staring down at the steering wheel. She was in shock. She wasn't expecting that to be the opening. Luckily, he kept talking. "Please don't deny anything, here, Bria. Here I am, thinking we had a meaningless, stupid little fight. But now, it feels like my gut was right. And I'm terrified that I'm about to lose the love of my life."

She felt her heart breaking in two. She couldn't see her future self with him anymore. She used to so clearly see herself in the backyard of some big house, much like the one he had just taken her to, with a few little Drews running around. But now it was all fuzzy. Now, the house was in Dalesville, and the man had a question mark for a face. All she knew was that he wasn't Drew. But she did love Drew. And she didn't want to see him hurt.

Bria didn't think about the down payment her parents had made to the venue, she didn't think about the guests that would need to be notified, she didn't think about what her future in-laws would think of her, and what her parents' friends would say. She just took his hand.

"Drew," she said, trying to steady her quivering voice, "I will always love you." Her voice was a whisper now. "I will always love what you did for me. And how you showed me my worth, and how hard you work. But I'm a different person, and I belong here. I want to be *here.*"

She thought she was going to die when she saw the tears rolling down his cheeks.

"Is it him?" he asked.

"It's not about him," she told him. "I'm just not ready for this, anymore. I'm so sorry. I'm so, so sorry."

They sat in silence for a few minutes.

"You know something," he finally said, "I think I knew, that night that we saw him at the bar. That look in your eyes. . .I think I knew then."

"Drew," she started to say.

"No, listen to me. I'm not sure what the deal is with you guys, but if he's it, please do something about it. Please don't let it pass you by, until you're engaged to some other guy someday, and it's too late. . . again."

He was looking her right in the eyes, and she knew he wasn't saying it to be malicious. He was saying it because he wanted her to be happy. Because she was still his everything. And she felt like nothing more than the soulless wench who was ruining his life. She nodded.

"Well, I can't believe this is the end," he said. And Bria didn't protest. Drew put the car in drive, and drove her back to her parents' house. For a moment, she felt like it should be more dragged out, like their six-year relationship should have caused much more pain and turmoil. More yelling and screaming and cursing. But it didn't. And she knew it was because she had learned over the last few months that she actually *could* live without Drew.

"Can you do me a favor? When you come to get your things, do you mind doing it during the day? I don't want to watch you move out," he said.

She nodded quietly. She reached for the car door, and as she unclipped her seatbelt, her diamond flashed in her eyes. They both paused to look down at it. She slowly wiggled it off and placed it in his hand.

"I'm so sorry, Drew," she whispered one more time. "I hope you have the happiest life. I really do."

He squeezed her hand and kissed it, with a faint, pained smile. Then, he was gone.

Bria wiped the tears from her cheeks and made her way up the porch steps. She stared down at her bare hand as if it were going to speak to her, tell her to run after him, that she needed her ring back. Her hand said nothing.

"Bria?" Sam asked, "that you?"

"Yeah," she said, her voice broken and shaky. Katie and Sam appeared around the corner of the kitchen. She took one look at them, and the tears came. She thought about the first moment she met Drew, and about the first time they made love, and about the moment she knew she wanted to marry him, and have kids with him. The night he proposed, the first time she called him her fiancé. The moment she had realized that Drew could be her escape; Drew would make sure that their kids got to go to college, and that if one ever fell ill, he could take care of them. But that warm feeling of security had faded over the last few months, as she realized she didn't need that kind of security anymore. Instead, she felt relief that she no longer had to pretend to want the life she had so eagerly pursued—a city life of private schools, and taking the

Metro, and eating at fancy restaurants in Dupont. She loved Drew, for what it was worth. But she was almost ashamed at the relief she felt, for escaping the future *she* had signed up for.

Her sisters stared at her for a minute, then rushed to her with the perfect amount of unspoken sisterly support. Bria had almost forgotten about the horrible things she'd said to Sam just a few minutes before, and from the way that Sam was holding her, it seemed she did, too. That's the thing about sisters. They can tell the difference between you and your demons. No apology, no explanation necessary. They just take it in stride, and move on.

"Well, looks like I'm moving back in," Bria finally managed to say.

"Oh, no," Katie cried. "It's all my fault! I'm so sorry, I should have kept my mouth shut."

"No, Kates, it's not your fault. It's no one's fault. It's just life. We just. . . we weren't right." Sam handed her a tissue.

They spent a few hours watching movies, curled up on the couch with one big blanket over them. Only this time, Bria's head was in Katie's lap, with her legs draped over Sam. Her sisters were everything. And at a moment like this, she couldn't believe that she ever wanted to be far away from them. After a few hours, her phone rang.

"Mom?" Katie must have called her.

"Oh, honey, you okay? What in the world happened?" Louise asked, frantically. But Bria couldn't bring herself to answer right away.

"I'm okay, mom. Really. It just . . .happened. But I promise to pay you back every dime you already put down. I'm sorry."

"Bria Kreery. After all you've done for us? Don't even think it. I just want to make sure you're happy." Bria smiled, feeling a little lighter. Her parents had been so focused on getting Katie well, that she forgot they could take care of Bria too. They made her crazy sometimes, but man, she loved her family.

"I will be, Mom," she said.

She waited a few more hours, expecting the regret to seep in. She waited to feel the heaviness of the huge mistake she had just made. But it never came. If this were any other guy, she would have called Knox.

Knox.

"Hey, where did Knox go?" she asked.

"He took off after you left," Sam said.

"Are you going to tell him you're madly in love with him, now?" Katie said. Bria scoffed at how quickly she had gotten over the Drew situation.

"What?" she asked. "Jesus, Kates. Drew and I have been broken up for ten minutes."

"Yeah," Sam said, "but you've been in love with Knox for ten years." Bria rolled her eyes, but the truth behind Sam's words hit her like a ton of bricks.

All these years, their timing was so off. It never worked out. And she was so afraid of falling victim to his charm, that she refused to let it even be an option. But as she thought about everything, every moment she had spent with Knox, she knew her sisters were right. It was time to put on her big girl panties and come clean. She stood up and grabbed her keys back off of the counter.

"I'll be back later," she said with a sly smile.

The whole way to Knox's, Bria was pretty sure she didn't take a single breath. She felt like she had just run five miles by the time she pulled up. She double-parked her car behind his and stared up at his door. Ten years later, and it was all coming down to this. She knocked on the door, a breeze in the air sending chills down her spine.

She heard some stumbling behind the door, and then it finally jolted open, Knox in a ratty old t-shirt, with his shaggy, jet-black hair falling perfectly in place on his head.

"Where's your fiancé?" he asked. And as he

wobbled a little bit closer to her, she could tell that he had been drinking.

"He's gone. And, uh, he's not my fiancé anymore." He said nothing, he just stared at her. "Can I come in?"

He stood still for a few more moments before opening the door.

Bria followed him up the stairs of his split-level to the living room, where he held his hand out, offering her a seat on his burnt orange couch. He plopped down next to her, emptying another can of beer into his mouth before slamming it back down on the table.

"I wasn't expecting company," he said, shrugging. "So what happened?"

"It just wasn't. . .he just wasn't what I wanted, anymore," she said, tugging at the hair tie on her wrist. She slowly looked up at him.

"I'm sorry to hear that," he said. She looked down again. What the hell was she supposed to say now? That she wanted to be with him? That she had *always* wanted to be with him? To her relief, he started talking again.

"You know, that one weekend we went up to the lake?"

She gave him a puzzled look. "Yeah, I remember."

"Early that one night, before things got weird with Darren. You were wearing this pink dress. And then you got in my bed." She remembered that night clear as day. The night that she had thought, that she had *hoped* something might happen.

"And I remember, Courtney and I were on the couch, and she was going on and on about how Chelsea Dunn kept screwing up every time she was inbounding the ball," Knox said, breaking into a slight smile. She giggled and rolled her eyes. "But as she kept talking, I couldn't take my eyes off of you. You were so. . .sexy," he said, with a chuckle, still looking down at his cup. "But I remember being in such awe at how effortless it was for you. All these other girls, they'd spend hours, but you, it was just natural. And I wanted you. So, so badly that night. And then I asked you to stay with me. I had all these intentions. All these horrible, dirty, intentions. Man, if you had only known what I wanted to do that night. But then I freaked out, because I had never really admitted to myself that I wanted you that way. " Finally, he looked up at her.

Bria felt her body tightening. She remembered that feeling, of forgetting to breathe, in disbelief that she was in the same bed as him, underneath the same covers. Before she could wrap her mind around what he was saying, he continued.

"But I knew that if we did it, one of two things would happen. The first, was that we'd stop talking, things would get weird, and I would hurt you; same thing that happened with any other girl I slept with. But the second option was that I'd want more. More than just sex with you. And I was fucking terrified. I didn't know how to. . . I *still* don't know how to do this. But Jesus, I wanted you that night." He was staring down at his hands, now. "And then, the other night, at the Café. Good *God.* That all came back to me, when I saw you dancing up there."

"Knox, I. . ." she started to say, but she felt her hands trembling. "Why didn't you ever say anything?"

"Because, Bria," he said, standing up now, and walking toward the window, "I guess I thought. . . I don't know. I guess I just thought it sort of went without saying. I mean, Jesus, I held your hand all the time, I'd touch you whenever I got the fuckin' chance. We were together all the time. . . with every other girl I'd been with, that was all it took. But you never took the bait like they did, and I guess I thought that you didn't feel the same way."

She stared at him in disbelief. All those times, all those chances. "There was one time that I was going to tell you. I showed up in College Park. I found out where you lived from Mari, and I showed up, hoping to surprise you.

And then I saw you, dressed for that date. . ."

Her jaw dropped. It was the night of her first date with Drew. The night she had been so pissed that Knox never called her, when he was really coming to see her.

"That night, when you were going on that date, I just had this feeling that I was losing you. So I didn't come back. I didn't tell you, because I don't know *how* to lose you. So I settled for just being your friend. Because I'd rather have had you like that, than not at all. Even if we stopped talking all the time, even if things weren't. . . the *same.* At least I still *had* you. There was no sad, dramatic ending to us that way. I had all the memories in my mind to revisit." The tears were pricking her eyes.

"So that's why you stopped answering me?" she asked. It all made sense now. He nodded.

"Yeah. It was getting to be a little bit painful for me. But I found that if I kept my distance, the pain eased up a little bit."

She heard what he was saying, and Lord knows they were the words she had secretly fantasized about for years. No, they were *better.* She looked at her friend, and she knew now why he never made a move on her. Why he would never pursue her, the way he had with so many other girls. And she knew it all too well, because it was exactly the same thing that kept her from doing it, too.

"Knox—" she said, taking a step toward him.

"But I see now, B. I see now that this can't work."

"W-what?"

"You want the same future you've always wanted. You want to get out of Dalesville. Your family, God love 'em, this town, it's weighed you down, B. I see all you can do outside of here, all you can have, and I. . ." his voice started to shake, and she felt her knees wobbling as she pushed herself to stand.

"I can't give that to you," he said. "It's not because I wouldn't try. It's just because . . . I don't want to. I don't want that. I'm not meant to be a husband, or a dad, or even a boyfriend, apparently. And you, you're meant for more than that. And you've probably known that all along." Her eyes grew wide again.

This was so *not* how this was supposed to go down.

"I *won't* hold you back from all that, and I won't do that to myself, either. I can't spend any more time just *wondering* if I would make you happy. I'm sorry about Drew. I really am, because all I ever needed to know was that you were happy. And I could tell, every time I saw you together, I had a feeling he had no idea what a Goddamn gem he had in his hands. But you have to find that guy. I can't be him. I think we missed our chance, B."

Bria felt like she was going to puke. She wasn't sure exactly what happened, but it felt a lot like Knox had professed his love to her and broken her heart, all in the span of five minutes. She said nothing; she just grabbed her bag off the table, and walked out of the house.

Her drive home was like one from a movie, where a highlight reel of all of their best times together played in her head. Of course, the low and sad Adele song she played in the background just added to the dramatic effect, but still.

She thought of every moment he had stroked her face, grabbed for her hand, called her a pet name. She thought of every moment that he had been there. She should have said something. She should have fucking said something.

And now, he was right: she wanted children, and a fucking future. But what he was wrong about was her needing to get out, and get away. That was her excuse for so long, but she had been so, so wrong. She felt like she had all the pieces to her life, but they were all out of order. And for an extremely brief moment between Drew leaving and her showing up to Knox's house, she stupidly supposed that he fit into that picture so perfectly. Her future right now was a puzzle with one huge-ass piece missing. But he wasn't the right piece. A round peg into a square hole, or whatever that stupid fucking saying was. And the worst part was, she *still* hadn't told him that she felt that way about him, too.

She actually clutched her chest as she drove. She pulled into the parking lot by the swings, the same lot she and Knox had parked in so many times, at so many different times in their lives. She plopped down on the seat with the shorter chains, as if he would be coming to take the better one, staring blankly ahead of her.

She would never admit it out of respect for Drew, but the moment it was over between the two of them, the moment Bria was "free," Knox's face popped into her head. She needed to try and find out what place he was supposed to have in her life.

But now, as she sat on the swings, on *their* swings, she realized that she and Knox, whatever they had, might be over. And those last words, that last glimpse of him, with tears in his eyes, could be the last time she ever saw him. She'd lost him, and he had never even been hers.

ONE YEAR LATER

TWENTY-FOUR

Bria plopped down on the couch with a bowl of cereal, flipping through the channels until she landed on House Hunters.

"Ew, those carpets are gross," she said to herself, but leaving the channel on. After all, she couldn't change it without knowing which house the adorable couple with seemingly no real source of income chose.

She looked around her own apartment. It was small, but she had slowly been adding her own little touch to it in the way of decorations and amateur paint jobs since she moved in a year ago.

It was in Dalesville, just a few miles from her family. Of course, after her split with Drew, and the end of whatever she had with Knox, Louise had begged for her to stay with them.

"Please, honey, think about it," she said. "You can save money, Lord knows we owe you some, and this way you don't have to be alone all the time."

Although the idea of moving back in full-time with her parents was slightly intriguing, she couldn't bear the idea of being a 25-year-old with a full-time job still living at home. She needed space. She needed to show herself that she could be independent.

This was, after all, the first time she had been single in over five years. According to Mari, she should be "living it up." But her idea of living it up was yanking her bra off the second she got home and sliding into the baggiest pair of sweatpants she had—the ones she got in high school with the stretchiest waist band. They had the perfect amount of give when she felt like eating an entire Chipotle burrito or a donut or two.

To Bria's surprise, this year had actually been pretty good. She had gotten another small promotion at work which came with a little bit of a raise, she'd bought herself a new car, and most of all, Katie was doing well. There was a scare earlier in the year; the doctors were concerned with some sort of infection, or some sort of reaction Katie had to a medicine.

To be honest, Bria didn't exactly know what the problem was. It seemed to resolve itself, and Katie was doing great. Sam had gotten a job, working about thirty minutes away, and the Kreery family unit was still as close as ever. And Bria was loving it.

But of course, every time she'd hear a certain song, or have an ice cream cone, she'd think of Knox.

And it hurt.

Although they'd had their "sabbaticals" in the past when they went months, maybe even years without talking, she always felt like he would be there if she did reach out. Their "friendship," or, what was left of it, had basically boiled down to one or two text messages every few months during those breaks, but at least she knew the basics of his life.

But this time, things were different. Bria couldn't

bring herself to reach out to him. She didn't want to know how he was doing. Because if it was bad, her heart would break. And if it was good, her heart would break again.

Besides, he hadn't contacted her, either.

Once, she and Sam almost ran into Mrs. Knoxville at the grocery store. But when they spotted her, they practically did a backflip down the next aisle, ducking behind displays of pasta sauce until she walked by.

Bria just couldn't. She didn't want to know.

Every so often her longing to see him, or hear him, the emptiness that she felt, would fade. Until the next time *Dirty Dancing* was on, or she was cold and needed a hoodie. God, there were so many things that reminded her of him. It was actually a little annoying. But still, for the most part, her life was good.

Then things started changing again.

Katie started complaining of back pain, and she was napping all day long. She dropped one of her classes, and was on the border of failing another. Some days, she had trouble catching her breath. One morning, she actually passed out while she was getting ready for class, and Louise and Joe knew it was time to take her back in.

All five of the Kreeries dreaded the "we better make an appointment" discussion, because it always ended in a not-so-good prognosis.

"I don't understand," Louise said, staring blankly ahead at Dr. Carmen. "She was fine a month ago. She's been fine for a year."

Bria sat on a rolling stool across from Louise and Joe in a tiny room as they waited for the nurses to bring Katie back in from her scan.

"Well, Mr. and Mrs. Kreery, I'm afraid I have some serious news. Looking at Katie's ultrasound results, I'm afraid she is experiencing end-stage renal failure," Dr. Carmen said, his tone extremely calm, despite the news he was delivering.

Bria watched her parents' faces, trying to get a

read on the exact emotions going through their heads.

"Kidney failure, my God," her father whispered.

"How did this happen? What would our options be?" Louise asked, panic oozing out of her. Dr. Carmen cleared his throat.

"Well, it's hard to pinpoint the exact cause, but I suspect it has something to do with the medications she's been on all these years. Or, it could be some sort of underlying infection . . . it's really hard to say. There appears to be some major damage done to them, and at this point, she's lost about eighty-percent of her kidney function. We will start her on dialysis right away to help remove some of the waste from her blood, but her best option at this point would be to look for a donor."

Bria felt her arms get heavy as she tried to lift one to put around her mother's shoulders. Luckily, her father beat her to it.

"Donor?" her mother choked out. "Jesus!"

"I know, ma'am, but I just want to make you aware of the current situation. I'm so sorry."

When Dr. Carmen left the room, Louise burst into tears. Joe held her tight, stroking her arm. For a moment, Bria forgot where she was, and all about the news she received. She watched her parents. Throughout the course of their marriage, she and her sisters had seen them struggle so much. The recession, layoffs, medical bills; money had not been a friend to them. She and Sam and Katie had just been drifting on the flood, watching their parents constantly tread water to stay afloat.

But as she watched them now, her mother leaning on her father, just as he had leaned on her in the past, Bria knew that *this* was what she needed in a partner. She needed a constant, a rock. And she wanted to be that rock for someone. She didn't need to be saved, because in all actuality, she knew she couldn't run from all the evils of life. She just needed someone to have her back. And she wanted to be that person in return. But she snapped back to reality when the door opened, the nurses pushing Katie's bed back into place.

"It's bad, isn't it?" Katie said, noticing her mother's tear-stained cheeks.

"Don't worry, kid," Bria said, stroking her sister's hair. "We're going to get you what you need."

As Joe and Louise sat on either side of Katie's bed to discuss the prognosis and her options, Bria excused herself from the room. She needed a breather.

She was resting her head against the big, white bricks of the hospital corridor when Dr. Carmen walked by.

"Excuse me, um, Dr. Carmen? I'm Bria Kreery, Katie's sister," she said.

He was a tall man, ruggedly handsome with jet-black hair and gray eyes. His skin was tan, and she couldn't help but think that he looked like a Ken doll she had once owned. She guessed he was only five or six years older than she, but the wrinkles around his eyes made him look older. Probably from the years of giving patients shitty news, she supposed.

"Hi, Bria," he said.

"Look, um, how do we tell if I'm a match for my sister? If she needs a kidney, I mean."

Dr. Carmen looked down at his clipboard, likely late for his next patient. But his face relaxed a little.

"Wow, Bria, that's very brave of you to ask. We have to run some blood tests to see if you're compatible. You should know, though, that donating a kidney isn't an easy procedure. It can be as long of a recovery for the donor as it is for the patient. If you want to get some testing done, you can call my office to schedule it."

She nodded.

Bria couldn't sleep that night. She had told Katie she'd stay at their parents' with her tonight, and she could hear her littlest sister tossing and turning in the other room. It broke Bria's heart.

After Katie's appointments, they had spent the rest of the afternoon watching Nicholas Sparks movies that Bria pretended to hate, but secretly loved. And now, she laid awake, staring at the N*SYNC poster that still clung to the ceiling in her childhood bedroom, wondering if her kidney would work inside of her sister's body. Wondering what would happen if it didn't. Wondering if her little sister would survive this.

And there was one person who *might* be awake right now. But she couldn't text him, or call him, or sneak over to his house.

Because he was wrong for her.

So she laid awake, silent tears rolling down her cheeks.

TWENTY-FIVE

Understandably, Katie was quiet the next few days. She smiled at her mom when she dropped two pancakes on her plate, but the smile didn't reach her eyes. Just then, the front door burst open.

"Hey, dudes," Sam said, kicking it shut behind her.

Bria beamed. These two girls were her world.

"Hey, Sammy," Bria said. Sam rolled her eyes. She *hated* that name.

The five of them sat at the breakfast table, listening to Sam's saga about her horrific new male coworker who hit on her every day for a week, despite the countless times she mentioned Abby and the fact that she had a *girl*friend.

Then they talked about this woman at Louise's office who was infamous for dumping the coffee grounds down the sink.

"And there isn't even a disposal in there! I am *so* sick of digging my hand down there to pull them out!"

Bria laughed and shook her head. As she stood to clean up, Katie plugged the speaker into the wall on the island, turning up Sam Cooke so the whole family could sing as they tidied up. Sam took the lead, while Katie and Bria were the backup singers. Eventually, though, Sam tossed the wooden spoon microphone to Joe so that she could scrub a pan. Louise played the piano, which made Bria hunch over in a fit of laughter—there was no piano in the song.

Then, Louise's phone rang, and the Kreery family went silent, a rare happening for them.

"Hello? Yes, Hi Dr. Carmen." Louise looked to Joe, then to Katie. "You want her to come in again? Yes, we can come in today." Louise hung up the phone. "Dr. Carmen wants to squeeze you in for your second round of dialysis today," she told Katie.

"Don't worry, Kates," Bria said, walking her to the front door.

"Yeah, dude. You got this. It's all gonna be fine," Sam said. But as they walked down the front porch steps, Bria and Sam looked at each other. This time, things really might *not* be fine, and they weren't sure what to do about it.

The two of them spent the day taking care of anything and everything they could think of to eliminate any extra stress on their parents. Bria called up and paid their cable and electric bills, Sam cleaned the house, and they gave Buster a bath. Then, finally, the front door opened, and Katie stepped inside. She looked up at her sisters, and ran to her bedroom.

"We've got to find her a kidney," her father said, looking down at the ground. "Mom and I went in last week to get blood work done, and it turns out, your mother and I are not matches."

When her parents excused themselves to go to

their room, Bria looked at Sam, and they both knew where they were headed.

They got in the car and drove twenty minutes to Dr. Carmen's office in complete silence.

"Hi, is Dr. Carmen available?" Bria asked the receptionist, who had a puzzled look on her face.

"He's here, but he's with patients all day. Do you have an appointment?" she asked.

"No, my sister is a patient here. And my other sister and I, we need. . . look I just really need to talk to him, okay?"

The receptionist looked from Bria to Sam, from Sam to Bria. And something in her expression shifted, Bria recognized the sadness, the sympathy in her eyes. She normally hated being patronized, she never wanted anyone to feel bad for her. But in this case, right now, she'd milk it for all it was worth.

"He has a fifteen-minute opening after this last appointment. I'll ask him if he can squeeze you in."

"Thank you!" Bria practically choked out as Sam pulled her toward a chair in the waiting room. Finally, Dr. Carmen appeared at the end of the hall.

"Ms. Kreery?" he asked. When Bria stood, he smiled, a sad, sympathetic smile. "Come on back."

"What can I do for you?" he asked, leading them to his office and closing the door.

"Well," Bria said, looking to Sam, "we'd like to be tested to see if either of us is a match for a kidney."

Dr. Carmen looked down at his desk.

"That's very brave of you both," he said. Then, looked right at Bria. "You're a wonderfully selfless big sister." She shifted in her seat. "Both of you are. But again, I must warn you, that even the process of testing to see if you're a match isn't an easy one. It's a three-step process; we'll first need to check your blood type. If that's the same, then we will need to do tissue typing, followed by cross-matching."

Bria felt her eyes cross and her ears turn off. She didn't give a damn what it entailed. She just wanted to get on with it. Finally, he paused. "Are you two ready for all that?"

They both nodded.

"Alright. Well, it will take some time, but given the rush, I'll have Kristina pencil you in first thing on Monday." Bria nodded as Dr. Carmen gave her a weary smile.

"What if neither of us are a match?" Sam asked.

Dr. Carmen sighed. "Then we keep looking."

"Well, how much time do we have?" Bria asked. He sighed again, gently shaking his head.

"It's hard to say. The dialysis will help, but I would like to get a new kidney in Katie in the next few months."

Holy shit. A few *months*. The words smacked Bria in the face. Her chest tightened and she suddenly felt like she couldn't breathe. Wait, no, she *actually* couldn't breathe. Then she blacked out.

When she came to, Sam was holding her head up while Dr. Carmen was standing over her.

"There ya go. Bria, can you hear me?" he said. The millions of tiny black dots she was seeing finally started to clear, as his perfectly square jawline came into focus. She nodded.

"Here, drink this," he said, handing her a juice box. "You okay? Can I walk you out?"

"We're fine," Sam said, "thanks, Doc."

As Sam stood at the front desk making their appointments, Bria felt a tap on her shoulder.

"Bria, look, I just want to tell you that I'm so moved by what you and your sister are trying to do here. I know this is rough, so if I can help at all, please, don't hesitate to give me a call."

He handed her a business card and put his hand on her shoulder.

"Thanks," she said.

"Jeez Louise," Sam said, pushing the button for the elevator, "why didn't he just ask you to marry him?"

"What?" Bria asked.

"Oh my God, come on. He was all over you with his eyes and his little 'oh, you're so brave, you're so selfless,' blah, blah, blah. Gross men and their gross penises," Sam said. Bria chuckled.

"No, you don't think he was, do you?"

"Good Lord, Bria. I know you got your heart broken, but it shouldn't make you totally oblivious to the fact that another man finds you attractive. In case you forgot, *that* is what flirting looks like," she said, pointing back toward the doctor's office.

Wow. Flirting. For the past year, it had seemed like such a foreign concept. She couldn't even wrap her head around it. She had no desire. She just wanted to heal, to move on with her life, and her career. And to fill that Knox-shaped hole in her heart.

The following week, Bria and Sam went to the doctor's office three times a piece, getting poked and prodded and scanned. Her mother had cried when they told her where she was going. They hadn't told Katie. As the nurse bandaged up the vein in Bria's arm, Dr. Carmen poked his head in the doorway.

"How ya holdin' up?" he asked.

"Oh, fine, you know."

"Well, listen. We will try and get you these results back as soon as possible. Sound good?" he asked.

"Sounds good."

Finally, it was Friday, and Bria was actually relieved to be back in the office and not being stuck by what felt like a hundred needles. Her office had been so understanding of the situation with Katie, and she'd been taking a lot of time off. Around lunch time, her phone vibrated on her desk.

"Hello?"

"Bria? It's Dr. Carmen."

"Oh, hi, Dr. Carmen," she said, her heart rate increasing.

"So I wanted to personally call you. We got the result of yours and Sam's tests. It looks like she has you on her HIPAA form, so I can give you both results, if you'd like."

"Yes, please."

"I'm so sorry, Bria, but neither of you are a compatible match for Katie. I hate to give you this news."

Her heart sunk, and then, so did she. She closed her office door and slid down the wall until she was sitting on the ground. She covered her mouth to stifle the cries.

"Bria? Are you okay? Is there anything I can do?"

"No, no," she sniffled, "I'm okay. We will find someone."

"Yes, I have no doubt. You don't seem like the type to give up easy," he said. This actually made her smile.

She thought about calling Sam, but she absolutely *hated* being the bearer of bad news, particularly when she didn't have a solution. And especially when she was breaking the news to her sisters. She took the rest of the day to immerse herself into her work, smiling at everyone, talking about the latest episodes of *The Bachelor*, and even scoring a new account. But when the workday ended, it was back to the brainstorming. The whole way home, she killed herself to come up with something, *some* sort of viable option. Some way to save her sister's life.

Just as she was about two miles from her parents' house, she got cut off by one of those assholes who goes ten under the speed limit on a single-lane road.

"Oh. My. God," she said, pounding her hands against the steering wheel. "Seriously? *Drive!*" But then she stopped. Drive.

She had an idea. She pulled out her phone and dialed Dr. Carmen.

"Bria?" he answered. "Everything okay?"

"Hi, Dr. Carmen," she said. "I have an idea that I wanted to run by you."

"Sure thing," he said. "I'm still at the office. Do you want to stop by?"

She turned around on Route 108, making a u-turn right there in the center of town while no cars were passing, and drove the twenty minutes to Dr. Carmen's office.

"I'm sorry," the receptionist said, walking toward the door to intercept her, "but we're actually closed."

"No, no, it's okay Jo," Dr. Carmen said, appearing from the back, still in his white lab coat, "I asked Bri—Miss Kreery to come in. You can head out, I'll close up."

Jo looked from Dr. Carmen to Bria, then nodded. This was the second time Dr. Carmen had made an exception for Bria, and she knew Jo remembered that.

"So," he said, leading her back to his office once again, "tell me about this idea."

Bria plopped down in the chair in front of his desk, her eyes opening wide with excitement. He smiled as she spoke, waving her hands from one side to the other, rattling off every single thought she had had while stuck behind the slowest driver in the history of fucking ever. When she finally finished, he sat back in his chair, touching his fingertips together lightly. Finally, he broke out into a wide grin, shaking his head lightly.

"You don't think it will work," she said quietly, staring down at her hands.

"No, no, that's not it at all," he said, reaching out and touching her hand briefly, then bringing it back to his desk. "I've just, I've never met someone like you. I mean, I've met my fair share of organ donors, but I've never met someone like you who is just so determined to fix things for the people she loves. And who is willing to do whatever she has to. You're just. . . you're pretty incredible."

She felt her cheeks flush. She shrugged.

"Well, I always said Katie was my practice baby," she laughed. "And she's family. We take care of each other." He nodded.

"You want kids someday?" he asked. The question jarred her. She barely knew him.

"Yeah, I do," she said, unapologetically. She was done belittling what she wanted. That seemed to get her in trouble before.

"Well, if this is any indication, I think you'll make an amazing mom one day," he said. Bria felt a smirk sneak across her face.

"Thank you."

"Well, Bria, if you can take care of the logistics, I'm all in," he said standing up and walking around to the other side of the desk. She jumped up out of her seat.

"Oh, Dr. Carmen! Oh, that is amazing news!" she said, reaching up and wrapping her arms around his neck. She felt his hands lay gently on her back, and she realized that she was in an awkwardly-long embrace with her sister's doctor. She slowly slid down off her tiptoes, bringing her hands back to her sides. "Sorry," she whispered. He smiled.

"Don't be," he whispered back, "and call me Eric."

As he walked her to the door, she felt his hand ever so gently touch the small of her back. But she didn't mind it. This man was a freaking Godsend.

"So, I'll call you when I nail down the details," she said.

"I'm looking forward to it."

Without thinking, she stood up on her tiptoes and quickly pecked him on the cheek. His eyes widened with boyish excitement. She smiled back at him, and walked out the door.

Bria ran from her car into her parents' house. Katie and Sam were already at the table, twirling their spaghetti while Louise and Joe made their plates.

"Guys. I have an idea," she said, slamming the door behind her.

"Yeah?" Sam said, slurping a noodle off of her plate.

"We can have a *drive.* A kidney drive! A kidney match drive!"

"A what?" Louise asked.

"We will post it all over town, and all over the county, and state, if we have to. We'll put Katie's blood type on everything, and we can host an event at the fire hall. We can have games and food and stuff. Dr. Carmen said his staff could volunteer for a day. They will test for similar blood type, and have those people come in to the office for the rest of the testing."

The four of them stared blankly at her for a minute.

"Well, God damn, that's a good idea!" Joe finally said. "We'll get a DJ, and some games!"

"Yeah, and I'll call Beth to see about donating some sandwiches!" Louise said.

"Great idea, B!" Sam said. She looked to Katie, who had tears welling up in her eyes.

"Thank you, Bria," she whispered, just as they fell.

TWENTY-SIX

The kidney drive was three days away, and Louise was starting to get into her pre-event panic.

"Watch out," Sam warned Bria when she got home from work, "she's on a warpath."

"Oh, lordy," Bria said. "Ma?"

"No, I need them there at five o'clock," Louise said, talking on the phone. "Five. Not six."

Bria shot Sam a look.

"This is crazy. No one can seem to get here on time!" Louise said, dropping her phone on the table.

"Mom, it's going to be fine. This is not about sandwiches, after all. It's about kidneys. And Katie."

Louise looked at her daughters and took a deep breath. "Man, I lucked out with you three," she said, kissing each of them on the forehead.

Finally, it was the day of the drive. The Kreeries had been all over town, chatting up neighbors about the event, tagging their friends on Facebook, and posting flyers in all the local shops and businesses. Bria arrived at the fire hall early to get things set up and wait for Dr. Carmen.

"Bria," he said, walking in with a team full of nurses and aids behind him.

"Eric!" she said, making her way to him and enveloping him in a hug. "I can't tell you what this means to my family."

He cleared his throat, his cheeks slightly pink. "Of course," he said, "I'm happy to help."

Bria smiled and walked him toward the back of the hall where his staff started to set up.

"Okay," he said, clapping his hands together, "I think we are good to go. What's going to happen today is just basic blood work. So we will take vials of blood from everyone who donates, bring it back to the lab, and see who matches. If their blood type matches, we will go ahead and call them in for the rest of the compatibility testing."

Bria nodded. This all sounded like it would take time, and she hoped it wouldn't be too *much* time. He must have seen the pain in her eyes.

"Don't worry, Bria," he said, putting his hand on her shoulder. "We will find someone as fast as possible." She gave him a look of thanks, placing her hand on his for just a moment.

Finally, the drive was open, and when Bria saw the line of people wrapped around the building, she wanted to burst into tears.

The thoughtfulness of her little town. Most people, granted, her family knew. But there were some new faces in the crowd too. And, here they all were, lining up to potentially donate an organ to save her sister's life.

Bria sat at the front table, checking people in and handing out medical waivers.

"How's it going?" she felt him whisper in her ear,

and she jumped.

"Oh, hey Dr. C," she said, "Yes, thanks, just sign right here," she told the woman in front of her. "Seems to be going well! How's it going back there?"

"Pretty good. Liza took the first batch back, and we actually already have one blood type match," he said with a smile. Bria's eyes brightened. "But, remember, it's a three-step process. We still have to do more testing. Look, I'm going to take a quick twenty-minute break to get some food. Where's good to eat around here?"

"Oh, um, Tom and Ray's is right across the street, there," she pointed through the large garage doors of the fire hall. "Do you want me to go with you?" she asked. It was the least she could do.

"I thought you'd never ask," he said, with that dazzling smile yet again.

"Thanks," Eric said, as the waitress put down a tray of fries for them to share.

"I'll be right back with your meals," she said.

"So, this is the Dalesville hangout?" he asked, taking a bite.

"One of them," Bria said with a smile. He smiled back.

"I like this place. It reminds me a lot of where I'm from, up in Pennsylvania. Small town like this."

"So, what brought you to this area?"

"Med School, and then a job," he said. She nodded. "But it didn't make leaving my family any easier."

She smiled again. A family man.

"Look, I want to thank you, again for all you're doing for *my* family." He smiled at her, then reached for her hand, holding it in his own.

"Bria, I'm happy to do this. And I hope we find our person today. But I also hope, when all is said and done, and Katie has that new kidney, that I get to see you again."

She smiled sheepishly, pulling her hand out from under his.

"Dr. Carmen," she said.

"Eric," he said.

"Eric. I really appreciate it, but I'm just not looking for anything right now."

"Oh, okay," he said. "Can I ask why?"

Bria got the impression that the smoldering doctor with ocean-like eyes didn't get told "no" very often. The truth was, she didn't know why she was turning him down. He was gorgeous, and kind. And her stomach had done a little flip each time he had politely touched her, or smiled at her. But she didn't feel ready. She just wasn't interested, and she couldn't put a finger on the reason.

Just as she was about to answer, she looked up and saw the car. The car she had ridden in so many times, pulling into the fire hall parking lot. And she lost her breath.

"I-I'm sorry. I have to get back," she said. "I'll see you over there."

She practically ran across the street to get back to the fire hall, making her way through the big doors. She scanned the room until she saw him. He was about to sit down in one of the chairs as the nurse was tying a rubber band around his upper arm.

"Drew," Bria said. He turned around slowly.

"Hey," he said, with a pained smile. She reached up and wrapped her arms around his neck. The hug lasted longer than she expected, but she really didn't mind. She actually *had* missed him.

"You're here," she said.

"Of course I'm here," he said. "I love your family. I love Katie. I still love you."

She looked down at the ground, unsure how to respond.

"Don't worry," he said. "I'm not here to try and win you back. I assume that my spot has already been taken, anyway. Where is Knox, anyhow?"

She looked up at him.

"I, uh, I don't know, actually." He looked at her quizzically. "We're not, uh, not together." She half expected him to smile in triumph. But he didn't. And if she wasn't mistaken, he actually looked saddened by the news.

"I'm really sorry, B. I really thought that. . ."

"I know," she said with a faint smile. "But it's okay. I'm okay. Are you?"

"I am," he said. "I'm seeing someone—it's new, but I like her. And I got the fellowship I wanted."

"Oh, Drew, I'm so happy to hear that," she whispered. And she really was. "I can't thank you enough for coming today."

"Of course," he said, squeezing her hand.

Throughout the rest of the day, she saw troves of people she knew. And she almost fell to floor when Mari walked through the doors.

"Let's get this blood pumpin'!" she shouted.

"Mari!" she cried out, running to her full force. "Mari! You're here!"

"Of course, baby! You know I wouldn't miss this! I'm home for a week. You, me, we're having a good old fashioned slumber party and listening to Fall Out Boy nonstop. Now, I'll see you after I get this blood drawn. Mwah!"

Finally, as the last of her friends, aunts, uncles, cousins, and even her grandmother funneled out of the fire hall, it was just her and Dr. Carmen.

"Hey," she said, walking over to him as he closed up some sort of medical case.

"Hey," he said back, not making eye contact.

"Look, about today," she started to say, but he held up his hand.

"No, no. I'm so sorry about today," he said. "I shouldn't have done that. It was so inappropriate and unprofessional. Man, I could lose my job for—"

"I would never tell anyone. And I'm flattered, really. And I can't thank you enough," she said, wrapping her arms around him.

"Well, Bria, if you ever need to talk, you still have my card," he said with a smile. "I'll be in touch as soon as we have results back."

She nodded. Just as she was closing up, her phone rang in her pocket.

"Hi my love," Mari said on the other line, "send me your new address. I'm headed your way in T minus ten."

That night, Mari lay across Bria's couch, fiddling with her iPhone while simultaneously flicking through the channels.

"So, how's L.A.?"

"Oh, God, it's gorgeous," she said. "If it weren't for you and my parents, I'd never come back to this side of the country. Seriously, I was made to live out there."

"That's great, Mari," Bria said, squeezing in next to her on the couch. "How are the guys?"

"They are hot. And tan, and they always smell like coconut oil and sunscreen. But we can talk about that later. What is going on with you?" she asked, turning her attention fully to Bria and dropping all electronic devices.

"What do you mean?"

"I mean, what's going on in the guy department? Have you heard from Knox?"

"Nope. Not for a year."

"Wow. I'm so sorry, hon. I hate to say this, but it still really surprises me. But look, maybe Knox was just a chapter in your life, you know?" Bria sighed.

"A chapter?" she asked. Mari nodded and took her hand.

"Yeah, maybe. A chapter you never got to finish reading," Mari said. She paused for a moment, looking

Bria up and down. "He messed you up, didn't he?"

Bria smiled faintly and shook her head. "I messed myself up. I messed myself up by keeping my mouth shut all those years."

"Well, hon, maybe it's time to start moving on. Knox probably isn't 'forever' material anyways, ya know?" Bria nodded. Yeah, she knew. And that's what hurt the most.

The next day, Bria called to get an update on the blood donors.

"We had twenty people yesterday who matched her blood type," Dr. Carmen told her over the phone. "They are all scheduled to come in this week and complete their testing."

"Great," she said. "That's great news. Thank you so much, Eric."

"You got it," he said.

Katie had a check-in that afternoon too, and Bria had offered to go along.

She watched, as she had so many times before, while Eric poked and prodded, the nurses stuck her and taped her, invading all her privacy and any dignity she may have had left. But it was like Katie didn't even notice, and that made Bria even sadder. She wondered if Katie would ever get to experience life the way she and Sam had. The way most people had. Not just in-between appointments. Not constantly waiting to feel better.

"Well," Eric finally said, typing one more note into his laptop before closing it, "I think we are all good to go for today. How do you feel, Katie?" he asked.

"I feel okay," she said.

"Okay, good. Well, keep your chin up. One of these donors will come around," he said, patting her on the back.

"Thanks, Dr. Carmen," Louise said. He nodded at Bria before they all left the room.

Her mother finished paying and making the next

appointment, and they made their way out the door and down the hall toward the elevators.

"Where should we get dinner tonight?" Louise asked. But in the distance, she heard someone calling her name.

"Mrs. Kreery! Mrs. Kreery!"

It was Eric, running toward them.

"Mrs. Kreery," he said, breathless, "we have a match."

TWENTY-SEVEN

"What? What?" Louise cried, her hands shaking as she reached for Dr. Carmen.

"Oh my gosh!" Katie exclaimed, jumping into Bria's arms.

Just then, the office door opened, and Drew walked down the hallway toward them.

"Drew?" Bria asked. "Was it. . .you?"

He looked at her, then to Katie, then to Louise.

"I'm sorry," he said, hanging his head, "it wasn't me. My blood type was right, but when they brought me in for the rest of the testing, I wasn't a match."

Bria actually breathed a silent breath of relief. Although she would have done anything to save her sister, she was really hoping that didn't mean taking a kidney from her ex-fiancé. Talk about things hanging over your head.

"Don't be sorry," Bria said, wrapping her arms around him, "I am forever grateful that you tried." He grabbed her hand and kissed it, then looked up at her with a sad smile.

"I'm so happy you found someone," he said to Katie, without taking his eyes of Bria. She smiled and nodded. This was probably the last time she'd see him, and they both knew it. As he walked down the hall, Bria watched him with a twinge of sadness, but yet, not an ounce of regret. She had loved him, but their time together had definitely expired. It was definite, with a clear start and ending.

"So, if it wasn't Drew, who was it, doc?" Katie asked, snapping Bria back to the much more critical situation at hand.

"I'm sorry, but unless the donor decides to sign a waiver, I can't reveal their identity." Dr. Carmen said. "I will ask at the appointment on Monday." Katie nodded.

"Who cares?" Louise said, choking back more tears. "All that matters is that we have a match! What do you want for dinner, Kates? I will make *whatever* you want!"

Bria choked back actual sobs. She couldn't remember the last time she was this truly happy. Well, she could. But she didn't want to. Instead, she wanted to focus on the fact that her little sister was going to survive. Her little sister was going to *live.*

That night, she and Sam cleaned up the whole house. Mopping, vacuuming, scrubbing; they channeled their inner-Louise and cleaned like she would.

They did all the laundry, prepared a few freezer meals for the week ahead, and made sure the DVD player was set up for Katie while she was recovering. In a few days, she'd be laying up on the couch, getting to know the new organ that would keep her alive. Finally, their mother walked in, carrying way too many groceries for one trip. Sam and Bria ran to help her. But Louise didn't seem to be in the same chipper mood that she had been just a few hours earlier.

"Mom? You okay?" Sam asked, dumping a bag of

Chips Ahoy! into the cookie jar.

"Yeah, yeah. I ran into Mrs. Knoxville at the store just now." Bria felt her spine straighten involuntarily.

"Oh? Is everything okay?" Sam asked, knowing that Bria would want her to. Louise paused from dumping the apples she had bought into the fruit drawer, and dropped her head. And then she started to cry.

"Ma? What did Mrs. Knoxville say?" Bria asked, reaching for her arm. Her heart was beating through her ears.

"It's Ben," Louise whispered.

"What? What's Ben? What happened?" Bria asked, frantic now. But Louise just shook her head. She finally managed to speak.

"Ben is the donor. He's giving Katie his kidney."

TWENTY-EIGHT

"B?" Sam asked, waving a hand in her face. "Did you hear mom?"

Bria nodded slowly, staring blankly at her mother.

"He goes in early Tuesday morning. And then Katie gets the kidney that afternoon," Louise said, just as Joe and Katie were walking into the kitchen.

"What's going on?" Katie asked. "What's wrong with Bria?"

But before anyone could answer, Bria was walking toward the door, grabbing her keys off the counter.

"I. . .I have to. . ."

"Go, B," Louise said, walking her to the door.

When she pulled up to his house, all the lights were out, but his car was still parked in front. Bria took a deep breath and stepped out, looking up at it for a moment. The last time she was here, things went so bad, so fast. But it didn't matter. Nothing they said—or didn't say—that night mattered. All that mattered was that Knox was giving up a piece of his damn body to save her sister's life. He'd made sacrifices for her in the past, but nothing, *nothing*, compared to this. That's why she was here. Focus, Bria.

She walked up the front steps and knocked three times, holding her breath. And then it finally opened.

He answered, to her surprise, wearing nothing but a pair of baggy jeans. As she feasted her eyes on his strong chest, she almost forgot to speak. She almost smiled at the fact that he still barely had any chest hair. He could never grow a full beard, or chest hair, or anything that could make him feel more like a *man*. She had playfully made fun of him for it for years in their teens. But now, his body was no laughing matter, and she was pretty sure she was actually salivating.

"Hey," he said, looking surprised—no—utterly *shocked*, to see her. She tried to speak, but she couldn't get anything out. Nothing seemed to fit the intense emotion she was feeling, the urge she had to hold onto him and not let go, combined with the overwhelming fear she had of rehashing the pain of the last night she saw him. "Bria? Are you alright?"

"Can I come in?" she finally asked.

He didn't say anything; he just opened the door wider to let her inside. As she walked up the steps to his living room, he grabbed a shirt off a pile on the stairs and pulled it over his head.

"You thirsty, can I get you a drink?" he said, motioning to the fridge. His place was still messy, as she would have suspected, but it was cozy. Just like him.

"I'm good, thanks," she said. He poured himself a glass of water and motioned toward the couch.

"I'm surprised to see you. So, um, how have you—"

"Knox," she whispered, cutting him off. "I know what you're doing for Katie."

His eyes widened as he set his glass down on the coffee table.

"You. . .you know? How? Jesus, isn't that shit protected by law or something? They told me no one would know."

"Our moms ran into each other at the grocery store," she said. He stood up, walking to the window, clasping his hands behind his head. She stood up, cautiously walking toward him.

"Aww, geez. Of course, ma," he said. He looked down at his feet. "I didn't want you to know."

"Why?"

"Because. . . I didn't want you to think I was doing it to try and. . . I don't know. I didn't want you to think I was doing it for the wrong reasons. I love Katie. I wanted to help if I could."

She nodded. Of course he wasn't doing it for her. He was doing it for Katie.

"And honestly, I couldn't bear to think of you being in pain for the rest of your life if something happened to her," he added.

Bria looked up at him, and the rush of feelings that came over her made her face red. She couldn't hold back anymore. She leapt onto him, wrapping her arms around his neck and burying her face into his chest as she had so many times before. And as he wrapped his arms around her tightly, she cried.

"Thank you," she whispered when she finally collected herself. "I don't know what else to say. I can't believe you're doing this."

He hugged her again, breathing her in for a moment longer.

But then she quickly remembered everything that had happened before. And she quickly realized that nothing else had changed. They still didn't want the same things. And she couldn't bear to hear those words coming from him again.

"Well," she said, taking a few steps toward the door, "I just wanted to let you know how grateful I am, and how grateful I will always be for you, Knox."

She smiled and touched his hand.

But he didn't smile back. Instead, he looked over to her, his green eyes looking glassy and wet.

"Bria?" he asked, with a familiar, cracking voice.

"Yeah?"

"You know my bad spells?"

She looked down at the ground and nodded. How could she forget? Some of her darkest times were when he was in the dark.

"This past year has been hell. It's been like one long, drawn out bad spell." She just looked up at him. She didn't know what to say. Hadn't he told her to stay away?

And then, suddenly, she wasn't afraid anymore. She didn't care if she spilled her guts, and he said nothing in return. She was so sick of wondering, of agonizing over what they should have been. She couldn't take it anymore. She didn't want to. Even if she had to pick herself up off the ground and drag herself out of his house, she couldn't leave without telling him everything she should have over a decade before.

"Knox, I. . ."

"I know I fucked this up. I fucked this up a million and one times. I should have said something when I was seventeen, or eighteen, or nineteen, or fucking twenty-six," he said. Okay, maybe he was going to beat her to it. "Jesus, I should have said something. And I want to kick myself every day because of it. And I know I still might not be good enough, and I know I said we were wrong. . .but. . .I'm just, I'm so sorry." He spun around, his hands clenched in his hair.

"No, Knox," she said, touching his arm again. Oh, shit. What was happening here? "*I* should have said something. I guess I thought the same way you did. That I didn't have to admit anything to you, and that you'd just know. But I was wrong. And I should have said something, too. And don't you *ever* say that you're not good enough. You're everything."

"B?" he whispered again.

"Yes?"

"Please don't leave again. I need you."

She stared at him, and she felt her knees go weak. Not figuratively, her knees *actually* buckled a bit.

She had stopped herself from making a move so many times with him, for fear of it not being reciprocated. For fear of being just another stupid girl who thought she might end up with Knox. But tonight, she wasn't afraid anymore. She'd been through a year without him, and not because she had someone else in her life. She'd been through a year without him when she *could* have been with him, and she had been killing herself to know what might have happened.

She'd stopped herself so many times, but she was pretty sure a stampede of rhinos couldn't stop her tonight.

She took a step closer so that her face was inches from his. She heard him swallow. She put one hand on his cheek, then the other, letting her thumbs stroke his face gently. She looked his face up and down, taking in his emerald eyes, his nose, his perfect lips that she had never seen so close. The same lips she'd dreamt about time after time, only to wake up denying it.

She leaned in and kissed him gently, and she felt his body tense beneath her hands. It wasn't the most perfect kiss; their lips didn't match up perfectly, and they were standing awkwardly like two teenagers kissing on a dare. But it was electrifying.

So *that* was what it was like to kiss Benjamin Knoxville.

She pulled away, looking into his bright green eyes. She leaned in again, this time wrapping her arms around his neck and pulling herself up onto her tip-toes. He wrapped his hand around her head, the other around her waist, pulling her in closer, so that they were chest-to-chest. She felt him consuming her, on so many levels. She jumped up, wrapping her legs around his waist, squeezing him tight.

She kissed him *hard*. Like, ten years-of-pent-up-sexual-tension hard. This time, she felt his tongue on hers, and she was overjoyed that he was holding her. She was pretty sure she would have fallen if not. They paused again and looked at each other, both knowing damn well that they weren't stopping here.

She pushed him back against the wall behind him, running her fingers through his hair, gently tugging it as she left her mouth on his. Now his hands were on her, but she was surprised at how G-rated he was keeping things. When she had pictured the two of them doing the deed, she had always pictured things to be a little more intense. After all, wasn't he supposed to be a pro at this? She pushed her chest against his, letting her groin grind gently on top of his. He jumped back, with an exasperated look on his face.

"Jesus," he whispered. She pulled his head back, gently breathing down his neck. Apparently, he was going to make her work for it. Although, she knew now, it was because he was scared. She let her tongue draw a line across the nape of his neck and up until it reached his lips again. She let it stroke his tongue gently, before she pulled away, keeping his bottom lip between her teeth gently. *Finally*, she could feel him letting himself go.

Suddenly, he popped off the wall and carried her to the couch, lowering her gently, him on top now. He kissed her hard, his hands lost in her hair. Yes. *This* was the Knox she had pictured a million times. He slid his hands beneath her back, letting them travel down to her butt, giving it a tantalizing squeeze. She reached up, yanking his shirt off and tossing it on to the floor. He returned the favor, gawking at her grown-up perfection. She was *so* glad she had chosen her lacy purple bra this morning. It was only because the soft, nude one she usually wore was in the wash, but he didn't need to know that. He stopped kissing her, picked her up off the couch like she weighed nothing, and carried her down the hall to his bedroom.

Setting her back on her feet, he reached behind her and unclasped her bra with little-to-no effort. If she wasn't so turned on, she probably would have giggled. *That* was the sexual prowess she had expected from him. She was normally shy the first time a guy saw her naked; there was that awkward feeling of being fully exposed, regardless of how hot the scenario was. But not this time.

Then she realized, Knox had seen her naked before, in a lot of different ways that no one else ever had.

Bria reached down and unbuttoned her jeans, letting them wriggle to the floor. Her matching purple panties were the sole survivor. He unbuttoned his pants and let them fall, his boxers following close behind. As she stepped backwards toward the bed, kissing his neck and chest, he paused for a moment, scanning her up and down.

"What?" she whispered.

"It's just. . . I can't believe we waited this long."

For half a second, she wanted to burst into tears. After all this time, to know that he'd been pining for it, yearning for it, just as much as she had, was too much for her. But nope, nothing was ruining this Knox-induced high she was on.

As she lay back on the bed, he reached down, gently sliding her underwear down her legs. As his hand made its way back up her legs, it paused between them, circling her most precious spots, and she felt like she was going to melt into a puddle. He climbed on top of her, entering her with one quick motion. She thought for a moment that she might actually die. She had never felt pleasure like this, never a connection this strong.

In all the hundreds of chick flicks Bria had watched, there always seemed to be some overdramatic, unrealistic sex scene where the couples ran into walls, knocked over vases and furniture, and tore up their homes in a fit of unwavering lust. She had always called bullshit on that. No sex was good enough to distract you from your best china and a picture of your grandmother crashing to the ground and shattering. Yeah, she definitely called bullshit.

Until Knox.

He moved her from position to position, skillfully navigating his bedroom. He yanked her off of the bed and pushed her up against the wall, her legs wrapping around his waist. Just as she got settled in their new location, he hopped off again, sitting her on top of his dresser. She arched her back, savoring the new angle. And where his impressive. . .ahem. . .*length*. . .wasn't finding her, his hands were. Holy shit. She definitely should have done this years ago.

"Jesus, Bria," he whispered into her ear, laying her back on the bed now. He let out a low groan, and she felt her insides bursting into flame.

"Yes, yes," she whispered back, digging her nails into his back. And it wasn't because she needed to overdramatize the effect his sex was having on her, like she had done so many times for Drew's benefit. It was because she literally couldn't muster up the brainwaves to say anything else.

As he moved on top of her one last time, they both exploded, collapsing dramatically onto the bed, like the couples in the stupid movies she had made fun of so many times.

TWENTY-NINE

When the sun crept in through the window, she blinked her eyes over and over again, trying to figure out where she was. And then she saw his arm, draped over her naked body, holding her close to his bare, hairless chest, and she smiled. She remembered everything, all that he had said the night before, all that they had done. And she curled into him, kissing his arm and hand.

"Mornin,'" he whispered, without opening his eyes.

"Morning to you," she said, kissing his neck and face. Finally, his eyes opened.

"Hey, now," he smiled, "careful. I'm still recovering from last night."

He stared at her for a moment, tucking her hair behind her ear.

"Ya know what's funny? This isn't even the first time I've woken up next to you," he said.

She smiled, remembering the time she had fallen asleep with him, in his parents' basement. The night that, unbeknownst to her, he had decided to save her and her family. The times she had laid with him all night until he smiled again. And the night in the hospital, and the night at the lake.

"True," she said. "Although, it *is* the first time I've woken up next to you naked."

He raised his eyebrows up and down, squeezing her sides and rolling over on top of her.

"Yeah, I don't mind that so much," he laughed, kissing the nape of her neck. He kissed her lips, and she felt like she was inhaling him. Like she couldn't get enough. Like she hadn't just had him, *all* of him, the night before. He smelled so good, so familiar. She wrapped her arms around his neck tight. Finally, he pulled off of her so they could come up for air.

"So," he asked, stroking her hair again, "what now?" She sighed, running her finger across his collarbone.

"Hmm," she said, "breakfast?"

He smiled. "Yeah, we can do that. But I meant after that."

"Well, I guess that depends."

"Depends on what?"

"On how long you plan on keeping your new flame around this time," she said, smiling as if it were a joke. But he didn't laugh. He didn't even crack a smile.

"Hey," he said, tilting her chin up with his finger, "that's not funny. You know that's not what this is." She looked down again. "You do know that, right?" he added.

Bria nodded, but if she was being honest, she didn't really know. After all, Knox rarely made it to a second date, let alone a full-blown relationship.

"Bria, I don't think you understood what I meant last night about how dark things got without you. I don't know exactly what I want, but I know I want you."

She pushed herself up on top of him now.

"I *need* you," she whispered, kissing him.

"So you're not going anywhere, right?" he asked, tucking her hair back, and running his fingers along the petals of the flowers tattooed on her shoulder.

"Maybe to the kitchen, but that's as far as I'll go," she said. He smiled and gently spanked her tush as she hopped out of bed. "Do you want pancakes?" she called from the pantry.

"Shit!"

"What? What happened?" she said, running back to the bedroom to see him pulling on his jeans.

"I forgot about my appointment today! I have bloodwork and prep for surgery."

"Oh," she said, a knot forming in her stomach as real life invaded on their sexy paradise. "Well, let's go!" She grabbed her jeans and pulled on one of his sweatshirts.

"You don't have to go," he said, looking at her.

"Are you kidding me? Look, tiger. After last night, you're stuck with me. Now let's go." He smiled as she led him out the front door.

"Hey," he said, a few minutes in to the ride, "you okay? You're awfully quiet."

Same old Knox. His world was about to be turned upside down, but he was worried about her.

"I'm good," Bria said, smiling and taking his hand. When the whole kidney donation thing had first come up, she knew she'd have to deal with the fact that her sister would be going under the knife, in pain, and recovering. But she never thought about the fact that she might also give a shit, actually, give a *lot* of shits, about the person giving up said kidney.

"So, after the removal, we will need to keep you in ICU for twenty-four hours," Dr. Carmen said, using his professional doctor voice, not the more familiar tone he had started to adopt with Bria. He had spent a great deal of the appointment looking back and forth between Bria and Knox, clearly confused.

"Then you'll be moved into a regular room where you'll stay for monitoring for another 24-48 hours, depending on how you react. Then, if all goes well, you'll head home. You'll be able to return to work after about three weeks," he said. "And you should make a full recovery by about six weeks."

Knox nodded. "Thanks, Dr. Carmen."

"Well, if there are no more questions, I'll see you tomorrow."

"See you then," Knox said, reaching for Bria's hand, and heading out of the office.

"Knox?" Bria said, as he reached for his keys in his pocket.

"Hmm?"

"Are you scared?" He looked at her.

"No, baby cakes, I'm not scared. Are you?" She looked down at her hands, just as he reached for one. "B, Katie is going to be fine. I promise." She looked up at him.

"Knox, I'm worried about you, too, ya dope."

He sat back, surprised. "Well, you have no idea how good it feels to hear you say that." He grinned, kissing her cheek before backing his car out of the parking spot and toward Bria's place.

As they pulled into her apartment complex back in Dalesville, Bria realized that she hadn't ever had a man besides her father in her apartment. Damn. She hadn't had sex in over a year, until last night.

"This is nice," he said, looking around at her insanely neat apartment. "It's very Bria."

"Thanks," she said. "Help yourself to anything in the kitchen. I was just going to hop in a quick shower and grab some stuff for tonight."

"Tonight?"

"Yeah. I thought that I would stay with you again tonight, and drive you in tomorrow morning."

"B, you don't have to do all this," he said, but she held up her hand.

"You are giving my sister an *organ*. I should be doing way more," she said. "I'll be out in a few minutes."

She turned on the water as hot as it would go and let it stream down her face for a few moments. She was feeling much more stressed than she was letting on. God, if something happened to him because of this. Or Katie. Or both of them. She shook her head. She couldn't bear to think about it.

And then she felt his hands on her waist, and she smiled.

"Hey, sneaky," she said, turning around to face him. But he didn't smile. He just pushed her up against the cool tile and kissed her everywhere. It didn't matter how many times he kissed her, the intensity of it still took her breath away. She wondered if he had kissed every girl like this, or if it was just her. Every time they kissed, he kissed her like he thought it might be the last time.

Back at his place, Bria was prepping for what looked like three months in an underground bunker. She was cooking, freezing, and baking food, unloading boxes of crackers and soup into his cabinets, and making sure his sheets were clean, and his laundry was done.

"B, you're making me feel a little guilty now," he said. She looked up at him. "But, I mean, damn, if I knew you were going to do all this, I would have given up my kidney years ago." She chuckled and shook her head.

"I just want to make sure we have enough stuff," she said, picking up a piece of green pepper she was cutting and putting it in her mouth. A goofy grin spread across his face. "What?"

"Nothin'. I just like being a 'we' with you."

Suddenly, Bria's phone vibrated on the counter next to her.

"Hey, mom," she said, holding it between her ear and her shoulder as she continued cutting. "Uh, yeah, I'm sure that's fine, but let me just check with him." She covered up the receiver. "My family would like to have you over for dinner tonight, as a little, thanks-for-giving-our-kid-your-kidney dinner," she said.

"I'd love to," he said, still looking much happier than the usual patient about to undergo surgery.

"Okay, we will be there. What time?"

She wasn't sure why she was nervous. He'd eaten dinner over a million times. He'd watched movies with her family, he'd come to her grandfather's funeral. But it was different. Because now he wasn't just her friend Knox. He was the Knox who had been on top of her the night before, and in the shower with her this morning. She caught herself staring into space as she replayed the X-rated happenings of the last twenty-four hours. Yeah, she'd be doing that again very, *very* soon.

"So," Louise said, coming into the kitchen to help cut up the vegetables for the salad, "did you have a good night?"

Her mother caught her off guard.

"It was. . .uh, yeah," Bria said. Her mother smirked.

"Honestly, I was always a little surprised that this didn't happen sooner between the two of you."

Much to her relief, the family dinner went off without a hitch. Everything was normal and natural, and despite their attempts, her sisters couldn't embarrass her. Not in front of Knox, anyway. He already knew everything. As she helped her mother do the dishes, Bria's heart felt full, thinking of how well Knox got along with her family. Her dad was laughing at Knox, and not just his polite, laughing-because-he-had-to-laugh chuckle, but his full, hearty, belly laugh that made his whole face go red. Knox helped gather the dishes from the table and wiped it down before asking what else he could do to help. When her mom told him to relax, he raced Katie to the living room for a quick game of Rock 'Em Sock 'Em Robots—her dad had found them at a yard sale years ago, and it was a family favorite.

"He's such a hoot," her mother said, watching them play.

"He is," Bria agreed, smiling.

After they were done with the dishes, she told her family that they would need to head out soon.

"Katie and Knox both need their rest," Bria said. She heard Knox saying his goodbyes to her sisters in the living room.

"Knox," Katie had stopped him, teary-eyed, "I am so happy that you are in our lives. And not just because you're saving mine."

He bent down and scooped her up, just like he had when she was a little kid, running to his car every time he pulled up. He kissed her on the cheek and placed her back down.

"You and me, Kates," he said, pointing to her as he walked away, "we will be bonded for life after tomorrow!" She laughed and waved goodbye.

Knox made his way out to the kitchen, putting his arms around Louise.

"Thanks for everything, Mrs. K," he said, "it was delicious."

"Oh, you stop with all those thank-yous," she said, patting his cheek lightly. "Joe and I, we will be thanking you for the rest of our lives for what you've done for our daughter. Both of 'em," she said, making eyes at Bria. He walked toward Bria, and she felt her heart rate pickup. Damn. The effect he had on her was a little unsettling.

"You ready?" she asked him.

"Ready, Freddie," he said.

The car ride back to Knox's was a quiet one. For Knox, it was casual, he was leaned back in the seat, one hand on the steering wheel, one hand on her knee, humming whatever song was on the radio. For Bria, it was filled with silent panic and anxiety. As he put the car in park, he turned to her.

"B," he said. She looked up at him. "I need you to stop worrying. Katie is going to be fine. I am going to be fine. We are going to all be fine. Take a few breaths."

So she did. And it helped a little bit, although they both knew that a little more oxygen wasn't going to fix her nerves. But she felt better knowing that he knew she wasn't okay. She was scared. And anxious. Her stomach was flipping. He leaned over and kissed her forehead, then rested his against hers for a moment.

"I love how much you care, Bria Kreery," he said, before getting out of the car.

That night, they moved in on each other like a pack of lions on its prey. She could remember a certain weekend in college, with Drew, where they had sex more than five times in two days. She hadn't gone nuts like this since then. But she couldn't get enough of Knox. And she was pretty sure he was feeling the same way about her.

As they lay in bed that night, him fast asleep on his pillow, she stared at him, stroking his hair, his cheek, running her finger along his collarbone.

THIRTY

"Morning, Mr. Knoxville," Dr. Carmen said, pulling the curtain open. "How are we today?"

"We are good," Knox said, looking at Bria and smiling. "But doc, do my legs look okay in this gown?" he said, pointing to the hideous hospital gown he had on. Dr. Carmen smiled and shook his head.

"Of course," he said. "Off-white with questionable stains is definitely your color. Now, before we get started, I have to ask you one more time. Are you willing to undergo surgery to remove your left kidney so that it may be donated?"

Bria felt her heart pounding. Knox looked at her for a moment and squeezed her hand.

"Kidneys are overrated. I only need one, anyway," he said with a sly smile. She let out the breath she didn't realize she was holding.

"Alright, then," Dr. Carmen said, "Josh here is

going to finish getting you prepped, and I'll see you in the operating room."

"Thank you, Dr. Carmen," Bria said.

"Of course," he said, smiling warmly back at her.

"There he is," Mrs. Knoxville said, coming into the room with a handful of magazines, her huge purse sliding off her shoulders. Mr. Knoxville followed close behind.

"How ya feelin'?" his dad asked.

"I'm feeling great. This place gets five stars from me," Knox said.

"Hi, Bria," Mrs. Knoxville said, giving her a peck on the cheek.

"Knox?" she heard a voice at the door.

"Hey, Kates," he said, cheerfully. "Come on in."

"I wanted to bring you this," she said, handing him a small blue gift box.

"Katie, you don't need to get me anything," he said.

"Open it." He took the top off the box and smiled.

"Uno!" he laughed.

"It's for when we are both stuck in bed. I thought that since you're giving me a kidney, I could let you win *one* time."

He smiled and reached his arm out to her. Bria wiped a tear from her eye. Just before Josh came back in to start prepping, the rest of the group stepped out of the room. When she stood up, he grabbed her hand.

"B, stay." She sat back down. "I actually have something for you." She popped up.

"What?"

"It's in my duffle bag," he said, pointing to the floor. She gave him a look, then unzipped it and pulled out a small stuffed gorilla holding a heart. The heart said "be mine," but Knox had covered it with a piece of paper. The paper read "your sister might be stealing my kidney, but you've stolen my heart."

Bria burst out into a fit of uncontrollable laughter as she collapsed on the bed next to him.

"Hey, you might not know this about me, but I am quite the romantic," he said, laughing. When she finally calmed down, he nudged her with his shoulder. "It's true, though."

The smile ran away from her face as she kissed him, long and hard.

"Okay, Mr. Knoxville," Josh said, pulling on a latex glove, "it's time to get you on up to the operating room."

"See ya on the other side, baby cakes," he said with a wink.

Then she stood in the doorway of his room as he rolled away.

After what felt like twelve years, Dr. Carmen appeared in the waiting room.

"Ben's surgery went great," he said, and she felt a load of panic immediately escape her body. "He's having some trouble coming back from the anesthesia, though, so we are keeping a close eye on him. In the meantime, Katie is being prepped, and we will start operating on her in just a short bit."

"Thanks for the heads-up, doc," Joe said, shaking his hand.

"I don't like that," Bria said.

"Don't worry, honey. He had the same issue after his car accident, remember?" Mrs. Knoxville said. "I'm sure he will be awake in just a little while."

But her heart was pounding in her chest. She closed her eyes. *Take a breath,* she could hear him saying. *Just breathe.*

She almost didn't wake up when Sam nudged her, until she heard her name.

"Bria! Wake up," Sam said, She shot up from the

chair. "Dr. Carmen is here."

"Well, folks, good news. The transplant went smoothly. We have both of the patients in ICU now, and we are monitoring them closely. All things are looking good."

Both families cheered loudly from the waiting room, and Bria slumped back into her chair. They were okay. They were both okay.

"Is Kno—Ben awake?" Bria asked him.

"He is. Unfortunately, neither can have visitors just yet, until they are moved to their regular rooms. We will keep you updated."

"Thank you so much," she said, grabbing his arm. He put his hand on top of hers before walking back behind the desk.

Hours passed, and they watched as the sun went completely down, then woke just as it was coming back up. Bria and Sam were sharing a plate of hospital-cafeteria nachos for breakfast when Dr. Carmen appeared in the doorway yet again.

"Bria?"

"Yes?" she asked, sleepily.

"Do you want to see him?" She practically leapt off of her chair, but she stopped when she saw her parents standing up. Katie.

"Katie's awake, too, if you'd like to see her," Dr. Carmen said, looking to her parents.

"You go see Knox," her father told her. "We'll check in on Katie."

Bria wanted to sprint down the hallway to his door, but Mrs. Knoxville was clicking next to her in her high heels, and she didn't want to be rude. When they got there, she took a breath before opening the door.

He lay in the hospital bed, eyes closed.

"Sweetie?" Mrs. Knoxville said, kneeling down to kiss his forehead, "how are you feeling?" Knox groaned.

"I've felt better," he said, barely above a whisper.

His lips were dry, and his eyes were still closed.

"I'm so proud of you," Mrs. Knoxville whispered to him and she kissed him one more time. "You look so tired. I'm going to run to the cafeteria, now that I know you're alright. Bria is here."

With that, his eyes popped open, and he turned slowly until he saw her.

"Hey, baby cakes," he said, his voice strained. She moved in closer to him and stroked his face, a tear rolling down her cheek.

"Hey, hey, no, no," he said. "I'm all good. And Katie. . . is Katie?"

"She's doing great, too," Bria said, wiping her tears on her sleeve, "thanks to you. I don't know how I ever. . ."

"Don't," he stopped her. But she kissed his face and leaned down closer to his ear.

"I don't know what I ever did to deserve you," she whispered, "but I hope I never screw it up."

Finally, the next morning, Knox was discharged. Katie would be going home the next day. Mr. and Mrs. Knoxville followed Bria back to Knox's house, him groggy in her passenger seat.

"I'll call you tonight and check in," she had told Katie earlier.

"Bria, stop worrying about me. You know mom and dad aren't going to leave my side. Be with him."

When they got home, Mrs. Knoxville dumped a bag of frozen something into the crockpot. She fluffed his pillows and made up a bed for him on the couch.

"Alright, now, is there anything else you need?" she asked. Bria looked at Knox.

"No, mom, thank you." She kissed his head once more.

"Okay. Please, Bria, make sure he gets some rest."

"You got it," Bria said.

"And call me if you need anything."

Bria showed her out and walked back up the steps to the living room.

"Your mom seems a lot more. . . present, these days," she said, lifting up the ottoman and moving it to the other side of the couch so she could sit down.

"She is. It's nice. But I really only need one nurse right now, and I kinda want the hot one to stay," he said, reaching his hand out. "Come here."

"I don't wanna hurt you," she said.

"Pshh. You could never."

She didn't realize just how exhausted she was, until she fell asleep on the couch, curled up against him, for almost five straight hours. When she finally woke up, he was still sound asleep. She guessed that losing an organ would make you a little tired. She quietly got up, went into the kitchen to get some crackers, and walked down the hallway to his bedroom. She dug through her overnight bag, trying to find a sweatshirt, but she had forgotten one. Or maybe, she had done it on purpose so that she could steal one of his. No one would ever know.

She opened his closet door, reaching up toward his sweat clothes and yanked one down. And down with it came a shoe box that burst open when it hit the ground, sending all sorts of things flying out from it. She knelt down to pick them up. . .the letter she had given him for graduation, the tickets to the Nationals' game they had gone to, and a picture. A picture of her in the woods. The one Knox took of her at Meade Lake.

"I've had that for probably, eight, nine years now," he said, startling her so much that she dropped the box again. He started to bend over to pick it up, but she stopped him.

"No, no, I'll get it. I'm sorry, I didn't mean to pry, I just knocked it off when I was snagging a sweatshirt," she said. He sat down on the bed, and she sat down next to him.

She remembered all the poses she had done for him that day, how hard he laughed. Out of all the photos he had taken, he kept the one of her, hunched over, laughing so hard that her nose was scrunched. The bottom corner of the photo was bent up, and it looked old. But she was so young.

"Wow," was all she could muster up.

"Yeah, I love that picture. I had it printed the day we got back from the lake that weekend," he said, looking down at it. "I still look at it, from time to time."

"You do?"

"Yeah. It makes me feel. . .calm, I guess."

"I can't believe you've had this, all these years."

"Yeah, well, I wasn't sure if I'd ever have *this* all these years," he said, putting his arm around her and pulling her into him. "I had to have something to look at when I needed you."

She rested her head on his shoulder. Man, if only she knew then.

He tilted her chin up with his finger, kissing her gently. Then harder, until she felt him pulling her up onto him.

"Ah-ah, mister," she said, pushing off. "Doc said no funny business for a few weeks. Lay back, and I'll make you some tea."

"Arghhhh," he sighed, covering his face with a pillow. "How am I supposed to wait *weeks*, when I have *that* waiting for me?"

She smiled at him, shaking her ass as she walked out of the room.

THIRTY-ONE

For the full two weeks after his surgery, Bria made Knox breakfast almost every morning, took him to the doctor for his follow-ups, and played games with him all night.

"I'm so happy everything is healing well," she told him, as she picked up his dishes and brought them to the sink.

"Me, too," he said. "Know what else Dr. Carmen told me?"

"Hmm?" she said. He appeared next to her at the sink, resting his chin on his palm.

"Funny business is a go," he said, raising his eyebrows.

Bria dropped the bowl she washing into the sink and dried her hands on a towel. She stood back, pulling her shirt off over her head and dropping it on the ground next to him.

"Your move, Mr. Kidney," she said.

He smiled, lunging at her and pushing her toward

his room.

It had only been a couple of weeks, but good *God* had she missed this. When they were finished, he rolled over to face her.

"I've been thinking," he said, running his fingers down her arm.

"Uh-oh, that could be dangerous," she said. He playfully bopped her with his pillow.

"And I think it's time we go on an actual date."

She felt herself catch her breath. She smirked.

"A real date, huh? You mean the last few weeks of us watching movies on Netflix and eating bagel bites don't qualify as 'actual' dates?" she laughed.

"No, as a matter of fact, they don't. Tonight. You. Me. I'll pick ya up at seven."

"Are you sure you're up for—"

"Seven!" he said. She smiled.

"Deal."

Today was only the second day she'd be leaving him alone at home, but she needed to haul her dirty clothes home and do some laundry. Plus, now, she had a hot date to get ready for.

"So, he's taking you out?" Sam asked that evening, standing in Bria's bedroom doorway, chowing down on a bowl of cereal. Her sisters had made it a habit of coming to her apartment whenever they felt like it. Each of them had a key, and sometimes, when Bria got home from work they'd be there, watching T.V. Bria kind of liked it.

"Yeah, guess so," Bria said.

"Oh, I found them!" Katie said, rummaging through her purse, and pulling out a pair of silver hoop earrings she had borrowed from Bria two years before. "I knew I still had them somewhere."

Bria's apartment was the only place Katie was allowed to go right now, aside from the doctor, just to get out of the house some.

"Thanks, Kates."

"So, where's he taking you?"

"Not sure. He won't tell me."

"That's so romantic," Katie said, staring at Bria as she curled her hair in the mirror.

"So, are you two officially together?" Sam asked.

"Not sure. I guess so. We haven't really talked about it."

Sam rolled her eyes.

"I swear, it's so much easier dating women. Know why?"

"Why?"

"Because we know what we want. And we aren't afraid to say it."

Bria smiled and shrugged.

"I prefer the uncertainty and anxiety that comes with heterosexual relationships, though," Bria said.

Sam giggled. A few minutes later, Bria could hear a knock on her front door.

"You look hot," Katie said, before walking out to let him in.

Bria was wearing the tightest dress she owned, with strappy heels and the hoops that Katie had given back to her.

"You do look awesome," Sam said.

Bria nodded. The double-sister approval was all she needed.

The look on Knox's face when she walked into the living room confirmed it. She had made the right wardrobe choice.

"So, where are we going?" she asked, pulling her seatbelt around.

"Well, my plan was to go to O'Reilly's," he said. She raised her eyebrows. O'Reilly's was one of the nicest restaurants in Bethesda. "But really, I just want to go somewhere where we can park."

"Oh?" she asked. "Why do you want to park?"

"So I can get you out of that dress as fast as possible."

She looked at him, giving him half a smile. She had put a lot of energy into her appearance tonight, but at this point, she couldn't care less. She just wanted him.

"Go to the farm," she instructed. He raised his eyebrows at her this time.

"Bria, I was just kidding."

"Well, I'm not," she said, running her hand up his thigh.

"Are you sure?" he asked.

"O'Reilly's can wait."

He did what he was told, driving to Beecher's Farm, a few miles away to the outskirts of town. Bria was finally going to hook up at the farm. The perfect spot to park and get her freak on. He pulled in, the dust from the tires blowing back behind them as they made their way to the furthest point of the dirt lot. As soon as he put the car in park, she pounced on him.

"Damn, B!" he said, laughing as she pulled him into the back seat. She kissed him everywhere, his lips, his neck, and his chest, once she had his shirt off. She shot him a sweet-but-devlish grin for a moment, until it was time to get busy. She hiked up her skirt and climbed on top of him. She had always wondered if the windows would really fog up like they did in *Titanic*. Well, they do.

When they were done, she made him blast the air conditioning in the car as she tried to salvage her hair and makeup, despite the fact that it was winter, and the air was bitter cold.

"Well, then," he said, clearing his throat and straightening out his shirt, "guess O'Reilly's is out tonight. We missed our reservation time."

"Worth it," she said with a smile, as she gave up on her hair and pulled it into a ponytail.

"Want to go to Regal's?" he asked.

"How about we just go to Andy's?" she asked. "I could just use a pizza."

"Love it," he said, kissing her cheek as he pulled away.

Andy's was loud tonight, which was uncharacteristic for a weeknight. They scored a booth in the back and shimmied in.

"So, how has work been?" he asked. The question sort of took her back for a moment. Drew rarely asked her about her day at work.

"It's going pretty good," she said, assuming he didn't really need any more information.

"Still liking the new position?" he asked.

"Yeah, I am, actually. It's going really well. Are you excited to get back to school? Have you thought anymore about applying for that position at Dalesville?" she asked.

"A little bit, but I haven't quite decided. It's weird because Mrs. Geiger and Mr. Kinney are both still there," he said.

"You're shitting me!" she said. "Aren't they both pushing like a hundred now?" He laughed.

"Something like that." He paused to take a sip of his drink and eat a fry. "This feels good, B."

"It does," she agreed. She looked back at him with contentment in her eyes, putting her hand on top of his before stealing one of his fries.

"So," he said, taking her hand as they walked to his car, "what do we do with this week we have left?"

She gave him a devilish smile, but in the pit of her stomach, she felt a little nauseous thinking about the end of Knox's bedrest and her return to work. The last two weeks were like a hazy teenage heaven. And soon they'd be ending.

THIRTY-TWO

She woke up the next morning, nose-to-nose with him. He was still in a deep sleep, and she studied his face for a few moments, memorizing every line, curve, and bit of stubble on it. Then came the panicky nausea again.

Wait, no. *Actual* nausea. She hopped off the bed and ran to the bathroom, closing the door behind her.

As she puked over the toilet, she could taste everything she had eaten the night before.

Dammit. This better not be food poisoning. The last time she had it was in college, and she was out for a week.

"B?" Knox asked, knocking on the door.

"Don't come in," she said, pressing her foot up against the door.

"Stop," he said. "Open up."

Reluctantly, she moved her foot, just in time to puke again.

"Aw, damn," he said, turning on the bath faucet and wetting a washcloth. He sat on the side of the tub and held the wet cloth against her neck.

"Looks like I'll be taking care of you this week," he said. "Come on, let's get up."

She wanted to say no, but she was so tired, she didn't even care to. She let him lead her to his bed, let him lift her onto it, let him fluff her pillow and pull the covers up around her.

"I'm going to go make some tea," he said, kissing her temple. "You rest." After a long nap, she finally woke up.

"Hey, you," he said. She turned over. He was sitting up in bed next to her, watching T.V.

"Hey," she said.

"Feeling any better?" he asked. "How's your stomach?"

She put her hands on her belly, and then her eyes shot wide open. It had been an *awfully* long time since dear old Aunt Flow had made an appearance.

And as she did the math in her head, she started to panic. For the past year, since she wasn't really having sex, she'd been super lazy about taking the pill. *Fuck. She'd been super lazy about taking the pill.* Had she taken it every night this week? This *month?* She needed the pharmacy pronto.

"I'm feeling better," she lied. "I need to run out and get a few things."

"Whoa, whoa, whoa," he said, pulling her back into bed. "Let me get them. Seriously, you should rest."

"No, really. I'm fine. It was probably just the grease from those fries last night," she said. "I'm going to grab some stuff from my apartment. I'll be back in a few hours."

"Are you sure? Do you want me to come with you?"

"No," she said, "you still need to get rest, too.

You've got 300 middle schoolers expecting you next week!" She kissed him and then ducked out.

As she scoured the shelves in the drugstore, she cursed every company that made pregnancy tests. Why did there need to be a million different kinds? She just needed one damn stick to tell her if she was knocked up by her best friend who didn't want kids in the first place. Oh boy, another wave of nausea. She shook her head, swallowing it back down, and eeny-meeny-miny-moed it. As she waited in line with the pregnancy test in hand, she prayed that no one she knew would walk in. Just to be safe, she grabbed a copy of *Vogue* and laid it over top of the box.

"Will that be all?" the cashier asked, in an obnoxious monotone voice.

"That's it."

"Do you want a bag?"

"No, I'm fine. I'll just take it, thanks," she said. As she hurriedly made her way to her car, she fumbled through her forever messy bag for her keys.

"What is that?" she heard Knox say. She looked up, and quickly dropped the tests into her bag.

"What. . .what are you doing here?" she asked him.

"I could ask you the same thing," he said. "I'm here to get you some antacids. Now, it's your turn."

She swallowed hard. "I. . .I'm thinking I might be a little. . . late."

"How much is 'a little'?" he asked.

"Like, a week."

His eyes grew wide. "I don't, uh. . . aren't you on the pill?"

"Yeah, I am, but I can't remember if I. . . "

"You can't remember? How could you not remember?" She leaned back for a moment.

"Are you kidding me? We had sex like twenty times in the last two weeks. You could have asked about protection then." Now he leaned back.

"Well, what do you do now?" She noticed the "you." Not the "we."

"Now, *I* go take this," she said, holding the box of tests up and getting into her car. He just stood there for a moment in the parking lot, looking completely lost. But then she sped off, back to her own apartment, literally leaving him in the dust.

"Mari?" she said over the phone.

"Hey, babe," Mari said, breathless. She must have been on the elliptical. "What's up?"

"Um, nothing. Listen, could you stay on the phone with me for three minutes?" At first, Mari laughed.

"Three minutes specifically? Sure," she said. "Why three minutes?"

"Well, um, I'm taking a. . . test." And then Mari was silent for a moment.

"Three minutes and counting," was all she said back. For the remaining two minutes and thirty-two seconds, Mari distracted her with a story about this new drink she had made the night before.

"You use cranberry vodka, rum, Sprite, and, uh, something else, I can't remember. Anyways, it tastes like juice, and oh my God, it's *amazing*!" Mari said. Bria laughed, just so that Mari would think she was actually listening.

Finally her alarm went off.

"Mari?"

"Yeah, hon?"

"If this is positive. . ." she started to say, but stopped herself. Despite the fact that they hadn't been able to get enough of each other for the past few weeks, she realized in this moment that she and Knox hadn't once spoken about what they were, where things were going, you know, the usual talks couples have. If that's even what they were.

And when they were younger, he never wanted to

talk about the future. He was noncommittal about *everything,* from girls, to school, even to what he was doing the following weekend. And she realized now that she had no idea if that was any different. She felt the panic setting in. "If this is positive, I don't know what will happen. I don't even know what he wants. Jesus, I don't even know if we are *dating.* Holy shit, am I just another dumb idiot who got in his bed? Oh my God, I am, aren't I? Oh, my *God!"*

"Bria, calm down. Take a freakin' chill pill," Mari said, using her stern, get-shit-done tone. "Now, first things first, you're a grown-ass woman. If this test is positive, you have a decision to make. And if I know you, that decision will result in a baby. And you'll rock the mom thing. You'll be a MILF if I've ever seen one. But you'll be amazing at it. It's all you've ever wanted. Second of all, I don't know what Knox will do if it's positive. And I don't know what you guys are, or where you'll be next week, let alone next year. But one thing I do know is that those feelings you felt, even the ones you hid at fifteen, those were *real.* And just because we were kids, that doesn't make them mean any less. You're not an idiot. If Knox just wanted to get you into bed, I have hunch that would have happened a long time ago. You two mean more to each other than that. It's okay to be scared. But don't ever regret feeling something, or acting on those feelings for the last few weeks. Not everyone gets that shot."

God, Mari was a freaking genius.

"Okay, babe," she said. "Look at it. I'm right here."

Bria took a breath. Her hands were shaking as she picked the tiny pink stick up off of the bathroom counter and flipped it over.

THIRTY-THREE

Bria sat on the couch, perched up with a mug of decaf on her knee. Her chestnut locks were in messy bun on the top of her head, and Knox's big sweatshirt swallowed her up. The television blared in front of her.

Why, oh *why* did they keep picking Blake over Adam? Aside from Adam's raw, sexy rocker thing, he was just *so* damn talented. Come on, Larissa from Pennsylvania. Get your shit together.

Bria jumped when there was a knock at her door. She walked toward the door slowly, looking through the peephole.

There he stood, his hood up, head down at the ground. She opened the door.

"Hi," he said. "Can I come in?"

She didn't say anything; she just held the door open wider for him to come in.

"How are you feeling?" he asked.

"I feel fine," she said, sitting back down on the

couch. He walked over toward her, slowly sitting down next to her.

"Bria, I'm sorry," he said. "I don't know if you've taken it yet or not, but I'm here now. And I'd like to stay with you, if that's okay."

She looked up at him, feeling the tears welling behind her eyes. No, she couldn't cry in front of him right now. Not about this. Not when he might be the source of her tears. He had come back. He had shown up, like an adult. She stopped him and held up the pink stick.

He looked at it, and his shoulders dropped.

"So, you're not—"

"I'm not pregnant," she said, putting both hands around her mug and taking another sip. "Don't worry. No little Knox or Bria coming along."

She saw him sink back into the couch, throwing his head back and closing his eyes. And even though he had let her down, all she wanted to do was hold him. Tell him it was going to be fine. That what she wanted didn't matter. But the way his shoulders had dropped, the relief he so visibly felt—it *did* matter. And then she felt that pit of anxiety burning in her stomach again.

"If it had been positive. . ." she started to say, swirling her coffee around in her mug. Knox leaned forward, clasping his hands together between his knees. He sighed.

"If it had been positive, I guess I would have taken a second job, and probably sold my car for something more kid-friendly. And, I don't know, I guess eventually one of us would have moved in with the other so we could save money. And eventually, maybe we'd get married?" She caught her breath as her eyes darted to his.

"How. . . how did you know I'd keep the baby?" she asked.

"Because it's you. I know you. I know that this is your biggest dream," he said, matter-of-factly. She blinked a few times, processing it all.

"And you would have. . .you would have done all that?" she asked.

"Of course I would. It's *you,*" he said.

On one hand, she was taken aback by the fact that he was actually thinking about it. He was actually making grown-up plans, he had figured out his next steps, he was planning on taking responsibility. But on the other hand, he didn't smile once. He wasn't excited about it. He felt obligated. She and the baby that never was, they would have been an *obligation* for him. She sighed, looking him up and down.

Bria hated this feeling; she recognized it so fully: disappointment. Something she had never, *ever* felt toward Knox in all their years. Heartbreak, sure. Each time he walked away, or left without kissing her, or grabbed onto another girl. But never disappointment. She knew she had put him up on a pedestal so long ago, but she didn't care. She liked him up there, because it meant he could never let her down. He could never break her heart. He could remain her perfectly sturdy Knox. And although she was pretty sure she'd never have a fire inside of her they way she did with him, she also realized something else.

"We really can't do this, can we?" she finally said, staring down into her cup. Her heart was thudding with such force, she felt her body trembling. This was the part where he was going to tell her she was wrong. And that he wanted what she wanted. And that the rest didn't matter because they had each other. He sat up, his eyes finding hers immediately.

"I don't. . .I don't know."

Okay, never mind. Guess not.

"It's okay, Knox."

She surprised herself at how calm she stayed; how adult she sounded, despite the teenager inside of her that was throwing a fucking tantrum. But he popped up off the couch, clasping his hands behind his head.

"How. . .how can this be? I mean, it's *you.* It's *us.* I

just don't understand. These past few weeks were so, *so* good. But God, when I saw those tests."

"I know, Knox. I know," she said. "These few weeks, they were *amazing*. They were everything I've been lying to myself about wanting since I was an awkward teenager. But I think I know *why* they were so good."

He looked at her, quizzically.

"They were good because life wasn't happening," she continued. "We were back in high school, doing all the things we never did, and saying all the things we never said. We didn't have jobs, family, questions to answer, bills to pay. Futures to have. None of that. It was just us."

He sighed again, looking down at the ground.

"Yeah, I guess you're right," he said. "It's like. . . it's like we got a chance to have that time we never took when we were kids."

She nodded.

"Yeah. And honestly, we're lucky. Some people don't ever get that chance. Or maybe, we're not lucky, we're just smart. Because a lot of people *get* that chance, but they never take it."

A sad smile flashed across his face, disappearing almost instantly.

"But I still don't know exactly what I want to do. I mean, before you got here, I wasn't even sure if I wanted to stay in Dalesville. You remember Craig Barrett? I ran into him in town a few weeks ago. And he was telling me about Teach for America. He's out in Colorado right now, and he's loving it. I was thinking of signing up, going out west for a while. I still don't even know if I want to settle down, or get married, or have kids at all," he said.

All she was feeling now was pure, sharp panic. She had never been so far away from him.

"I know," she managed to whisper.

"And you still do." He said it like a statement, but she could tell he was really asking.

"I know that, too. Sooner, rather than later, I want

a family."

It was true. She couldn't bear the thought of being without Knox, but she also couldn't stand the thought of putting off the life she wanted. She didn't need to travel, she didn't want to see the world anymore. She wanted to be here, in Dalesville. She wanted kids that could grow up down the street from their grandparents. She wanted them to pass a farm or two on their way to school. She wanted them to grow up helping their neighbors shovel the walk during a big snowstorm or playing tag down by the creek.

They were both quiet for a moment.

"Last year, after Drew and I split up, when I came to your house, I thought I was going to tell you then. Tell you how I felt about you. That's *why* I came. And then when it didn't happen, Mari, she said that maybe you were just a chapter in my life. And I just never got to finish reading you."

This made him smile.

"A chapter, huh?"

She nodded.

"Well, I will re-read this chapter for the rest of my life," he said, reaching his hands around her head and pulling her in for the most bittersweet kiss she'd ever tasted.

"This is it, for us, isn't it?" she whispered between kisses, with a tear rolling down her cheek.

He answered her with another kiss, one that was hard, and intense, and soul-searching, and perfect. She wrapped her arms around his neck, and her legs around his waist.

He carried her toward the kitchen table, pushing off anything that was in their way. For a second, she almost laughed; this *totally* would have been something she would have made fun of in a movie.

She tore off his shirt, pulling him down on top of her as she kissed his neck.

He did the same, tearing off his sweatshirt that she

was wearing, and the shirt that was underneath it. He clawed at her bra until it was off, kissing her chest over and over again.

He picked her up again, carrying her back to her bedroom, where he laid her down gently on the bed. He stopped to tear open a condom. And as they both lost whatever clothing remained, there was a single moment where she wanted to cry. She couldn't believe this was it. This was the last time she'd see him naked. The last time she'd lust like this. The last time he'd make love to her. Because she knew now, that that was *exactly* what he was doing.

The sun crept in through her bedroom window, and she could feel it beating on her face. It cast a pinkish-orangish glow on her bedroom walls, and with the birds chirping out of her window, it was like she was inside of a flower. The sun was lighting up his face beautifully when she rolled over. He was so painfully perfect.

Then a car alarm blared in the distance. And she could hear the woman downstairs hollering at her kids. The pit in her stomach formed again, as real life snuck back in. He blinked a few times before turning to look at her.

"Morning," she said, smiling and running her fingers through his hair.

"Mornin', baby cakes," he said, kissing her wrist. She so badly wanted to climb back on top of him; pretend they hadn't had the discussion they had the night before. But she knew she needed to rip the band-aid off and face reality.

"I guess I need to get my stuff from your place," she said. He nodded, thoughtfully.

"Okay," he said. "But not just yet. I just want to lay here. I just want you to be mine for a little while longer."

And as she curled up next to him, she was sure she could physically feel her heart crumbling inside of her.

When they got back to his house, she was surprised to see how much of her shit had actually accumulated around his house over just a few weeks. Since the operation, they'd practically been living together, and it showed.

He bent over to pick up a pair of her shoes and handed them to her, helping her open her huge duffle bag.

"Oh, wait," she said, sliding his gray hoodie off over her head and handing it back to him. "Don't forget this."

"That's yours," he said. "Keep it."

She smiled, pulling the hoodie into her and clutching it.

"B?"

"Yeah?"

"Will I still hear from you?"

The corners of her mouth lifted slightly as the tears welled up a little. She knew that if she kept in touch with him, that each time they spoke, it would kill her a little bit. She felt a fleeting moment of panic as she stared at him. She remembered her favorite line from *Dirty Dancing*, the one that crushed her to her core every damn time she watched it. The one where Baby tells Johnny that the thing that scares her the most is never feeling about anyone else the way she feels about him. Yeah, that soul-crushing, heart-tearing line.

She was Baby. And she was about to lose her Johnny. And she swallowed, hard, facing the painful fact that she just might never feel quite like this, ever again.

"Yeah," she said, dropping her things. She walked toward him and put her arms around his wide back. "You can't get rid of me that easy."

He smiled back as his arms found their way around her.

"And if you're feeling like you're, ya know, not

yourself, call me. Anytime. Please." He looked down at the ground and nodded. "And I will tell you about this kid I knew once, named Ben Knoxville, who saved me a hundred times."

He smiled, and when he blinked, two tears fell from his eyes.

She wiped them with her thumb. "And I will always, *always* be your best friend," she whispered.

"No, baby cakes," he said, kissing her forehead, "you're it for me. Maybe down the road, I'll find someone. But you? I mean, I know I don't know a lot about this. But I'm pretty sure you're the love of my life."

EIGHT YEARS LATER

THIRTY-FOUR

"Stop! Jack, that's *mine!*" Bailey said, swatting at her brother and reaching for a straw that he had picked up off the ground.

Bria looked down at her children, in a bit of a haze. She was so used to their arguing, she sometimes didn't even hear it. Everyone had said that Jack was her twin; he had chestnut brown hair and eyes ever since the day he was born. And Bailey, with hair as dark as the night, was the spitting image of her father. Bria stroked Bailey's long braid with an absent-minded smile. Man, they were beautiful.

"Enough, you two," she said. "If you behave, we can get Happy Meals on our way home."

She watched as they both stood at attention, as if she had put them under some sort of spell. But it didn't last long.

"Bailey!" Jack yelled at his sister, reaching for the straw back. It blew Bria's mind that a freaking straw was the object of their desire, so much so that they were willing to go to physical battle for it. A *straw*. Finally, they reached the head of the line.

"Thanks for shopping with us, Mrs. Carmen," the young cashier said, handing her a receipt.

"Thanks, you, too," Bria said.

Shit. You too? She hated when she did awkward shit like that. It happened *way* too often. Eric had loved it; on their first date, when the ticket taker at the theatre had told them to enjoy their movie, she had said, "thanks, you, too." She thought Eric was going to lose his mind with laughter.

The memory seemed so far away, so distant now, as if it happened in another life. And it quickly disappeared with the sound of Bailey shrieking.

"Enough!" Bria said, snatching the straw and unlocking the back of her Dodge minivan. "Hop in the car and turn on the T.V. I'll be done in a second," she said, beginning to load the bags into the back of the van.

It was a beautiful Spring day in Dalesville, and despite the bickering of her children, the breeze brought a smile to her face. Until the last bag ripped, sending cans of Spaghettios rolling around the ground behind her car. She looked around quickly, as if to make sure that none of the other moms, the judgy ones who meal-prepped and made all their children's food from scratch, saw the canned abominations she was bringing home to feed her children.

"God dammit," she said, sighing as she reached down to grab them.

"You look like you could use some ice cream," she heard a voice say. She felt her spine go straight, and a few goosebumps made their way down the back of her neck. No effing way. She turned around slowly.

"Jimmie Cone?" he asked.

There he was, his face with a little more age to it now, but still covered by boyish stubble. She smiled. He never could grow a full beard. Out of the corner of her eye, she noticed his ring-less ring finger as he knelt down to pick up the last of the runaway cans. A few years before, she'd seen on Facebook that he was engaged. She deleted her account shortly after that.

"Knox," she said, barely above a whisper. He said nothing, just smiled at her, green eyes flashing as he handed it to her.

"How have you been? How's the good doctor?" he asked, still smirking. His eyes darted toward her finger, also ringless. They'd said they'd keep in touch, be there for each other. But as time moved on, so did they, and she realized just how out-of-touch she and Knox had grown. She swallowed and shrugged.

"I'm sure he's doing just fine," she said. "He moved out about a year ago, when I caught him with his nursing assistant."

Knox's eyes widened, eyebrows up. She could see the anger and hurt behind them. She knew that after everything, he'd never want her to be hurting.

"Oh, shit. I'm so sorry, Bria," he said. "How are the kids handling it?" He eyed the van.

"They are actually handling it pretty well," she said. "Luckily, they've gotten used to it. I don't think they know any better; they're still young."

He smiled, taking a step closer. She felt the breath run from her lungs.

"They are. And so are you," he said, his eyes finding hers.

"Well, what about you? How's married life?" she asked. He gave a half-smile, holding up his bare hand.

"We didn't end up. . .ah, making it to the altar."

Bria nodded, eyes wide.

"I'm sorry," she said, looking down at the ground.

"And I'm sorry you're hurting, Bria." And without a moment of hesitation, he stepped closer, wrapping his arms around her, pulling her head to his chest like he'd done so many times before. She let her shoulders fall and her guard drop, the guard she'd had up for a year, now, ever since she saw the text on Eric's phone.

Did you decide if you're going to tell Bria about us? Or do you think she already knows?

Those two stupid questions would be ingrained in her memory forever. Because, no, Eric probably wouldn't have ever told her. And no, she was too blind, too stupid to have known without seeing the text.

But now, for the first time in a year, it didn't matter as much. It didn't weigh on her as heavy as it had before. She wrapped her arms around Knox tightly for another moment, breathing in his familiar scent. And then she remembered she wasn't alone.

If she were, she might have pounced on him. She might have wrapped her arms and legs around him, letting him spin her around the grocery store parking lot. But there were two sets of little eyes that could see her, and although they understood that Mommy and Daddy weren't living together anymore, they might not be quite ready to see Mommy draped over another man. Hell, they might not *ever* be ready for that.

But for the first time in a year, *she* was starting to feel ready.

"So, about that Jimmie Cone invite," she said with a sly smile as she pulled away from him slightly. "The kids go to Eric's on Friday. Are you busy?"

He looked down at her, another smile creeping over his face now.

"I'm not anymore," he said. "I'll see you then." He turned to walk back toward the store, and she called out his name.

"Isn't it funny?" she asked.

"What?"

"That after all this time, here we are, right back in Dalesville. Together."

He smiled again, reaching back to gently scratch the back of his neck.

"I told you years ago," he said, shrugging, "you're

it for me."

She smiled, closing her eyes for a moment to soak in his words. When she opened them again, he was still there, that dangerous grin now spread across his lips. He winked at her. "See ya, baby cakes."

Had it been any other man that she'd made plans with, she probably would have panicked. It had been almost a decade since she'd been out with anyone besides Eric. But this wasn't just a random guy, or some blind date.

It was Knox.

The beautiful, tragic, wonderful, terrifying roller coaster of Knox. She could feel her stomach swirling with butterflies. The pain she'd been through when they had parted ways was something she had never fully rid herself of, even through the happiest points of her marriage to Eric. But if there was one thing those years away from Knox had taught her, it was that the pain was worth it. Even if there would always be a small Knox-shaped hole in her heart, the few moments when he was hers made it all worth it.

And as she watched him walk away, suddenly, she was fifteen again, singing at the top of her lungs, her hands outstretched through his sunroof, breathing in the sun, the air, and him.

Acknowledgements

This book would still be just a document on my computer without the people who are always behind me, telling me to "just do it!"

Little, thank you for always kicking my butt into gear whenever doubt sneaks in. I'd be lost without you.

Will, thanks for sitting with me night after night, while I plowed through each chapter, waiting patiently for me to come up for air. Teamwork makes the dream work.

To my family, you are truly my rock.

Lizzy Bee, thank for you every minute you spent on this book. You put as much heart into your edits as I put into writing it, and I can't tell you how much it means!

K&S, thank you for ALWAYS being there for every up and every down.

To Mr. & Mrs. B., thank you for being great sports and for putting up with all my poses. Little Blue is famous!

Anne, my mentor and my friend. Thank you for being with me every single step of this journey. I want to be like you when I grow up :)

To B, thank you for being my inspiration always. I love you.

And to all the bloggers, readers, and fellow authors who gave my debut novel a chance, I am grateful to each and every one of you. Thank you for loving love!

About Taylor

Taylor Danae Colbert is a romance and women's fiction author. When she's not chasing her toddler or hanging with her husband, she's probably under her favorite blanket, either reading a book, or writing one. Taylor lives in Maryland, where she was born and raised. For more information, visit www.taylordanaecolbert.com.

Follow Taylor on Instagram and Twitter, @taydanaewrites, and on Facebook, Author Taylor Danae Colbert, for information on upcoming books!

Note from the Author

Dear Reader,

I can't tell you what it means that you've decided, out of all of the books in Romancelandia, to read mine.

If you enjoyed reading it as much as I enjoyed writing it, please consider leaving an Amazon or GoodReads review (or both!). Reviews are crucial to a book's success, and I can't thank you enough for leaving one (or a few!)!

Thank you for taking the time to read IT GOES WITHOUT SAYING.

Always,
TDC
www.taylordanaecolbert.com
@taydanaewrites

CPSIA information can be obtained
at www.ICGtesting.com
Printed in the USA
LVHW09s0019171018
593878LV00001B/253/P